CRICKET

CRICKET

a novel by

NATHANIEL LANDE

NAL BOOKS

NEW AMERICAN LIBRARY

TIMES MIRROR

NEW YORK AND SCARBOROUGH, ONTARIO

Published simultaneously in Canada by
The New American Library of Canada Limited

The author wishes to thank the following sources for permission to
quote material in this book:
    New Directions Publishing Corporation for material from
SELECTED POEMS by Federico García Lorca. Copyright 1955 by
New Directions Publishing Corporation.
    Random House, Inc., for material from ULYSSES by James Joyce.
Copyright 1934 by James Joyce.

 NAL BOOKS TRADEMARK REG. U.S. PAT. OFF. AND FOREIGN COUNTRIES
REGISTERED TRADEMARK—MARCA REGISTRADA
HECHO EN CRAWFORDSVILLE, INDIANA, U.S.A.

SIGNET, SIGNET CLASSICS, MENTOR, PLUME, MERIDIAN
and NAL BOOKS are published *in the United States* by
The New American Library, Inc., 1633 Broadway, New York,
New York 10019, *in Canada* by The New American Library of
Canada Limited, 81 Mack Avenue, Scarborough, Ontario M1L 1M8

Designed by Julian Hamer

Library of Congress Cataloging in Publication Data

Lande, Nathaniel.
    Cricket.

    I. Title.
PS3562.A4753C7   811'.54   80-26059
ISBN 0-453-00392-3

First Printing, February, 1981

1 2 3 4 5 6 7 8 9

PRINTED IN THE UNITED STATES OF AMERICA

For Andrew

I wish to thank and acknowledge my graceful friend Paige Rense for helping the author through his first novel with encouragement and editorial excellence.

To my editor, Joan Sanger, and to Sterling Lord and Susan Buchanan, a warm and special thanks.

And, lastly, to the editors of Time-Life whose written words implemented the research and the making of this book.

El Niño Mudo

The little boy was looking for his voice.
(The king of the crickets had it.)
In a drop of water
the little boy was looking for his voice.

I do not want it for speaking with;
I will make a ring of it
so that he may wear my silence
on his little finger.

In a drop of water
the little boy was looking for his voice.

(The captive voice, far away,
put on a cricket's clothes.)

—García Lorca

THE THIRTIES

It was a shuffling time of trailer parks and dust, of mice and men and migrant workers. Women huddled under long coats and pulled-down hats. Adventure came in cereal boxes with magic rings and badges, and forty million radios were tuned to One Man's Family.

The young wore saddle shoes and beanies, wished upon a star, and danced to "Moonlight Serenade."

Cole Porter was de-lightful and de-lovely and a bunch of Ink Spots told us they would never smile again.

It was a time of café society and debutantes, when cigarettes and cocktails and being bored were chic. When two-lane highways joined towns of all-night diners with five-minute Cream of Wheat and tourist cabins under the trees.

The thirties was Life *magazine and Packard cars.*

Fountain sodas and ice-cream sundaes.

Shirley Temple and Fireside Chats.

Whitman Samplers and Arrow shirts.

Burma-Shave signs.

America rode the Superchief, flew in a DC-3, and crossed the Atlantic on the Queens.

We discovered beer cans, ball-point pens, and Alka-Seltzer, and for the first time, out of WXYZ Detroit, came, "A fiery horse with the speed of light, a cloud of dust, and a hearty hi-o Silver."

Bobby Jones was our grand-slam golfer and Joe DiMaggio hit out grand-slam homers.

We were proud when Jesse Owens took four gold medals in Berlin.

We wept during the Kristalnacht when the German SS looted, demolished, and burned 30,000 Jewish shops, homes, and synagogues.

Thousands of families tried to escape into Switzerland; others tried to emigrate to freedom on boats like the St. Louis. *Lindbergh led the isolationists, Adolf Hitler vowed to protect ten million Germans living outside the Reich, and marched across Europe. A concentration camp, Buchenwald, opened overlooking the Weimar, and the world would never be the same again.*

1

"She sells seashells by the seashore."

"Shr shenls sheashen ai he sheeshon."

"Again."

"Shrin shells shheshells an she sherrnshore."

"Now . . . The big black bug bit the big black bear."

"Trn ig ack bg hit thr big ack air."

Speech therapists said that learning to speak and be understood was a matter of training, but I would never be able to talk. The doctors told my mother that I was born without a palate. "Maybe in time, with new techniques in reconstructive surgery, we'll be able to build him one." I had many operations.

Hospital after hospital, operation after operation to form a palate, a bridge for making sounds. Alone, terrified, in pain. Unable to speak. Disfigured by stitches and scar tissue. I knew something was terribly wrong with me. I remember the look on my mother's face—a mingling of revulsion and embarrassment. I can't remember how young I was, but I couldn't have been more than two or three when I felt that she and my father didn't want me, or even like me.

I wanted them to look at me just once kindly, not even with admiration or pride, but just kindly. That wish became almost an obsession. Thousands of hours of vocal exercises and speech training, dozens of reconstructive operations, all so that one day I could say, "I can talk. And look at me. You like me, don't you?"

I wanted to speak like the other children, with their pretty lips. I wanted to sing a song, recite a sonnet, shout with joy, express wonderment. I wanted to ask a question, to give a reply. I wanted to ask directions. I wanted to speak on the telephone. All the things that other people did without even thinking about it, without even knowing what it was like to talk.

At school it wasn't so much trying to talk as it was trying to be understood. The anticipation of talking to someone was as frightening to me as the moment when I heard my name. "Jonathan, answer me!" my mother demanded. I responded through my nose, with nasal sounds. "I don't understand you. You can do better than that."

My father would take a key word and enunciate it, moving his mouth in exaggeration: "Jon-a-than."

"Shan-a-hun, Shan-a-hun," came my reply.

"Try harder, try harder," he'd say. I would, but it never helped. I tried with my mother, too, but when she still couldn't understand me, she would always seem to drift off, remembering something she had forgotten, handing me a book, turning her attention elsewhere. She did not know what to do.

My mother was tall, with long black hair, high forehead, chiseled nose, and deep indigo-blue eyes. She was always in high fashion. She was too beautiful, too young, too privileged to deal with the inequities of life.

When a speech therapist said, "We've been working with him for six months and there is no improvement—he'll never be able to talk—you must accept that," my father's answer was to get another therapist. In his dark flannel suits and with his quiet manner, he looked like a professor, and in fact he was. But this did not help him to face the reality of his son. "The boy will be all right," he would say, "he'll be fine." And he would escape back into his work.

And off I would go for the same exercises all over again, sounding the same letters from A through Z, the same combinations of letters AA, AB, over and over and over again. Only the names changed. From Mrs. Sherman to Miss Clark to Mr. Pekingell to Miss Tate to Mr. Schumann—AA, AAH, AB, AC, AD, AAA, AD, AE, TA, TE, TI. Crying out the vowels A-E-I-O-U, grinding out the words. Throwing out the air so it wouldn't go up the nose. Breathing from the diaphragm.

"Peter Piper picked a peck of pickled peppers."

"AA, AAH, AB, AC, AD, AE, BA, BE, BEB . . ."

Four afternoons a week, speech camps every summer, year after year.

6

And at the end of every summer: "I'm sorry, Mrs. Landau, Jonathan will never be able to speak clearly."

But mute, I *was* learning how to *listen*. My friends' voices were young and flat—short and inexperienced—but they would change. Children's voices were always free and spontaneous. I could easily detect adolescent insecurity and the studied control of middle age. Voices said everything to me. Each sound was unique. It was rarely I found two voices alike. If they were similar, they were usually within the same family. Inflections from darting instructions or calm assurances were clues to what a person was like. It was always the tone of what was said—the tone told it all. Insecurity, ease, gentleness, anger, sarcasm—all in the tone, not in the words. And if I listened really hard, I could hear when someone was telling a lie. Facial expressions and the quality of the voice indicated to me the quality of the person. Discipline and habit taught me to hear in an unusual way, and I did not know if other people heard the same. It was just another thing that set me apart from them.

There was no emotional shelter for me. My feelings were all jumbled up. I was captive and alone. My feelings hurt. I didn't feel wanted. It was a desperate solitude. And I hid and stayed mute. I knew that a lot of the time I didn't feel very good. There was frustration and anxiety in not being able to talk. From a very early age I learned to write simple things. There was a shoe store in Augusta that advertised "Jonathan Shoes." I very carefully learned to write "Jonathan" before I went to school, and I wrote other words, like "yes" and "no," "please" and "thank you." I kept a small notepad with me at all times, and if I were left without it, I felt lost. It was part of me; it was through writing that I could be responsive and included in the world. Little one- and two-word notes would be dispatched. Of special importance was food, and I studied the labels on the cans in my mother's kitchen. Then I passed notes to our cook. I learned to spell, copy, and draw my needs. I was able to manage quite nicely. I could get what I wanted; it was my way of being understood.

There came a day when my mother took the pad away from me, and I was terribly frightened at first. I said nothing when I needed something. Then slowly I would try again, and people would frown in misunderstanding. Their faces would get all squashed up and contorted as if they were in pain. "What was that?" "Say that again." Eventually they would figure out what I was saying by instinct, and just a syllable would provide a clue. The grown-ups were patient but the other kids my age would laugh and tease me, and again I felt alone and apart from them. I didn't feel love and hadn't learned to love. I thought it was all my fault. Who could love someone like me? I looked always for someone or something that would make life wonderful and happy. I looked to other people to help heal the wound, but they never could, and abandonment became a familiar trial. Rejection cut deep and left jagged edges. It was like constantly having something that makes you feel good pulled away from you, just out of reach. I wanted some affirming sign that I was all right. The feelings today are the same as when I was four, fourteen, twenty-four, forty-four.

I was six when the fathers at the William Robertson School told my mother I could enroll there. Even though I was a "special child," they would look after me. They had had a deaf child once, and he had managed quite well. He had difficulty adjusting at first, but in time he became one of their most promising boys.

Although I couldn't talk, I could listen and read, the fathers said. And if I applied myself, they were sure I would do well. All the students attended chapel every morning. It was required. My mother saw nothing wrong in this, even though we were Jewish. After all, Grandmother had been raised in a convent in Austria.

I was scared my first day at school. I didn't know how to act, what to do, where to go. I was behind walls in unfamiliar territory.

Several kids came up to me and asked me questions. I didn't answer. "What is your name?" they asked.

I reached for my pad, which that morning I had carefully put with my things. It wasn't in my pocket; I didn't understand. Where was it? I could write "Jonathan"; they would easily know my name. Now I had to talk to them, and the words were chilly, so like my father had drilled me, I finally took a chance. "An-na-hun."

8

"What?"

"An-na-hun," I said, trying to enunciate. But it sounded like nasal putty.

"What did he say?" they asked each other.

"He said An-na-hun." They laughed.

"An-na-hun," they chanted over and over, making faces and jumping up and down.

"Ease op!" I pleaded, meaning "Please stop!"

"We never heard anyone talk like you before. What's wrong with you? How come your lip is so funny?" came the children's questions. I retreated into silence, and there were jeers. The playground went out of focus, colors and objects ran together. Father Martin came outside, looked away, pretending not to notice. He shepherded us in to mass and into solemn litanies.

"Omnes sancti Angeli et Archangeli . . . orate pro nobis . . . ab ira, et odio, et omni mala voluntate . . . libera nos Domine."

The fathers chanted solemnly, responding, swinging the incense. The light streamed through the stained glass, spilling patterns on the wooden altar. In chapel no one spoke—the only place in school where I felt comfortable.

One afternoon Father Martin called me to the blackboard to work out a problem in long division, then left the room, saying he would be back in a few minutes. I was still at the blackboard when Jimmy Ellison snatched the chalk I was going to use. I backed against the board and tried to say "chalk": "Shal, shal, shal," I said over and over. Jimmy echoed, "Shal, shal, shal." The children teased and laughed. My eyes welled with tears.

Butch McCoy, who was to become my best friend, grabbed the eraser and threw it across the room, hitting Jimmy squarely in the mouth, and Jimmy ran out of the room yelling, "Ou, ou, my outh," and for a moment he couldn't talk either.

Later, in the cafeteria, I was sitting alone, drinking my milk through a straw, and some of it came through my nose. I looked for a napkin. I panicked, because I couldn't find one. The milk was dripping all over my face. Butch handed me a napkin. I smiled and tried to thank him. He put his arm around my shoulder. "Don't worry, Jonathan, we'll be friends."

I felt so good having a friend, I ran home to tell my mother. Dashing inside the house, gathering momentum and enthusiasm, I blurted to my mother, "Shal, shall huch il e ay in the outh my fren."

"Talk slower, Jonathan," my mother said. I did, but when she still didn't understand, I wanted so much for her to share in my happiness that I ran out into the garden and picked as many fresh flowers as I could carry to give to her. But I didn't know how to pick flowers, so I just pulled them from the ground—tulips and daffodils—and carried them in my arms to present them to her.

"Not now," she said, as she stepped into her car and drove off. I felt alone and abandoned. I had wanted to give my mother flowers, and she hadn't even noticed. When my mother came home, she saw the garden all pulled up.

"What have you done!" she screamed.

I tried to explain to her, but when she turned away I cried and went back out into the garden and uprooted more plants in anger. When my father came home, he hit me. He had never hit me before. It was so painful that I forced myself not to think and I tried not to feel. I couldn't understand how my father could hit a part of *himself*.

I was young enough to be confused, yet old enough to sense that this was without reason and could never be forgotten.

From the outside my family looked like a happy one, and I used to wonder why I didn't feel happy inside. My feelings were shadowy and undefined, and somehow connected with never being able to please my mother, who couldn't accept her conspicuously less-than-perfect child.

She lived in a world of bridge bids and ringing telephones, Lily Daché hats and long Pall Mall cigarettes. My baby brother, Edward, pink, plump, smiling, and happy—whom everyone called Dizzy—had been my mother's favorite ever since I could remember and demanded a lot of her time. I didn't call him Dizzy—or anything else—because I didn't talk to him. My father got mixed up and called *me* Dizzy sometimes.

10

My parents' friends visited our home, and asked me, "Hi, what's your name? How old are you? Where do you go to school?"

I wanted to talk. I wanted to talk and be like them. In my mind I said, "My name is Jonathan. Nice day. Would you like to see my toys?" But I wouldn't say anything. I used my notepad instead.

Once my mother *insisted* that I say something, that I say, "How do you do?" Unintelligible, guttural sounds came out from my nose. Everyone looked away in studied embarrassment. I knew they were as uncomfortable as I was. They didn't say anything more. What could they have said? "Nice going"? "Beautiful child"? "Just like his dad"?

I wonder what it must have been like for my mother. I never knew. I never felt her closeness. I wondered if I would ever be all right. If I were, then she would like me and I would feel good—I knew I would.

It must have been as hurtful for her as it was for me. Inside I was angry.

The house we lived in looked rich. It was French in architecture, old brick in construction, formal in style; a graceful setting. The slate roof and large green shutters gave the home distinction. When the house was built a hundred years ago, it stood alone as a centerpiece on four acres of gardens. Commerce and community were now close by.

My mother's foyer looked out into a garden. There were long slender windows meeting highly polished wide-oak-beam floors. The furniture was French. A lot of old pieces. The fabrics were tufted, quilted, and new.

The entrance hall in our house was two stories high and the fireplace was so big that when I was six I could stand inside it and my head didn't reach the top. My mother liked to give parties and was always changing the decor to keep in style. It was fashionable to have a hyphenated name and my mother attached her name to my father's and they became known as Landau-Grunwald. But in time the Grunwald seemed cumbersome and was dropped.

My father was a doctor and a professor at the Medical College of Georgia. He did not make as much money as he would have had he been in private practice. My mother was concerned with the way things looked. My father was concerned with the way things were. Our house, along with the Daimler, belonged to my mother. The car had been a present from her father. He came from a family of bankers who left Europe and had gone to Canada in the twenties.

My father left Canada's McGill University to do his residency in Georgia, partly to get away from the cold Canadian winters. He liked the climate of Georgia, and he never left it.

The town of Augusta was a golfing community with 60,000 people that included only one hundred Jewish families. Sixteen golf courses broke the pattern of the town, and every few miles were well-groomed and manicured green lakes of assorted shapes and sizes. The finest golf course was the National. We did not belong.

On Sunday mornings my father played golf at the Lake Forest Hotel course, and he used to take me with him. "Fresh air and exercise make you fit," he'd say. He played with three old men—Lee Blum, a large man who owned Stark-Empire Laundry & Cleaners; frail and gentle Moses Levee, who had the largest building-supply company in Augusta; and Dr. Sam Simons, who prided himself on being a superb golfer. Sam Simons' mustache was always neatly trimmed, and he looked like a leading man in the movies.

Except for Sam Simons, the foursome wore white pants and sweaters. He wore tweed knickers. As they walked along poking fun and hustling each other with bets, they were always nice to me. They didn't walk as fast as my father—who strode ahead impatiently—and I couldn't always keep up with him.

Sunday mornings were the only times I really saw my father.

The best times, anyway. The other times I remember were when he would call me in, sit me down, and announce that I was going to have another operation. These operations were vivid snapshots of my childhood. Apart from them, I recall only glimpses and random episodes from these early years. There must have been much more than that, which has been forgotten.

I remember being wheeled into different hospitals and looking up at the overhead lights in the ceiling and listening to the

12

pages for different doctors, bounding echoes through the corridors, a monotone: "Dr. Dunning," ding, ding . . . "Dr. Foreman," ding, ding . . . "Dr. Phillips," ding. They all looked and sounded the same. In a long narrow elevator, the gate shut; here I was again. I heard a humming and a bursting ricochet as the elevator reached its predestined floor. Into the operating room, where there were more doctors, all wearing gowns like my father wore in the theater at the medical college. There was the familiar scent of ether, which smelled sour and made me nauseous. I fought with a vengeance, and the nurses and doctors held me down. Here Dr. Dunning, whom I had seen so many times before, told me it would not hurt and to be calm, but it did hurt and I couldn't be calm. I grabbed the cloth they put over my eyes and then the rubber mask that I thought would make me throw up. I thought I was going to choke. Finally I was strapped to the table, and I couldn't move, the cloth covered my face and the mask placed over my nose and mouth, and I heard the hissing flow from a valve that emitted the gas and took me to unconsciousness. Then the doctors would begin the long process of taking tissue from under my tongue and the lower part of my mouth, and cut precisely and stitch the red tissue to the gums, forming a roof on both sides of my mouth. Nylon threads penetrated the skin and knit the sides together. On each subsequent operation, a little more tissue was added, sometimes over smooth bone, until a roof was built. My lip was cut and sandpapered to diminish the scar. I could not utter sounds for a few months following the operation. The pain felt like hundreds of needles and pins and caused my eyes to tear. I could eat only soft foods, like eggs and Cream of Wheat. It was mostly a liquid diet, not right away but in a few weeks after the operation. There was one good thing, though —that for three or four months my mother let me use my pad, so I didn't have to suffer any embarrassment. I could ask for the things that I wanted; I could write down my private thoughts and descriptions. I never wrote down more than a sentence or two, notations that would follow me for the rest of my life and became very important. I wrote: "Someday I will talk like everybody else."

With each operation, as I grew older, the surgeons added more tissue to my palate, slowly bringing it together so it would form a natural arch. The same surgeons also slowly repaired my lip, making it an even vermilion, finally sewing the stitches so that it would leave an unnoticed scar. Still, I dreaded the operations, less because of the anxiety I felt beforehand or because of the unbearable pain in my mouth for weeks afterward, than for the moment when I returned to school.

I remember after my third operation, there were several kids waiting for me outside school when the last class let out on my first day back. Jamie Fitzpatrick and David Phillips, who were much bigger than me, were among them. "Where you been, Jonathan? Cat got your tongue? Hey, Jonathan, what's your name? Let's hear it. Come on. An-na-hun." Jamie pushed me. "You don't belong in this school. Why don't you go somewhere else?" He pushed me again. "My daddy says you're a Jew, and this is a Catholic school."

"Uch-off."

"What?"

"Uch-off."

He swung at me. Rather than flinching from the pain, I absorbed it. "You creep. Come on, you're a piece of shit." He swung at me again, and I ducked. When I dropped my books and hit Jamie in the chest, David Phillips came up from behind and held me while Fitzpatrick pounded me over and over again and busted open my lip. Blood gushed through my fingers when I tried to stop the bleeding. They ran away. I walked home alone.

When I arrived, my mother was hysterical and drove me to the hospital, where my father was waiting. "What happened?" he said over and over. But the pain of what had happened was too strong to try to talk. I was rushed into the white rooms and familiar glaring lights. When I woke up later, I wrote in my notebook: "Someday I will be all right. Someday I will talk better than anyone else in the world."

Then Butch McCoy came into the room. "I'm sorry, Jonathan, that wasn't fair."

While I was getting well, we played together. Butch and I used to go to my father's laboratory at the medical college. It was an old, dark, Victorian building that smelled of alcohol and formaldehyde. The photographs of people on his office walls showed a different side of him that I did not know until

14

later. They all had white coats and microscopes. They had all written inscriptions. Framed window boxes held medals: the Lasker, Fleming, AMA, Royal College of Surgeons, Legion of Honor. There were awards from Belgium, Holland, Brazil, Argentina—where he had been honored for his work in medicine. My father was a great surgeon.

I'd climb on Butch's shoulders to reach the textbooks, which always smelled of must and dust, ink and high-gloss paper, to pore over the pictures of endocrinology malformations.

"Jesus, look at that."

There were pictures of fat, naked women.

"Hesus," I said.

"Say it again, Jonathan. Jesus."

"Ge-Ge-Ge . . . ," and I tried. "Geshus."

"That's good," Butch said. "See, you can do it when you want to."

I figured that I'd become a doctor, too, that my father would accept me and like me a whole lot more. Yes, maybe if I became a doctor, I'd be like him. I wanted to be like him; he seemed to do good things, and I longed for him to hold me like Butch's father held him when he came home from work.

I felt more confident. We looked at every case history we could find. Every breast, thigh, vagina. There were slides and tissues and cells magnified between the pages. Dots and circles in different colors—reds, pinks—forming satellites.

"Jesus," Butch said. "That's what we're made of."

"Yesh," I said. My eyes were wide open.

After our textbook education, we entered the practice of medicine with Jill Downing. She was our age and she liked playing nurse. Often we went over to Jill's house to play doctor. One day we started up the stairs to her mother's room.

"Ont nu hink we should use he gararge?"

"No," Butch said, "it's cold down there. Let's go upstairs." So into her mother's room we went, where Butch persuaded Jill to take off her clothes.

"I'll show you mine if you show me yours," he said.

"Sure," she said.

We looked at her small and delicate vagina. I touched it.

15

"What are you doing?" Jill said.

I dispensed some cinnamon hearts that our cook used for decorating cakes.

"Here, take these pills. You'll feel better in no time," Butch said.

"But I feel good now," Jill replied. The edges of her lips were red from eating the candy.

When her mother came in, Butch and I had our penises out showing them to Jill.

"Oh, my!" she shrieked. "Oh, my!"

She reported us to my father.

"Is this true?" my father asked me. I nodded yes, and soon afterward he gave me a black bag he used to carry with him, filled with chrome instruments, rubber hoses, and brown glass bottles. I think he felt I had a bent toward medicine.

With our newfound interest, my father invited Butch and me to sit in the surgical amphitheater at college and watch operations. We'd sit on the top row with several hundred medical students dressed in white, some with stethoscopes around their necks, others with notebooks, most with glasses. And down on the floor, beyond a glass wall, around the operating table, stood a forum of doctors and nurses in white masks and rubber gloves and caps. All you could see was a circle of eyes. I could always recognize my father's. They had a warmth to them, and once or twice our eyes met. The surgeons and interns communicated with darting looks as he performed. I watched and looked down at a body, draped in white. Each time he leaned forward with his scalpel, the audience in the theater instinctively bent forward as one moving body. It was cold and precise and logical—and held no magic for me.

Afterward Butch and I would climb the rickety, dusty wooden stairs to the third floor, where they kept the cadavers that the medical students worked on. Anyone with a name like Butch should be fearless, but he'd say, "Are you sure we won't get into trouble?" Because of my father, this was my territory. I'd shake my head, and up the stairs we'd creep. Pulling back a green canvas, we'd look into a lifeless face and wonder if the person was in heaven or hell and if the streets were really paved with gold or running with fire, like when I'd heard a preacher shout when I took long walks and passed by the House of Prayer.

Mrs. O'Flaherty, the mother of my father's secretary, who watched over me, was up there one day waiting for us, a willow switch in hand. "You're not to be up here." Her voice was as dry and crackly as walking in fall leaves, and she whacked me across the back of the legs. She carried that switch as if she were out to do the world's work, and I stayed away from her—and the third floor—from then on.

2

After a few years in school, when I knew more words, I'd use my pad to make notes of the special things that happened to me during the day. Sometimes I'd jot down my feelings, the hurt I felt, especially the time when I thought my parents didn't want me and the times when something wonderful happened, like the day Andrew came.

He appeared one day. A black man, tall and young—in his early thirties—impeccably well-mannered and impressively dressed in a dark suit and tie, he appeared at the door looking for work. My mother interviewed him in the foyer downstairs, and I sat in the corner of the room watching with wide brown eyes. I didn't say anything. My lip still hurt a lot from the latest operation.

She explained to Andrew that she had plenty of help and didn't need anyone just now.

He looked at her and smiled and said, "I know, ma'am, but I can cook."

My mother said, "I have a cook."

"I can garden."

"I do most of that myself."

"I keep a good yard."

"We have a man who comes twice a week."

"I can shop and I can drive."

Every once in a while Andrew looked at me and smiled, and I pretended not to notice. I felt his warmth.

By the end of the interview, for no apparent reason, he was hired, and I was very pleased, though I didn't know quite why. I didn't know that Andrew would become the most important part of my life. It was like being welcomed into a warm embrace. He didn't pay much attention to the way I talked, and make-believe was as much a part of his life as it was of mine.

My mother dressed me as if I were the young Prince of Wales—long gray flannel pants, Eton shirts, regimental-striped school ties, Buster Brown shoes. Andrew liked the way I dressed.

"You look very natty," he said. "You dress well, you dress real nice."

He waited for a response.

"They call me the King of the Crickets," Andrew said. "That's my name. You want to know why?"

Of course I did, but I was hesitant. The King of the Crickets, I thought. I nodded my head, and Andrew revealed a shining gold snapper in his hand.

"Know what this is?"

I shook my head no.

He clicked it. "It's a cricket. Do you know about crickets? They're very special. They stay awake all night chirping and singing."

King of the Crickets, I kept thinking. My eyes were wide. I wanted to know more, and Andrew knew it. He stopped.

"This is what they sound like. Crick-it . . . Ca-lop. At night when everyone is sleeping, the crickets are there. When you hear them, you know that everything is all right in the world."

I was fascinated.

"Would you like to be a cricket?"

I shook my head yes.

"You can, 'cause crickets have a special way of talking, and they feel a lot. If you want to find your voice, the King of the Crickets is sure to have it. I'll help you find it, and when you do, you will talk better than anyone else in the world. Remember that—because you really will."

And that's what he said to me. I hoped he was right—it didn't seem possible. And then Andrew said something quietly which I didn't understand at the time.

"But around your voice will be a ring of silence. The only sound that can break the circle is crick-it . . . crick-it."

Andrew gave me a little cricket snapper, and that night when it was dark, we went outside. It was way past my bedtime, and my parents were out. We were in my mother's garden.

"Now, you stay here," Andrew said. "When you hear the sound of the cricket, see if you can find me, and I'll do the same. I'll see if I can find you."

He disappeared. I was scared. It seemed darker and there were ominous shadows around the house. The minutes passed and it seemed like a long, long time. And then I heard "crick-it, crick-it," and then I pressed mine. Into the night we went. The garden seemed like a magical forest with dark giant trees. "Crick-it." I heard it over and over again, and around bushes and over the lawn I went. I pressed my cricket and Andrew would respond in the distance, and slowly the cricket got louder and louder. I would press mine and Andrew pressed his, until Andrew and I were together. We found each other. I didn't feel so alone anymore, and I started to smile just a little.

"I like you, Cricket," Andrew said.

That made me feel good—"Cricket." It was affectionate and seemed comfortable to me.

Cricket seemed to catch on with my father, too, who began to call me that. To my mother, of course, I remained Jonathan, in a tone that had an edge to it and was always somehow a threatening link to her.

I lived in my own world. When I'd finished my homework, I would close my door, reach into my desk drawer, and open the pages of my imagination to Dick Tracy, Superman, Captain Marvel, Batman and Robin. After reading them, I'd take a pen and write myself into every strip, revealing all my real feelings into a secret diary. Little scraps of paper became notepads, and pads became notebooks. I didn't know at the time how important it was to be able to write down my thoughts. Not only did it help me to remember, but it helped me to express my feelings and my fantasies. With each entry, I became more careful with words, until they became accurate and effective descriptions. I learned early that to be effective is to be simple, but that to be simple it had to be just the right word, so from that time on there were times in my life that became a search for words and appreciation for language. But now all I wrote was, "Andrew is wonderful. I'm glad he's here."

Andrew knew about escapes, too. They were natural to him, necessary for him. Only, he escaped into *roles*—playing them with flourish and in uniform——black cap for chauffeuring my mother in the Daimler, white gloves for serving at her parties, blue-and-white-striped apron for gardening. He also lost himself in Noël Coward records, which my mother imported from England and played over and over again on the Victrola that Andrew kept wound as he washed and polished, cleaned and served. When no one was watching—no one but me—he'd dance around the mop, clip azalea bushes in a clickety-clack rhythm.

Sometimes Andrew came to school and surprised me. Outside my class just before the last period ended, I heard the crick of the cricket. It broke the silence. I knew he was out there, and as soon as the bell rang, I ran outside and clicked my cricket and Andrew responded with a big smile. "What's that?" David Phillips asked Andrew. "It's a cricket," Andrew said. "Oh," David replied, and Andrew took me by the hand to the car and we drove off.

Andrew also escaped from domestic quarantine into fantasy of his own making. Whenever we went shopping for my mother, which was as often as he could find reason to go, he took the long way around, sitting up tall in her four-door convertible, driving through the streets where he had grown up.

He said to me, "Cricket, we all have a problem sometimes. When I was little, I didn't even have a mama. And I lived in one of these houses. This is where the King of the Crickets used to live."

He drove slowly so all the people could see him and know that he had prestige, and because he knew I liked looking at the houses and the people: women in cream-colored satin slips sitting on wrought-iron balconies drinking iced tea, old ladies rocking on the front porch of cottages shelling peas and stringing beans, wash on the line, dogs sleeping at their feet. I liked looking at the kids lounging on sofas discarded in the weeds. I saw people's lives in a narrow frame, one moment at a time. It was only after I read Faulkner and Capote, Williams and Caldwell, that my life by comparison began not to come out the short end.

One day Andrew and I left the house before dawn to drive to an open field. From a distance I saw giant lights and boxes on tripods that Andrew said were Technicolor cameras.

"They're doing location shots for a picture," he said.

"Maybe *Gone with the Wind* or *Tobacco Road*."

We watched and waited for just the right moment when the sun rose above a clump of trees, for clouds to move across the sky, for the angle of the sun to shine on a field. Andrew held my hand in his and the rising sun cast a warm glow over everything. The director shouted, "Okay, let's get started! Dawn doesn't last all day."

"Those cameras take pictures of life," said Andrew, "and the pictures move. You can take movies of anything you dream of."

But the camera, like me, recorded only what it wanted to see, and the illusion of life seemed to be easier than life.

I don't know when I saw my first movie, but I was seven when they became an important part of my life. They had more meaning to me than anything that was going on around me, more at least than anything my family was saying or doing.

By the time I saw *The Wizard of Oz* and *Love Finds Andy Hardy*, I had come to think of Hollywood as a place where worlds were created to suit the creator and everyone lived happily ever after.

At about this same time, Andrew gave me my first advice on Hollywood and New York. For some reason it was important to him to lump the two cities together.

"You go to Hollywood with gold in your pockets and a handful of stars," he'd said. "And in New York people don't get anywhere if they're a nobody. That's where the buildings reach the sky. We're going to be somebodies, you and me. We're going there together. New York, New York, and then Hollywood!"

We had stopped in front of Davidson's Fine Foods, the only store in Augusta, Georgia, that carried imported caviar, according to my mother. I climbed out of the car and waited on the sidewalk for Andrew to come around. He did a kind of shuffle, tapping his high-polish shoes on the street until he came to the curb, then up down, up down, up down, his arms high in the air for balance, the way Bill Robinson danced with Shirley Temple in *The Littlest Rebel*.

Andrew could do anything—he could sing and dance and

perform and talk easily—and he was King of the Crickets. He could make the magic. I wanted to be exactly like Andrew.

I remember when the line between fantasy and reality became blurred. Andrew and I had come out of Davidson's and were walking two blocks to the Forest Hill Bakery. Andrew was singing "A Room with a View," which he had just learned—"There won't be anyone to hurry or worry us." He smiled.

"You know, Cricket, when you and I go to Hollywood, you're going to put the pictures together. You're going to get the music going and the dancing started and the stage lit up. You're going to make the magic. You're going to those premieres and get out of a big long shiny black car, a spotlight will turn on you, and the announcer will say, 'Ladies and gentlemen, the man responsible, the genius behind the show . . . Jonathan Landau.' "

I saw the crowd in the bleachers stamping and shouting and clapping their hands.

Andrew stopped in the middle of the sidewalk, held up his hands, clapping and shouting, "Bravo! Bravo!"

I was dizzy with excitement, a million miles away—a band played—people reached out to me as I walked down the red carpet toward the theater, slowing to scribble my name in autograph books, interrupted by:

"Hi, Andy."

"Hi, Cricket."

"Hi, Ginger."

"Hi, Cricket."

Flashbulbs and microphones were thrust in front of me. "Just a few words, Mr. Landau—how does it feel to be in Hollywood?"

Warm sweet air swept over me. The applause evaporated in the smell of fresh peach pie. On the way back to the car with the pink boxes, I wanted to ask Andrew how you made the magic, but I didn't. When I opened my mouth, I didn't always know what sounds would come out. I would lose control of my voice and thought better of trying to talk in public.

I learned early to affect the game of make-believe—to

23

present an impassive face and affected calm, except to those I felt close to.

At home alone, in my silence and the privacy of my mind, I started making movies of my own. My belief in make-believe became real. I swam with Esther. I sounded the bugle for Gunga Din. I commandeered the Good Ship *Lollipop*—up and over the waves, and not a bit seasick.

As I grew older, my world of make-believe grew, too— beyond the movies. A half-forgotten verse of song—"You went away and my heart went with you"—was all I needed to create a memory . . . "a million or more times." I was more comfortable with the characters in *Lux Radio Theatre* than the people in my own life. In my mind there was only Andrew and me at home. I'd forget about the others until Illona, the cook and self-appointed top sergeant, would take command. That was usually on the day of a party. She'd turn to me and say, "Sugar, you go run and play and stay out of the way. You lunch will be ready when that nurse of your brother's gets down here to give it to you." Then she'd turn to Andrew. "You get busy with the silver, and then you can get started on polishing the glasses. We need the water and the . . ."

I climbed on the high stool in the pantry and watched Andrew polish the silver bowls and platters and flatware.

Sometimes after Andrew had finished waxing the floors he'd say, "Cricket, come on. It's Saturday morning," and he would drive me down to Broad Street, the widest street and the main street in downtown Augusta. In the middle of a green park at the heart of town was a statue of a general from the Confederacy. He sat on his horse pointing to the Miller Theater across the way. It was here that Andrew would deposit me safely in the balcony with popcorn and a Baby Ruth candy bar, and I became as tough as Edward G. Robinson, sang along with Bing Crosby, kissed Betty Grable, laughed with Abbott and Costello, and rode into sunsets with Roy Rogers and Hopalong Cassidy. I eavesdropped on romances between Garfield and Turner, Gable and Lombard, Powell and Parker. I danced with Fred and Ginger and conducted with José Iturbi at the Hollywood Bowl. I watched other people—studied them—how comfortable they were. I sometimes spent hours before the mirror, practicing a look, a walk, a posture. I'll be like everyone else. Then I'll be accepted.

24

Then later at home I put a record on my mother's Victrola and pretended to lead an entire orchestra. Andrew made a box for me to stand on and said, "You're in charge, Cricket. It's your orchestra—make it happen." I'd stand in the middle of the room and wave my arms and listen to every instrument. When the violins played, I waved them on with my right arm, and when the music finished, Andrew would laugh and applaud.

"Cricket," he'd say, "you're somethin' else." Then he'd take me by the hand and lead me out to the stables on the other side of town. He knew I had a secret affection for horses ever since I read *National Velvet*.

The first time Andrew took me to the stables, I was scared. "Horses are nice people," he said. "They won't hurt you."

There were long rows of paddocks in a low white building with open beams and a green ceiling. On a grass track with whitewashed fences were a few colts that had just been born. Alice Minnick, who looked like a shampoo ad that I had seen in magazines, was married to a man who played polo. "Give the horses a lump of sugar," she said, handing me a cube. Alice knew all about horses and kids.

I liked to ride. Horses didn't talk, either. And it was a lovely thing to have a favorite horse. Mine was Princess. If you gave the horse a lot of love, it felt nice. I was sure that Princess loved me.

Posting up, down, up, down, along the trails, finally I gave up my fear and learned to canter. In time I was as comfortable on horseback as I was walking—and that was because of Alice. She never expected too much, and let me progress in my own time.

The days in Georgia had a stillness to them. Pine trees would stand without a breeze. A solitary leaf would skip and tumble now and then across great green rolling hills bordered by wildflowers—blue cornflowers and clover—that would reach to a far horizon. When I wasn't at school or off somewhere with Andrew, I would go exploring by myself. My walks took me to tree houses, isolated pockets of childhood suspended upon the limbs of a great oak. Here I could climb high above the ground, defending myself in my high fortress against the attacks of Indians and waiting for the cavalry, which would always arrive in time to rescue me. Sometimes an old tire hung suspended from a tree on a rope, and I would swing back and forth, back and forth. There was gentleness in the motion. In bed at night I would try to duplicate the rocking—turning again and again, back and forth, thinking that someday I would feel better inside.

My walks often took me far enough from home to reach the National. It was several miles away. I would look through the old wrought-iron gates with coach lamps and watch lawn parties entirely in white. The people were pretty. Ladies wore long dresses and large summer hats, and the men wore seersucker suits. I listened to the thwack of tennis balls sailing over nets and the clink of golf balls coming home from a putt. There were flowers all around, and acres of magnolias and Carolina cherries and peach trees.

In school the kids always talked about the National. I wasn't sure what it was. But it sounded like a club.

"Hey, Jimmy, you going to the National Saturday night?"

"Yeah, I'll be there."

"See you there."

"Did you ever go to the National?" Butch asked me while waiting for Andrew to pick me up after school one day. I shook my head no. I had never been invited. It was obviously a place you had to be very special to belong to, but once you did, everything was good. Life was better. It was like the movies. I often thought how much I would like to belong, and that maybe we didn't because something was wrong with me.

I was sure of it a few weeks later after school when a group of ten kids formed a circle around me, standing in a ring all holding hands, with me in the center. When I ran, the ring followed me, and all the children produced popping steel crickets in their hands and started to click them furiously. It sounded like a thousand crickets, and then they mimicked me: "Hey, cricket, cricket!" They laughed and yelled and shouted at me, interspersed by the sounds echoing back and forth, responding to each other, then all of a sudden the King of the Crickets—Andrew—appeared.

"That's enough." The running ring stopped. "Now, you leave that boy alone."

There was a long silence. Then Jamie Fitzpatrick and

David Phillips started talking through their nose. "You talking to me or to Cricket?" Jamie said.

Unleashing controlled and instant anger, Andrew picked Jamie and David up by the collar and held them against the wall. They were about four feet off the ground, their faces turned red, and their eyes bulged. The ring broke into small groups.

"You boys better tend to your learnin'. 'Cause if I ever catch you two poking fun or hurting that boy again, you know what's gonna happen?"

"No, sir."

"I'm gonna go to jail, that's what's gonna happen. And you wanna know why?"

"Why is that, sir?"

" 'Cause I'm gonna bash your heads in two, that's why, and see if there's any sense in there. Now, apologize, you apologize fast."

"Sorry," they said, and Andrew let them down. They looked at him and walked away. They were a good distance away when they turned.

"You nigger, you goddamn nigger!" they yelled, and ran away.

On the way home Andrew bought a pair of boxing gloves.

"You've gotta learn to protect yourself, Cricket."

The gloves fit easily on my hands; they were much too big for me.

"Now, you stand here with one foot ahead of the other. It gives you balance. Never side by side, but one foot ahead. You rock into it, you punch into it, and rock back. Now, move side to side, see, got your balance? Always keep your right hand in front of your face, bobbing, nodding, just like Joe Louis. And throw the left jab, throw that left arm straight out, fast. Zing it out, just like Sugar Ray, out, like lightnin', you can do it. Left. Left. Keep that right up, just like Gene Tunney. Push that left out. Now, if somebody's pushing you, hitting you with a left, back off, dance, duck, move wide, side by side. But when you get your opening, push with that left, like Jack Dempsey, try to get 'em to open up. And when they do, come around with your right, a right uppercut. And as you get 'em, follow through with a left in the chest. Put all your weight into it. And keep your guard up, cover that lip."

Andrew and I practiced a few times, enough to teach me self-defense, but I didn't like boxing very much.

Every Sunday I pored through the funny papers, from the latest exploits of Flash Gordon to up-to-date leapin'-lizards episodes of Little Orphan Annie. In the comic kingdom of heroes and heroines, I was part of every adventure. I belonged to that common ground of virtue. Good, clean living held unlimited rewards. And during the week, I was at my regular five-o'clock post, listening to the radio when it blared, "Won't you try Wheaties? Won't you try Wheaties? Wheaties is the best food of man."

"Jack Armstrong, the all-American Boy!" The radio announcer shouted those magic words and a male chorus would swing into the Hudson fight song. "Wave the flag for Hudson High, boys, show them how we stand. Ever shall our team be champions known throughout the land." Jack Armstrong's mission was to overcome all the bad guys, and although I didn't know it at the time, to peddle Wheaties. With each installment my hero fired off a barrage of sales pitches in behalf of trinkets, toys, and his favorite breakfast food. I had sent him two box tops from the twenty boxes at home on the shelf, and Jack sent me back his picture, smiling. "To Jonathan, from your friend, Jack Armstrong."

Another two box tops had brought the Chart Game, which was a game of chance that took you on a Pan American Clipper to Manila, and then through China. A turn of a cardboard wheel, back ahead, and extra spins took you down to India, Burma, and then to Siam and the South China Sea with Uncle Jim, Billy, and Betty. Then came an exciting new offer—two more box tops for Jack's magic-whistle ring. I sent away for it immediately. It arrived soon after Andrew taught me how to box. The instructions read, "One whistle, *attention.* Two whistles, one short, one long, *be on guard for trouble.* Three whistles, one long, two short, *in danger, come at once.*" It wouldn't hurt to play it safe, I thought.

During the next night's episode, I remember, a Tibetan monk said to Jack, "Tell the boys and girls in the United States, this world is theirs. If they have hearts of gold, a glorious new golden age awaits us. If they are honest, riches shall be theirs. If they are kind, they shall save the whole world from malice and meanness. Will you take that message to the boys and girls of the United States, Jack Armstrong?"

I thought about that. That was an important message. I thought about it all evening and all night. The next morning when I went to school, I wrote down that message and showed it to everyone. I also took Jack's picture with me and showed it to Jamie Fitzpatrick and David Phillips. When they read where it was inscribed "To Jonathan, from your friend Jack Armstrong," they laughed and beat me up. I tried to box like Andrew had taught me, but it was two against one and hard to fight back. I blew three whistles, one long and two short, "In danger, come at once." I blew it over and over again, but no one came.

Feeling a deep sense of personal betrayal, I stopped listening to Jack Armstrong for several weeks. To pass the time before supper, I started wandering up to the attic and rummaging around in an old armoire which I knew contained boxes of old photographs. I'd never looked at them before. Lying among the feathered down cushions that had been put up there for storage, I sank into them every night and looked at the snapshots. My mother and father in funny old bathing suits at the ocean. Another that said "Old Orchard Beach, Maine." A picture of my father playing rugby, the team all wearing the McGill letter "M"—my father with a mustache. My mother's wedding picture with long white trains of pleated lace. Postcards from the *Queen Mary* sent by aunts and uncles. The pictures were old and faded—and in Victorian sepia.

I looked through box after box, hoping, I suppose, to find something from the past to give me a present identity. There was the lake house, and my grandmother's cocker spaniel, and a picture of me with my Uncle Laurence kneeling in his flannels and blazer, holding me close and smiling. I looked like a little boy of three—standing with short pants and trying to smile. It must have been taken at Grandmother's house in Montreal. I looked at my hair, and it was long and blond. Could I have really had blond hair? It was dark now. Then I saw the lip—it was swollen—and I knew it was me.

There was a picture of my cousin Lily. Lily was an artist in

Paris. Every summer she came for a visit to Canada, where we spent long warm days in my grandmother's house on the lake in the Laurentians. Sometimes she would be waiting for me after I got out of the Royal Victoria Hospital. She was in her twenties. She was tall, with long brown hair and eyes with the longest lashes I had ever seen. My mother used to say we looked alike. We'd take long walks in the woods, and it wouldn't be until the house was in sight that we realized we hadn't had lunch. Then we'd empty our pockets on the library table with what we'd gathered—stones, birch twigs, leaves, bits of moss. They were very personal treasures.

She didn't care about the same things other people found important. She didn't spend time with people she didn't like, no matter how much help they could give her in her art. And unlike my mother, she wasn't always changing clothes every five minutes, for lunch, for tea, for dinner. Sometimes she wore the same long dress two evenings in a row.

We'd sit together on the dock, which creaked and swayed with the lapping of the water against the pilings, and she'd tell me a story with pictures and say, "There are lots of ways to communicate, Jonathan. Drawing is one, writing is another. Feeling is also communicating. Sometimes what we can't put into words or on paper is more important than those things we can."

I knew exactly what Lily meant. I could write down my thoughts and feelings. I remember writing about her voice. It had all the kindness and openness a voice could have. Her words created a cushion that made life more comfortable for me. I put the pictures away and hoped I would see Lily soon.

3

I was very young when my father decided to send me to a speech camp held by the University of Michigan. My father took me and we stopped off at the Shubert Theater in Chicago, where we saw *High Button Shoes*. A friend of my father's was the producer and we watched the show from backstage. During intermission we went to Nanette Fabray's dressing room. "Jonathan, do you like the show? Are you having a nice time?" She didn't wait for me to answer, but went on talking and smiling. "If you stand over on top of the grid in the wings, I think you can see it a little better."

There I was way up watching the Model T roll onto the stage, humming along with "Papa, Won't You Dance with Me?" and tapping to the "Keystone Kops Ballet." It was loud and brassy and I loved it, and I sang the songs in my head all the way up to Travis City in northern Michigan, where my father dropped me off before going back to Chicago to deliver a lecture to the American Medical Association.

The camp was run by Dr. Hubbard, who believed that character developed from self-denial, and that cold showers were the way to virtue. He believed that we had problems because we screwed up, and didn't try. It was there that I heard my own voice on a recording for the first time. Until then I had thought that people who liked me understood what I said. But when I heard myself talk on the tape, *I* couldn't understand what I was saying. I didn't like how I sounded and I felt bad about it. I wanted to go home. I missed Andrew. Even in the middle of summer, I felt cold. The reality of being surrounded by people with impediments, defects, and handicaps at least as bad as mine wasn't comforting; it hurt too much to endure. I wrote my father asking if I could come home. He wrote back, "Stick it out, you'll get used to it." After another two weeks I was still not used to it, but they wouldn't let me use the phone. So one afternoon I ran up the road to a café with three dimes in my pocket. The café was crowded, but no one was using the phone. I dropped in a dime.

"Operator," a voice said.

"Augusha, Gorogia," I said.

"Please repeat that."

"Augusha, Gorogia."

"I can't understand what you're saying."

"Augusha, Gorogia." Click. My dime fell back into the slot. I tried again.

"Operator."

"I-want-to-maaa-a-ollect-all-to Augusha, George."

"Agusha, Agusha? Would you speak clearer, please? I can't understand you."

"Agusha."

Click. My dime dropped again.

This was the first time I had used a phone. If I wanted to get through, I knew I would have to ask for help, but there was just one very busy waitress, and the man behind me was waiting.

I went back to camp. That night I went to bed with my clothes on, and after bed check I crept out of bed into the kitchen. I put a package of graham crackers, two apples, and a pint of milk into my knapsack—along with four dollars and my portable radio—and walked to the highway. It was dark. Trees on either side of the road loomed high. Were there bears in Michigan? I walked fast. And soon I saw the lights of the café. I would try the phone once more. But when I reached the door, a sign said "CLOSED. PLEASE CALL AGAIN."

I walked on. There was no moon or stars. The black sky and the black of the trees became one. I sat down beside the road and ate part of the graham crackers and drank half the milk. Then I got up and walked on. I had planned to hitch-hike. I knew how from the movies. Just put out your thumb and a car stops. "Hop in," the driver says. "Where ya headed?" "Augusta," I say. "It's right on my way," he says. But there were no cars.

I don't know how long I walked, but finally I stopped and finished the milk and ate one of my apples. I looked down the highway. The white stripe went over the hill and disappeared. Then I saw Nanette and Eddie Foy, Jr., and the cast from *High Button Shoes* in a Model T coming down the road. They were singing, "Cricket, won't you dance with me, please dance with me, oh, dance with me." They came closer. I stood up, reached out. They passed by and disappeared into the night.

Suddenly there was a truck barreling past. People were standing up in the back—cherry pickers. It must be close to five o'clock. They would be getting up at camp soon. I wished a car would come. I'd do anything for a car. I looked over my shoulder. No lights. I hurried on. Someone at camp would miss me. They might come looking for me. I'd hide in the trees until night again.

Darkness faded into a gray dawn. Reds dotted the green trees. Then I heard a car. I shifted my portable radio to my other hand and stuck my thumb out. It came closer and closer and slowed beside me. It was the camp wagon. The door opened. "Get in." It was Dr. Hubbard. He swung the car around and started back to camp. I want to go home, I thought. We drove all the way in silence.

"Run the baseball field twenty times," he said when we arrived, standing near home plate. I ran to first, to second, to third, and as I passed home plate he hit me. He hit me until I cried. Harder and harder with a strap. Please don't. I was trapped in an angry world. If only I could hit him back. He hurt me. I was sore. "You're deformed and I can't stand you," he said. "How dare you leave without my permission?" He slapped my face and I thought about picking up a brick and throwing it at him. He looked at me sweating and breathing hard. "Don't you throw that, you little bastard." I threw the brick and it hit his shoulder. He started to beat me again. What had I done? Why was he so mean? Please, I want to go home . . . please. I ran on back to first, walked to second, and on third I stopped. Dr. Hubbard looked at me from home plate. "Come here," he said. I shook my head no. I didn't want him to hit me again. He finally walked away. I sat on third base for a long time. Eventually my counselor appeared, walked out to third base, and took my arm. "Dr. Hubbard has called your parents and requested that you be sent home," he said. "I'll help you pack."

I had a Pullman berth, an upper. I played with the lights

and switches until I fell asleep. Next morning I changed trains in Chicago. My mother and Andrew were on the platform in Augusta. I was glad to see them. Then I looked at my mother's face and the old churning in my stomach began again.

"Jonathan, you don't appreciate what we're doing for you. You're hurting us and yourself," she said as we drove home. "You're a disappointment. Your father is very unhappy about your leaving camp. Why can't you be like Dizzy? He gets along with everybody."

I thought how he was sent to the principal's office four times last year in school, but Andrew looked at me pointedly in the rearview mirror. I didn't have the courage to quarrel with my mother. That would have taken a feeling of acceptability which I didn't have.

When we got home, Andrew and I carried my bags up to my room. "Wasn't so hot up there, eh?" he said.

I shook my head. "She doesn't understand that," I said.

"Your mama's only trying, Cricket—only trying."

That night after supper, Andrew said, "I want to show you what I've been up to while you were gone." We got in the car. "I know you must have been unhappy up there at that speech camp—and lonesome. You probably cried yourself to sleep every night."

"No, no, I dent-ent rye at hall," I said. I wouldn't cry, I thought. I wouldn't want the others to hear me. We stopped at Louise's Snack and Chat, a café in Andrew's favorite part of town.

Kerosene lamps glowed, and the patrons sat around large tables covered with flowered oilcloth and paper napkins, eating pork chops smothered in pan gravy, black-eyed peas, collard greens, sweet potatoes, carrots, pickles, and cornbread. Family-style smiling and friendly conversation illuminated the pleasures and pastimes of the day. Louise made the best chocolate cake I'd ever had, with lots of icing, and banana pudding with Nabisco vanilla wafers. I had two desserts at once. This was the best place in the world.

The people who ate there were black. Andrew introduced me to his friends. There was Robert, a butler; Matthew, a Pullman porter; and Sammy, a waiter at the country club. They all wore smiles, and around that warmth were white coats, brass buttons and red caps.

"The boys and I have a little surprise for you," Andrew said. "Hit it, Sammy."

The quartet gathered around the piano and sang "Boo-hoo." They sang about how they were going to tell their mama on me. They mimed and played all the parts.

I laughed until there were tears in my eyes.

This was the beginning of Andrew's new career. I didn't know it at the time, but a few weeks later the "Red Caps" were singing for dinner parties and at the club. Everyone liked them, and I couldn't wait until I heard them sing again.

4

Andrew was one of the elders in the House of Prayer for All People, and when it was time for their leader, Daddy Grace, to make his annual visit to Augusta, Andrew led the parade to church down Walton Way. It was a Saturday afternoon. I skipped along beside Andrew, leading a band playing ragtime by Scott Joplin. Behind the band marched Daddy Grace himself,·in a black suit, black silk top hat, and white spats, with a gold chain hung across his round stomach. The late-afternoon sun caught the glint of gold on his fingers as he strutted down the road, an aide holding a big black umbrella over him. Keeping time to the music, they were followed by three elders, also dressed in black, followed by local maids and cooks in long white dresses that swept the clay country road. They wore white turbans and carried parasols in blue, pink, lime, yellow, orange. The black congregation, dressed in their best, waving their arms, swinging their hips, sashayed on behind.

When they reached the church, the band parted in the middle and the congregation stood with them on both sides of the walk, stepping in place to the music as Andrew swung open the double doors. Daddy Grace swaggered in, down the center aisle, and took his seat in a high-back chair in front of the altar. The procession moved up the aisles behind him, chanting.

"Oh, sweet Daddy! Sweet Jesus! Amen! Amen!"

The elders seated on either side of Sweet Daddy nodded in benign approval as the people, nodding and crying out, shuffled by the altar, dropping dollars in a basket.

On and on they came—the young and the old—until the last one passed on tired legs, sure that their salvation was in the future.

"Ahhhhh, Sweet Jesus, Sweet Daddy."

"A-men."

As long as people marched around the inside of the altar, they dropped in dollars and the band played. Like high-rolling musical chairs, the players dropped off, and the last one standing received a special dispensation from Daddy Grace.

And then there was silence.

Finally Daddy Grace rose, a sweet smile spread across his cherubic face, his eyes sweeping back and forth among the rows of chairs until they came to the very back and rested upon me.

"Ahhhhh, we have a little boy with us tonight," he said in a deep melodic voice. "Georgia's on top tonight—for all people, black and white." He stepped from the altar and moved down the aisle. Heads turned to follow him.

People whispered, "Who is that boy?"

"That's the Landau boy."

"Georgia's on top tonight—prosperity has come . . . to all people. . . ."

Daddy Grace stopped at the end of my aisle and held out his hand. I walked to where he stood.

"What is your name, son?" he asked.

I looked up and smiled.

"Don't be shy, son."

No one said anything. Then Daddy Grace took my hand and led me up the aisle, saying, "Silence is sorrow. There is a silence in the main street of the soul, and a silence of the spirit. The silence of this little boy is the silence in the highway of the spirit. The silence of this little boy is the silence of the heart."

We mounted the platform. Andrew smiled, and I could see the gold tooth in the side of his mouth.

"Just let in your thoughts," said Daddy Grace, "let them flow sweet, clean, and clear. Close your eyes and visualize. The Lord, Sweet Jesus, can make it happen. He can give it to you right here and now. No more washing. Thursdays off, all the carfare you want. But you got to do your share. You got to think about what it is that you want . . . on your way to glory."

The band struck up and voices sang:

"O precious Lord, take my hand
And let me stand . . .

From that day on, I became special to all the maids in town. I could take any route home from my speech therapist, because in every house, on every block, there was a sentry of maids to protect me from Jamie Fitzpatrick and David Phillips and all the other big-time bullies who had tormented me for as long as I could remember.

I wondered how you lifted up your soul and made it happen. "Close your eyes and visualize." I thought of the girl whom I'd just met. Her name was Lady Meredith, and although I was just ten, I was sure I was in love with her. I met Lady one day while I was taking the long way home from my speech therapist's, to keep from meeting David and Jamie, who lived on the direct route. She sped out of a driveway on a bicycle, and we practically bumped heads. "I'm sorry," she said breathlessly. Her butter-blond hair was pulled back, and she was pretty, with violet eyes. "People call me Meredith, Lady Meredith," she added, turning her bicycle around and speeding on up the road without another word. I thought about her all the way home. I confessed this to Andrew. He understood, as always, and helped me write a letter inviting her to come for a walk the next afternoon at three o'clock.

I dropped the note in her mailbox, and the next morning there was a reply in *my* mailbox: She would be glad to come and see me. My excitement gave way to terror. How could I talk?

"Never mind, Cricket," Andrew said. "Just leave it all up to Andrew. It'll work out fine—just fine."

Andrew could make things happen. He could create illusions almost out of nothing.

I was ready at 2:30, waiting by the side gate. I made sure I had a paper and pencil in my pocket.

"You let me bring her back here to you," said Andrew. "Then you take her for a walk. Just keep walking and leave everything to me."

Precisely at three o'clock, Lady came down the driveway and followed Andrew around the veranda to where I was waiting. I was terrified. Would she walk away from me like my mother? Would she like me? She was starched and combed, more beautiful than anyone else I had ever seen. As we started down an old brick path to the garden, I heard the muffled sounds of music. I couldn't figure out where it was coming from, but it sounded like Andrew singing. Draped over the camellia bushes, the branches of white dogwood and magnolia trees, a green hose wound through the garden and ended in a large funnel. Out of the funnel he sang "A Room With a View." The song was about just the two of us, gazing and dreaming what life was all about.

We didn't have to talk. How Andrew knew we had come to the end of the garden, I don't know, but he appeared with a tray of lemonade and a plate of napoleons and French pastry.

"Well, my word, look who's here—Mista Jonathan and Miss Lady," he said in a most exaggerated way. "Here's some refreshment for you. Yassah. Now, you just sit there and enjoy yourself," he said, putting the tray down between us on the stone bench and going back through the garden.

I watched him disappear, and once again the soft refrain continued.

I wrote a note to Meredith: "Do you like the music?"

She took the paper and wrote back, "Yes, and I'm glad to be here." She then drew some flowers. Then she leaned over and kissed me on my cheek. I felt elated. I knew she liked me.

We finished eating and followed the hose to the house— through the French doors, across the polished floor and the Aubusson rug, over the sofa to the piano, where it ended with another funnel, into which Andrew was singing dreamily.

My mother appeared in the doorway. "Andrew, what is this hose doing in the house?"

Andrew was at the piano. "This is one of your favorite songs, Mrs. Landau, and I thought I'd fill the garden with music. It's just such a beautiful day." Andrew started winding the hose over his arm, backing slowly out of the room.

"I don't understand why you . . ."

"Don't you worry about a thing. Everything's taken care of just fine, Mrs. Landau," he said. The funnel on the end of the hose got caught on a chair as he was backing out the French doors, and he had to stop and pull it off.

"I don't think a house is a place for a hose, and I hope . . ."

My mother had a way of missing the point.

"Don't you worry, Mrs. Landau, you just leave everything to me." Andrew began singing softly again as he slipped the hose off his arm and put it on the ground outside.

Lady Meredith held out her hand. "I had a wonderful time and I love your garden," she said, walking across the patio and out through the gate.

I had planned to walk her home, but she was gone too quickly. For a girl living in the South, she moved rapidly, decisively, with quick fleeting movements—like a fawn.

Still, she and I seemed to communicate without saying anything. Maybe that's what Lily was talking about that day on the dock when she told me: "Sometimes what we cannot put into words is more important than what we can."

But one time Lady tried to trick me into speaking. It was at one of the tea dances that was held on the last Saturday of every month by Miss Price, who taught Augusta's children how to dance. For the tea dance, green palms were dotted strategically throughout the big glass-domed conservatory and Miss Price wore a long white lace dress and carried a silver cane and wore her red hair—which people said was dyed—up in sweeping curls.

I went up to Lady Meredith for the first dance, bowed low, and held out my arm. She said, "You're supposed to ask me to dance." It wasn't Lady I minded, but Jamie and David, somehow always close by, ready to sneer and mimic me in whispers. I took both of Lady's hands, placed them over her ears, and moving my lips, mouthed the words, "May I have this dance?" It was situations like this that taught me early to think quickly. Dealing with my greatest shame gave me my greatest asset. We went gliding over the polished floor, keeping time to Miss Price's tapping on the edge of the piano. Glide, two, three; glide, two, three; glide, two, three. Glide . . .

5

It was never a relief when school was out, for it meant another long summer in Canada, and this year I wanted to stay
home with Lady. But it was time for another operation at the
Royal Victoria Hospital. Andrew wanted to drive us up, but
my father said he should stay and look after the house. The
morning we were to leave, Andrew drove me to Lady's house
and I gave her a spoon I took from my mother's silver,
wrapped in white tissue and tied with a blue bow. She gave
me a box of pencils with my name imprinted on the side, a
book about the Bobbsey Twins, and a package of Double
Bubble Gum.

When I got home, my father was checking the straps on the
luggage rack. My mother had put a Lily Daché hatbox, a
silver-fox jacket, and Dizzy in the backseat. I gave Andrew a
hug, climbed in next to Dizzy, and we were off. I peered out
the back window, waving to Andrew, waving and waving until
the trees hid him from view. A lump rose in my throat and
stuck there, dry and hot, forcing tears into my eyes. Andrew
and Lady Meredith were mixed up in my head. I didn't know
who I was missing most. I chewed hard on a stick of bubble
gum and the radio played and my mother sang along: "I'll be
seeing you . . ."

I remembered Miss Price's dancing class. ". . . a sentimental
journey familiar places . . ." Walking in the garden with
Andrew's music coming through the hose. "You've got to *ask*
me to dance." ". . . embraceable you . . ." "You gotta go to
Hollywood with gold in your pockets and stars in your
hands." ". . . till time goes by . . ." I wanted to forget. I
put my head on my mother's soft fur jacket and cried. I tried
gulping down a sob, but it came out along with the wad of
pink gum, which rolled into the fur and stuck. I pulled at it,

but pink strings tangled in the long hair and stuck to my fingers. I grabbed the gum and the fur and pulled again. Tufts of silver hair matted together with the gum came out between my fingers. I squeezed my eyes shut, hoping I could disappear. Hoping I would die. Hoping that this wasn't really happening.

The song finished and my mother lit a Pall Mall. Smoke began to fill the car. "Open the window back there, will you, Jonathan?" my mother said. It was then that she turned and saw the coat and shrieked. My father slammed on the brakes and nearly swerved us into a ditch.

"Oh, my God, moths!" she cried.

Dizzy pointed his finger at the coat. "No, Mama, bubble gum."

My mother reached over the backseat and slapped me across the face. I turned my head to the window and shut my eyes again. I was a long way away. On the radio was Walter Winchell, and I thought I heard him say, "Good evening, Mr. and Mrs. America, and all the ships at sea. Another exclusive. Jonathan Landau was just slapped by his mother, Mrs. Landau, for no good reason." I kept my face to the window for most of the trip, looking at the passing telephone poles and the Burma-Shave signs.

> Hardly a driver
> Is now alive
> Who passes
> On hills
> At 75
> Burma-Shave.

I felt the changing weather, and I watched the countryside change from weeping willows and dogwoods to maples and the green and white of birch trees. Occasionally an orange roof would dot the countryside, and we'd stop to have an ice-cream cone at Howard Johnson's. Out of twenty-eight flavors, I rarely picked anything but chocolate or vanilla. My mother made me finish the cone before getting into the back of the car.

We arrived in Montreal at four in the afternoon. Everyone hugged everyone else and I was glad to get lost in a crowd of aunts and uncles, great-uncles and cousins—and my Grandmother Rachel. It was teatime, and silver chafing dishes steamed with creamed chicken. Silver trays were heaped with pastries and cakes and little sandwiches, bowls piled high with strawberries and clotted cream, and shakers with powdered sugar.

The Landaus were rich and influential. They were accepted by the Canadians as Europeans rather than as Jews. It is not surprising that instead of giving her children traditional Jewish names—Solomon, Joshua, Abraham, Jacob, Ruth—my grandmother gave them grander-sounding names. There was Bernard, whose wife, Millicent, was from an old Canadian family called Seagram. Uncle Bernard collected art and moved leisurely through committee meetings raising money for worthy causes. Uncle Laurence had degrees from Oxford and the Sorbonne, endowed a chair at McGill, and had been knighted by the queen. Uncle Philippe, a banker, had married a gentile from Michigan whose family owned General Motors. My grandmother pretended she was Jewish.

Grandmother Rachel was still a very beautiful woman. She had been born in Vienna, and her father had been a director of the opera. She sang beautifully, and often she talked about life in Salzburg, where as a child she had listened to Haydn and Mozart, Brahms and Strauss. She always wore a diamond necklace and had blue-gray hair which matched her eyes. Her manner was polite, and servants attended to her as if she were royalty.

My uncles were all very formal. They had all been educated at Oxford and Cambridge. Their suits tailored by Hawes & Curtis, shirts fitted by Turnbull & Asser, luggage crafted by Crouch & Fitzgerald, marmalade preserved by Fortnum & Mason. They did not follow the strict principles of Judaism. They went to synagogue twice a year, and rather than walking on the Sabbath as was the custom, they parked their cars two blocks away and pretended they had walked all the way from their homes. But they were champions of Palestine, a dream that went back to the year when my grandfather Honour Landau joined Theodor Herzel and Louis Brandeis in Paris for the Dreyfus trial and watched a mob attack the Jews. A few years later, Grandpa met Brandeis and Herzel at the first Zionist council in Switzerland for the purpose of winning support for a Jewish homeland in Palestine, and they worked with Arthur Balfour, the British foreign secretary. My family's heritage was their life, and I had whole forests in Palestine named after me.

In dramatic contrast to my other uncles was Uncle Moe, who wore plaid suits and introduced himself as "Uncle Moe from Buffalo." He was a large man with jowls, droopy eyes, and a Havana cigar always between his lips. He couldn't sail, ride horseback, fence, or talk as well as Bernard, Philippe or Laurence, but he talked to me, and made me feel important.

"When are you coming to Buffalo, Jonathan? I spoke to the mayor and he's waiting to see you. I've arranged a special boat for you at Niagara Falls. The *Maid of the Mist*, a beautiful ship that will take us through the falls under the rainbow. I will be so honored and pleased if you come and visit me." I knew I would.

One dark and rainy afternoon, I went into the library. There was no one around. The servants were in the back of the house. I looked through some of my grandmother's record collection—there were mostly operas by Verdi and Puccini—until I found one by Johann Strauss. I wound up the phonograph. The music was gorgeously romantic, and I waved my arms, conducting the orchestra. The drums and the French horns, the bassoons and the violins. All in perfect order and precision. I conducted over and over. I was happily keeping time to the music when I saw a large shadow from the corner of my eye. I turned and thought I saw my Uncle Moe looking at me. Embarrassed, I stopped and went over to the door and called out to see if there was anyone there. There was no answer, and I saw no one. Just my imagination, I thought. I stopped. It was quiet, and a summer rain splashed outside.

I wondered when Lily would come. This summer she had given up her holiday in Canada to help our cousins escape from Austria. Across the Swiss border she went carrying $50,000, the price of safety. Then the Swiss stopped immigration and our last hope of getting them out of Europe was on a ship—the *St. Louis*—which was leaving Hamburg for Havana. The money for their passage—even more than $50,000 —came from the family's fortune, which was considerable. They had done well as bankers in Europe, though not as well as the Rothschilds. My grandfather did not like such comparisons. "The Rothschilds stayed in Europe, we did not," he was fond of saying. Everyone knew my grandfather had arrived in America with no more than he could carry—not a carpetbag of shabby belongings, but a sizable quantity of diamonds, which he had traded for the gold from his vaults. Stones were easier to get across borders.

Grandmother's house smelled of furniture polish and lavender and fresh starched linen. My room was on the third floor next to the nursery. But I never stayed in it. There were always so many people around, and even though I didn't like to talk, I wanted to stay in the midst of things. I liked sitting in one of the library's great chairs in front of the fire, which burned even in summer. Canada always seemed to be cool enough for a fire. There by the hearth, Uncle Laurence would read Blake and Tennyson to me. He and Uncle Moe were the only people I tried to talk to—besides Andrew—about my difficulty in speaking. Uncle Laurence saved me from feeling sorry for myself. "Everyone has problems, Jonathan. What is important is how you handle them."

Often at dinner, sitting at the long table, someone would ask me a question, and unless it could be answered with a yes or a no, I would simply shake my head. Later, when we were alone, Uncle Laurence would urge me to try to speak.

"If I alk, eple urn away," I told him once. I had seen the pain on their faces. The embarrassment, the coughs, shuffles, and how they pretended to look at their plates.

Uncle Laurence reached over and touched my arm. "But you see, that is their weakness—not yours. Try to know that there are people in the world who are not strong. Besides, how do you know your family here would act that way? You've not tried. *I* don't do any of those things." He went into an exaggerated movement of shuffling his feet, looking furtively around the room, shaking his hands in the air, and going into a spasm of coughing, until we both laughed.

My mother does some of those things, I thought, embarrassed.

"It must be very difficult for you," he said softly, putting an arm around my shoulders.

I nodded in acknowledgment, and for the first time felt something like a strength of my own.

* * *

A few days after we arrived in Montreal, we left for Mont Tremblant, where my grandparents had a house on a large lake. There were five cars filled with family and servants, trunks strapped on the back. The caravan wound its way through the mountains up to the clean, cool air that blew across the lake. Two servants had gone ahead the day before to open up the house, and before we reached it, I could see the windows gleaming with light and smoke curling out of the chimney in the dusk. It was a big house with windows on all sides. My grandfather saw no reason to shut out the world, and would have had a glass house if he could. I remembered my cupboard bed, with its eiderdown comforter, and the smell of wood burning low in the fireplace.

One morning two weeks later my mother came into my room carrying a suitcase. I would be leaving for Royal Victoria Hospital the next day. As I packed, I missed Andrew. Packing was always something he would do and make a game of it. "Now, let's see, shall we take the yellow flannel pants and the blue checked jacket?" As he knew very well, I never wore anything but Eton suits and gray flannel pants, shirts, and sweaters. But once I had saved eight dollars and bought a pair of yellow pants, like Andrew's Saturday-night stepping-out trousers. When she saw them, of course, my mother forbade me to wear them ever again, and my father said they made me look like a sissy. I wonder what he thought those Eton suits made me look like. My mother packed three of them.

The next day I was driven up to the gray-stone hospital for my sixth operation. Shortly after she signed me in, my mother left with Dizzy to catch a train for Ottawa, where she would spend a month shopping and visiting with old friends. "You won't be lonely, darling. Your father will be here tonight, and Aunt Helen-Vera," she said, kissing me on the cheek as she hurried out the door.

I was in the children's ward, six beds, and four were empty. Mine was closest to the window. I lay looking out at the rolling green lawn. The white clouds moving across the sky got lost behind the trees, then reappeared again.

"Hello, Jonathan." A nurse in a blue-and-white apron and a winged cap stood by my bed. She put a thermometer in my mouth, held my wrist, and looked at her watch. I affected calm as the only way to endure the terror I felt. She took the thermometer out of my mouth and introduced me to the other patient, a boy a year or two older, who had leukemia.

The next morning, I was wheeled into the operating room in a foggy daze, and when it was over I awoke just long enough to see my father, my grandmother, Uncle Laurence, and my Uncle Moe standing over my bed.

"I brought you some music," said Uncle Moe. He produced a small portable record player. "It also has a radio. It's made by Philco. They have a plant just outside Buffalo." It looked like a small suitcase. It opened up into a turntable.

"I also brought you some records, Jonathan." He put on a familiar waltz by Strauss. I smiled a thank-you and shook my head.

"You like music, Jonathan?" he said. It played softly.

Then my eyes drooped and I fell back into oblivion—which I welcomed. I was sorry when it faded and I was up drinking through a straw again. My mouth hurt terribly, and I wished that my mother were there.

The day after I got back to the lake house, a new speech therapist showed up. His name was Mr. Balmain, and he carried a black case. It was about four feet long. He opened it into a big screen and plugged it into a socket. "I want you to look at the words on the screen, listen with the earphones, and then say what you hear and see."

He flipped a switch. A voice said, "Cow."

The picture showed a brown-and-white cow.

"Oooouuu," I said.

"K-k-k-k-k," said Mr. Balmain.

"K-k-k-k-k," I said.

"Ow," he said.

"Ow," I said.

"Now, put the two sounds together—Ka-ow."

"Kou."

"No, throw the air out—Ka-hahahahahahah ha hah hah."

"Hah hah hah hah."

"Now, Kahah-ou."

"Kaaaou."

"Good! Good! Again."

"Kaaou . . . Kaaaou."

The next picture was "horse," then "mule," then "donkey," then "duck."

I had learned to look pleasant and eager, but it was like wearing borrowed clothes. On the inside I felt that it was hopeless, and to keep from being disappointed, I didn't really try. I had been to so many therapists. But at least this was better than the camp with Dr. Hubbard. But I kept on saying the words. Mr. Balmain's magic machine, as he called it, started flashing two words at a time.

"I o. I ent. I came. I ike. I ove."

"Again," Mr. Balmain said.

"It's hard."

Mr. Balmain put his hand on my shoulder. "Try harder," he said gently.

"Ut I oo try."

"I understand," he said.

"I an't."

"You can if you *will*. Now, again . . ." he said.

"I o. I ent. I came. I like. I love."

"Say them faster."

I did.

"Slower."

I did.

"Throw out the air."

I did.

He turned the volume up, and the words echoed in my head: "Horse." "Cow." "Duck." "Dog." "Bird."

Then came longer sentences.

"I am happy." "I am sad." "I am hungry."

"The dog ate a biscuit."

The words flashed on faster and faster.

Mr. Balmain started his metronome. I learned to talk in rhythm. And we played a game. "Tell me how many objects you see, and name them in sequence," he said, and flashed pictures of a horse, a hat, a smiling baby and a sailboat on the screen. I repeated what I saw, and then made up sentences using the words. Over and over we went. I could recall twenty and thirty images at a time.

One afternoon when we finished he said, "Jonathan, I'm beginning to understand you." I really didn't believe him. But whenever anyone but Mr. Balmain spoke to me, I returned to

48

my old habit of not talking, or talking so that no one could understand me.

"You'll talk to them clearly in time," he said. But fear still walled me away. Sometimes it took all my effort to conceal my panic and present an earnest face. I practiced saying names: Uncle Laurence, Lily, Grandpa Honour.

Every day they talked of Lily and the *St. Louis* and wondered when she would arrive with our relatives. We played croquet on the lawn and I listened to talk of concentration camps. I drank tea and ate lady fingers and heard that Jews were loaded into freight cars and shipped to Auschwitz, Dachau, Treblinka. My father came home on weekends from the McGill University laboratories, where he was studying the effect of hormones on fertility and working on a formula to enhance conception. My mother brought me suits from Simpson's and then disappeared to visit her friends again.

One afternoon a cable came for my grandfather from the Joint Distribution Committee, an organization to facilitate the reimmigration of refugees on the *St. Louis* when they reached Cuba. It read: "SERIOUS DOUBT ABOUT VALIDITY OF PASSENGER DOCUMENTS." President Federico Laredo Brú of Cuba had signed a decree voiding the landing certificates of the passengers. When he received the cable, grandfather left immediately for Havana to appeal the decree with Fulgencio Batista, a friend of his who worked for the president.

From Havana my grandfather cabled us: "PEOPLE COME EVERY DAY TO THE DOCK FOR GLIMPSES OF THEIR FRIENDS AND RELATIVES ON THE SHIP. IN LAUNCHES THEY CIRCLE THE SHIP, WAVING, SMILING, SHOUTING GREETINGS AND ENCOURAGEMENT. ABOARD THE BOAT, LILY HAS ORGANIZED THE GERMAN JEWISH CHILDREN'S AID AND IS CONCENTRATING ON ARRANGEMENTS FOR THE HOUSING, SCHOOLING AND WELL-BEING OF THE ST. LOUIS PASSENGERS. I SHALL CONTINUE TO NEGOTIATE WITH LAREDO BRÚ AND BATISTA, BUT NOW THE PRESIDENT HAS ORDERED THE SHIP 'BEYOND THE TWELVE-MILE LIMIT.' "

That night, another cable came from my grandfather, who had meanwhile offered a million dollars for the passengers' safety: "THE ST. LOUIS HOVERING IN CUBAN WATERS. THE PRESIDENT AND HIS GENERAL DISAGREE ON WHO WILL RECEIVE MONEY."

A few days later, Uncle Bernard said that the *St. Louis* was steaming up the Atlantic coast, having given up on Cuba as a sanctuary, and Grandpa was on the way home. He said Grandpa sent a telegram to Franklin Roosevelt asking for help for the passengers and the children. There had been no reply.

When he arrived home, Grandpa asked the prime minister of Canada to lunch, hoping that he could arrange for the passengers on the *St. Louis* to land in Canada. Tables were set up on the lawn with white cloths and silver bowls filled with summer flowers. The men wore dark suits and wing collars and the women wore long dresses in flower prints and white linen. My grandmother, who had been reared in a convent, always invited several nuns to gatherings like this. Today it was Mother Theresa, who became silent after a glass of sherry. I felt united with her and spent my time by her side.

Prime Minister Mackenzie King patted me on the head and flirted with my mother and grandmother in florid French. *"Vous êtes belle comme les fleurs dans votre jardin et dans le monde, Madame Landau."* After lunch, I followed him, my uncles, and my grandfather into the library, where they lit cigars and sipped brandy and I sat on a chair in the corner. My grandfather thought it was good for me to be in on his meetings as long as I didn't make a disturbance. As soon as everyone was settled, he told the prime minister about the *St. Louis*. Then he asked if Canada would open its doors, and guaranteed that the nation would suffer no economic hardship. "Aboard this ship are fine people, physicians and craftsmen, scientists and artists, and children," he said.

King nodded in understanding, and replied, "Canada is sympathetic to the plight of those aboard the *St. Louis*, Honour. But our policy is the same as the United States'. We have a quota. We must take care of our own needs first."

"But, sir," said Grandfather, "it is hard for us in a free society to know what it is like for families to be driven from their homes in terror. It is hard for us to understand the bitterness of exile beyond a faraway frontier. These people are floating by our shores."

"We cannot relax our regulations."

"You're speaking of regulations, and I am talking about *life*."

The prime minister looked away. "I have tried—God

50

knows I have tried. Unfortunately, it seems to be seen by the government as a matter of private concern," he said finally.

Later I asked my grandfather why a boat couldn't just go to the ship and take Lily and the others to shore. Lily and some of the children could come here, I told him. There are an extra five bedrooms that no one is using.

He said, "I'm afraid life isn't as simple as that, Jonathan. It has to do with politics. It has to do with war—between countries and between people." I didn't understand. There was something about my uncle's look that made me know that he didn't understand either.

I asked Grandma if Lily would be all right. She said she didn't know. Then she started to weep. I said I didn't want to make her cry. She said I hadn't. She said she was crying because she was sad for Lily and all the people who had no place to go.

We left for home soon afterward, passing through New York and Delaware on the first day. I sat alone in the back seat of my father's car and counted telephone poles in a pollen-hazy light, dappled in shades of late-summer greens and yellows, splintered by tall white birch trees. In Virginia we stopped for the night at an inn on the coast, and after supper I lay in bed propped on my elbow listening to the sound of a foghorn, counting the number of times the beacon swept across the water in a minute—ten, eleven, twelve. On one of its sweeps, I saw a ship caught in the light. I leaned into the window, my nose pressed against the screen. Lights were strung across the top of the ship like diamonds. It was cruising slowly and it was close to shore. I knew it was Lily's ship. I bolted out the door and across the sand to the water's edge.

"Nanan nahll nahllly nahlll," I yelled, waving my arms. "It's mmmeeeem mimi mi mi mi commmmm baaaaaa commmmmbaaaaa."

"What are you saying, little boy?" I heard a man's voice. "What do you want?"

"Nananilll nahill nahillly. It's me mi mi mi mi mi An-na-hun. Nailll on that ship!"

"I can't understand him at all. What is he saying?" the man asked a woman standing near him. She shook her head.

I pointed to the ship, "Nahilly's on that ship."

"I think he's trying to say Lily," the woman said. By this time half a dozen people had gathered on the sand.

"Nahilly nahilly nil ni nil le le le lil lil lil lil lily lilee lileee!"

"He said Lily!" the man cried. "What about Lily, son?"

"On the ship, on the ship!" I said. I looked back at the people. My father was hurrying across the beach.

"You spoke!" He cried, hugging me.

My father understood me for the first time.

"Lily's on that ship," I said clearly.

"No, son, I don't think that's Lily's ship." He shook his head slowly and held me close to him.

6

From then on I began to speak, falteringly at first, but by the time we got home my mother and father didn't have to try to guess what I was saying.

Finally we turned into the driveway. Andrew must have been watching for us, because by the time we reached the porch he was standing ready to open the doors.

"Hi, Andrew!" I yelled.

"Oh, Cricket, Cricket!" He hugged me.

I smelled the familiar scent of the cologne that Andrew usually saved for his nights out. "You sound good. You sound real good," he kept saying over and over as he unloaded the bags and trunks and carried them into the front hall.

"I can talk, Andrew! Listen to me." I danced up and down and Andrew danced with me. "I'm Jonathan." I spoke slowly, but plainly and clearly. I felt an inexpressible sense of relief.

The next day for Sunday dinner Lady came over for a celebration of fried chicken, sweet potatoes with marshmallows, green beans with almonds, biscuits, and iced tea made with freshly ground mint from the garden. Earlier that day, Illona had become the proud owner of my mother's silver fox, and she modeled it for Lady. "Honey," she said, "when they see Illona in this fur coat, they'll know that *style* has come to town."

After dinner Lady and I talked. "You really sound okay, Jonathan," she said with admiration. I still didn't say too much to her. I noticed that her dress had tiny little flowers embroidered on the skirt and her hair was clean and straight with a bandana and her eyes were still clear and blue and she laughed with easy spontaneity. There were a lot of things I *wanted* to say, but even though I could be understood, I found it hard to express the feelings *behind* the words. I could write a note to her. I had to tell her somehow that I cared for her so much. So I excused myself and went shopping through the house to see what I could find to give her: a piece of lace, a silver napkin ring, a bracelet of my mother's, a quilted pillow, a silver bowl—something small, delicate, pretty. Andrew was reluctant to assist me. My mother had often wondered what had happened to her seventeenth-century silver spoon with the shell. This time I picked a small painting of flowers that Lily had painted. It would be the perfect gift for Lady. And some-day Lily would paint another one.

I wrapped it in one of the blue Tiffany boxes in the attic and tied it with a white ribbon and presented it to Lady. She said she thought it was beautiful, and she leaned over and kissed me. I was very self-conscious. A few days later, my mother quizzed Andrew about the missing painting, which had been in her dressing room, and Andrew replied to my mother that it was absolutely mysterious but he never remem-bered seeing it. He succeeded in persuading her not to worry, because it had to be somewhere—and indeed it was. Lady called me and thanked me again for the lovely painting, which she had hung in the most favorite place in her room.

I had never been so happy. Then came the first day of school. As I entered the classroom, David Phillips yelled, "Hay, An-na-hun, An-na-hun! Where you been this summer?"

I felt the familiar rage, but I walked on in, pretending not to hear him, and sat down. Each year at school the same fears had always engulfed me—fear of ridicule, rejection, being made to feel a fool. I thought they were behind me. But they all rushed back in an instant. "Hey, An-na-hun, let's hear you talk—talk like this," said Jamie Fitzpatrick, imitating me by talking through his nose.

Everything snapped inside, and I lunged at him, swinging wildly and blindly with both fists. He was sent home bloody, but so was I. When I tried to explain what happened, my mother couldn't understand me. I had lapsed back into my old ways. She decided I should return to Mr. Balmain. The night before I left for Canada, Andrew was helping me pack. "I've been thinking a lot," Andrew said. "I was thinking that while you were in Canada, the boys and me would try our luck and get things going up North in New York."

54

"No, Andrew," I said slowly and as plainly as I could. "Don't leave me! Come with me to Canada." My speech was nasal and uncontrolled, the words unformed. But he understood.

Andrew put his arms around me. "I'll never let you go, Cricket. I was just going to get things ready for us."

But I felt this safe refuge slipping away and I was numb with panic. I shook my head. "No, I'll be so alone up there in Canada, Andrew. I don't have any friends and I'm scared. I'm always being sent away." I cried uncontrollably.

Andrew looked at me and stroked my head. "You been talkin' so good, Cricket. You just need more trainin', and I can't always help you. Remember what I said about Hollywood and New York? Well, I mean that. You and I are gonna go there together, and when we do, you'll talk real fine, better than anyone else in the world. And everybody will listen to you. And I'll be there, and we'll do just about anything we want to do. No, Andrew's not leavin' his boy."

He pushed me gently away so he could look at me. There were tears in his eyes, too.

"You're crying, Andrew."

"Now, ain't that just a shame? That's just 'cause I love you, Cricket. I love knowin' you're around. You make me feel real good."

I held him again and smelled the clean starch from his white shirt, which blotted my tears. "Once you get speakin' straight, you can sing with the Red Caps. We'll make you the conductor. Yessir, Conductor Jonathan Landau."

"That'll be a long time."

"Not so long, Cricket. You and I got a lot to do. The time will go fast. You just gotta get your education and learn to talk. You're going to be all right."

"I'll feel bad without you, Andrew."

"Oh, Cricket. I'll write you and call you and think about you all the time."

"I'm going to miss you, Andrew."

"You're going to be a fine boy, Jonathan." Andrew paused and looked at me. "Don't ever forget, the cricket always breaks the silence." Then he gave me his gold cricket. "I want you to have this." He put it in my hand and told me that someday I would be king, and when you are King of the Crickets, remember this gold cricket will remind you that all is well in the world. That was the last thing he said. I held his gift tightly.

Andrew couldn't talk anymore, and he finished packing without another word. But the next morning, after stowing my bag in the trunk of the car, he gave me another hug—a long one and a hard one.

As we drove away, I was terribly scared. And I thought about him all the way up to Canada, remembering what he had said to me. I looked at my shiny gold medallion with the cricket engraved on it. I would keep it forever. It was my greatest treasure.

Back at my grandmother's house in Montreal, a tutor came at eight each morning, and I learned reading, English, French, geography, history, and mathematics until noon. Then lunch, and Mr. Balmain from one to four. In time, reading became thought, arithmetic became mathematics, French became literature. Words became thoughts, and thoughts became conversation.

The winters were cold, and the long days overlapped into one another. Late every afternoon I looked out at the barren trees through icicle villages, waiting for the mailman to make his way up the long hill. Postcards from Andrew were frequent, and I received a letter every week from my mother; they were always about her dinner parties and her garden, fashions and redecorating rooms. She sent an occasional clipping about a family accomplishment, and sometimes news about my dad, who had gone off to war and was somewhere in the South Pacific on an attack transport. She never asked about me.

I wanted very badly to hear from my dad, and just when I was about to give up hope, I received a letter from him. It was the first he had ever sent me, and it would be the last. But it meant more to me than any letter I've ever gotten, even before I opened it. With trembling hands I pulled it out of the envelope and began reading:

Dear Son,

    I've been thinking about you, and I write because I have not done so before. I do so now for moments and circumstance help me recall a store of things that matter most. I recall a thousand separate feelings. The important, the familiar, the remarkable. Causes to which we are committed, interests to which we are drawn, people to whom we belong. I'm sorry I can't be there to talk to you. I had so many opportunities to do so when we were together and I saw you growing up, but I didn't. Your mother and I just did not know how. My viewpoint was one of medical history; I saw to it that you had the best surgeons with each operation.

I know the physical pain is slight compared to the emotional wounds you endured. It sometimes leaves a deep scar, and we physicians sometimes forget about feelings. We become condemned and conditioned to pain and disease, so much so that we rarely allow ourselves a deeper compassion. This is partly because we are afraid to lose our objectivity, because if we look at life squarely we will become too involved in the tragedy to be effective at our jobs.

But I was too preoccupied, Jonathan, and I'm sure my distance was interpreted as rejection and indifference. I was optimistic, and I tried to help—but I was too involved with my work and I wasn't there to support you with gentle praise. Forgive me. The madness of this war has changed my thoughts. I want to express the respect I have for you. I want to let you know that I love you. We're somewhere in [Censored] and heading toward [Censored]. We are under constant attack and several boats [Censored]. We operate on forty-eight-hour shifts on napalm-burned bodies, disfigured limbs, blood and guts. The loss of human life is terrifying. I am so close to death I couldn't take the chance of not having told you. Through this war there is an indomitable spirit to survive.

I am all right. We have been under [Censored] and [Censored]. The admiral's [Censored].

In the final analysis we just have each other, and I know now something which I never said before. I write to you balancing as best I can my intentions and concerns, caring about much, and seeking to let you know that I'm proud of you, Jonathan. I feel your loneliness, and I wish I could somehow make life easier for you. I wish I could be there now. But I can give you only my words. In these next years, Jonathan, learn hard, learn well. For what you learn now will be the foundation for the rest of your life, and with a father's expectations, I know you will grow into a stunning man. It is up to you.

Your father

By the time Mr. Balmain came for my next lesson, I had decided that I would learn to speak, once and for all, before the end of the winter.

"Breathe, breathe from the diaphragm, Jonathan, and let the air pass slowly, forming words. Let your mouth guide the air and form the sounds. Through the mouth, Jonathan, slowly, deliberately, clearly."

He had me grind the sounds in my head, "Woo-wah-woo-wah," and louder, and then to the M's, "MMMMMMM-MMMMMM," as loud as I could. And project "Peter Piper picked a peck of pickled peppers" into a candle held a foot away from my lips until I could extinguish it with my enunciation. If I got sloppy, Mr. Balmain would take me upstairs to the attic and make me shout, "Can, could come, be, be, ban, better, bring, brought, Britain, no, now!" He was unmerciful, hour after hour, a thousand words a day.

After four hours one day, I asked if I could stop. The drill was too maddening. He looked at my palate with a little penlight. It had grafted back together. "There is no reason why you cannot speak clearly, Jonathan. No excuses will be accepted. One more hour."

The maids in the house hid when Mr. Balmain was there, and my grandparents made a point of going out. Words bounced off the walls. We were in a boxing ring of vowels and consonants. He would not let up until I finished each round clearly and perfectly.

When I was tired, he yelled, "You're not trying!"

"I *am* trying!"

"Then *speak*! Follow the principles, the procedures—air from the diaphragm, pass through, project, out through your mouth!"

I would try again, and sounds would fumble and mush into unformed words.

One day he became enraged at my "laziness" and slammed the door so loudly that the second floor shook. I thought a cannon had gone off. He locked the door and threw the keys out the window. "You're not leaving this room until you can talk!" he yelled.

I yelled back, "I've been trying!"

"Not hard enough!" He was red with anger. "We're going

58

right back to the beginning, Jonathan. Every exercise until you're a master of language."

"It's impossible."

"You can and you will. You can do it." He turned up the volume on his goddamn machine, and the metronome ticked back and forth through full sentences.

"I don't understand you!" he'd shout. "Clearer! Follow the system!"

Finally I took my earphones off and threw them down. "Pish off!" I screamed.

"The word is 'piss,' p-i-s-s. Not a sibilant s. Not 'pish,' 'piss.' Hold the s."

I stood up, fists clenched. He pushed me down. I stood up again. He pushed me down again. I hit him. He assumed a defense. Up went my guard, and I looked him squarely in the eye; rocking back and forth, around we went.

"I'm bigger than you are, Jonathan," he said.

"I don't want to do th-h-hish."

"The word is 'this,' Jonathan. T-h-i-s. Now, say 'sequentially sequestered, sequentially sequestered.' "

I picked up my chair and threw it against the wall.

Mr. Balmain grabbed me and held me, restraining me until I calmed down. Then he made me read a passage from Shakespeare: "To persevere an obstinate condiment is a course of impious stubbornness, 'tis unmanly grief, it shows a will most incorrect to heaven. A heart unfortified, a mind impatient."

"Again," he said.

"To persevere an obstinate condiment is a course of impious stubbornness, 'tis unmanly grief, it shows a will most incorrect to heaven. A heart unfortified, a mind impatient."

"Excellent," said Mr. Balmain.

I couldn't believe my ears. Or my eyes. He actually smiled at me.

I spoke. I spoke clearly. And when I spoke clearly, he would insist on clarity and diction and manner and style, until it was effortless, and a part of me. I emerged from the third-floor room victorious, pounded and pummeled by discipline and drills, exercises in diction and style, broken apart and put back together again.

"You're making good progress, Jonathan. By next year you

will speak perfectly, and no one will ever know you ever had an impediment." I ran outside and shouted wonderful words through the falling snow. This time I was really going to make it! This time I was going to really speak at last!

During my next vacation, when I was eleven, I felt so good about myself that I accepted my Uncle Moe's invitation to visit him in Buffalo. He met me at the train station and I ran to meet him. Delighted by my clearly enunciated greeting, he turned to the conductor and said, "This is my nephew Jonathan Landau. He's come all the way down from Montreal to visit your city of Buffalo."

"How do you do?" I said, just like anyone else, extending my hand to shake his.

On the way home, Uncle Moe introduced me to everyone he knew, and even passing strangers. When he was talking about the Buffalo Bills baseball team, he would do so with enthusiasm, and enlist any willing ear to support his civic pride. He made events out of details. The next day he took me to a baseball game, and afterward took me down to the dugout and introduced me to the team. "Jonathan has come a long way to see you boys play." I beamed with pride, and one of the players gave me his glove. In the days that followed, we took long walks together and he showed me Niagara Falls and we rode on the *Maid of the Mist* with yellow slickers.

Then one evening Uncle Moe and Cousin Regina invited me to dinner at a supper club on Park Lane. The restaurant had polished silver and flowers on each table. On a bandstand beyond the dance floor was a twelve-piece orchestra all dressed in white dinner jackets. In the center, high on a platform, was the drummer, whose sign painted on his bass drum announced: "The Sam Miller Orchestra." The orchestra played, and couples danced the foxtrot. Halfway through dinner, the drums rolled and Sam Miller said over the microphone, "Ladies and gentlemen, Mr. Jonathan Landau will now lead the orchestra." What? I didn't believe what I had heard.

I snuggled with embarrassment into Uncle Moe, but he pulled me to my feet and walked me up to the stand. It had been him watching me that night at grandmother's house in Montreal. Before I knew what was happening, Sam Miller had handed me his baton and I was waving it in the air. Immediately the band began to play, and I tried to keep time with the music— "Put your arms around me, honey, da-da-dum . . ." But I found that when I waved it slower, the band played slower. Soon I found the right tempo and was tapping my foot. I was beginning to enjoy myself, and I didn't even get scared when I looked over my shoulder and saw that all eyes were fixed on me. It was a wonderful evening, and I wrote a postcard to Andrew about my show-business debut.

Soon afterward, I got a card from him: "Dear Cricket! We stopped in New York on our way to Hollywood. New York is big. We have our first job singing with Cab Calloway. See you soon. . . . Love, Andrew."

When I returned to Montreal, I spent most of my time studying with my tutors, and the rest thinking about Andrew and Lily. Finally I found out from Grandpa what had happened to the people on the *St. Louis*. The Belgian minister of justice had accepted 200 passengers, Queen Wilhelmina announced that Holland would welcome 194, the British said they would probably accept 250, and Georges Bonnet of France agreed to several hundred more. We got a letter from Lily in Paris saying that all of the passengers had found countries. It was a short note. She said she'd write more later. Then Hitler marched into Belgium, France, and Holland, took them all as prisoners, returned them to Germany—and sent them to the concentration camps. We never heard from Lily again.

THE
FORTIES

The forties smelled of Tabu and wore red lipstick and hair over an eye. The early years praised the Lord and passed the ammunition and created a new worktime called swing shift. Round-the-clock radio played "Don't Sit Under the Apple Tree" by the Andrews Sisters, "White Cliffs of Dover," and "When the Lights Go on All Over the World," and canteen romances bloomed. GI became a new word and jeep a new way of transportation. Stars hung in windows and telegrams arrived with greetings or without.

It was an era of acceleration, "cool" wasn't invented, escapes were to beach parties, jukeboxes, and drive-ins. Rockwell moved America to Main Street. Esquire introduced us to air-brushed calendar girls. Frank Sinatra made bobby-soxers out of teenagers and moved them to hysteria.

There were round-the-clock ports, New York and San Francisco, where friends made friends on the street, in penny arcades, or in bars. All-night neons hyped the fun—grab one moment as the whole—with hurry-up marriages to girls in bottled stockings and pompadours. And the movies told us these were "the best years of our lives."

Hope, Crosby, Lamour took the road to Morocco and Rodgers and Hammerstein took words and music and made new places out of Oklahoma and the South Pacific.

7

It was 1941, and it had been two years since I had been home. Luck and hard work had given me the grace to speak well at last. My father was still a fleet surgeon stationed in the South Pacific. He would have been proud of the way I talked.

The South was swept with a wave of blind and mindless nationalism. Everyone was going to military school, and my mother decided to send me to The Fortress, the West Point of the South, to join the long gray line of model cadets who had worn the honorable star of accreditation on their sleeves for 122 years. High on a bluff above a narrow river in South Carolina were tall oaks sheltering the rolling green landscape of the venerable citadel that had graduated George Patton, George Marshall, and Stonewall Jackson.

As a freshman, I was the traditional slave to upperclassmen. I shined their shoes, cleaned their rooms, washed their laundry. And I was the weather man, because I was tall and everyone wanted to know how the weather was "up there." I always sat in the back, always stood at the end of the line. I endured it all—as my punishment for God knows what—for being a first-year plebe, for being in the South, for being part of life. But in the rowdy fellowship of rank, there was a kind of forced camaraderie among the underdogs—and a shared hatred of all upperclassmen.

None was more hated than Jamie Fitzpatrick, the pride of The Fort. I couldn't get away from him. After being the junior-club gold champion at the National for several years, he had gone on to become the star of The Fortress's vaunted golfing team. He could hit a very long ball and he was being groomed to someday play the circuit. Since Jamie practiced all the time, he had to have someone caddy for him—and he chose *me* to be his caddy. A plebe had to obey every upper-classman's command, so four times a week I was given the honor of carrying his bag eighteen holes. Sometimes, when there was a foursome, I had to carry *two* bags, while my friend Daniel, another freshman, and the only other Jewish boy in the school, carried the other two. The bags were heavy, but the worst part of the task was the battery of insults and demerits we faced en route. If Fitzpatrick lost a ball in the pond, we would have to roll up our pants and wade knee-deep in the water and mud to find it. And once Daniel had to look for a ball for three hours in the woods—after I saw Fitz-patrick pick it up and put it in his pocket.

"Golf is a gentleman's sport," Fitzpatrick would say. "It's not a game for Jews." Then he would tee the ball up and instruct me to hit it, and I would bend my arms and try to swing, and the ball would bounce a few feet off the tee. Usually he would do this in front of the clubhouse, teeing up one ball after another and taking bets on how far the ball would go—five feet, ten feet. Daniel and I took turns as Jamie and the others laughed at our failing efforts. We laughed, too—not out of fun, but out of the pain of trying desperately to belong. They referred to us as "the double bogies." Once, after Fitzpatrick had showed Daniel how to hit the ball, he bet that he would hit it at least fifty feet. When Daniel hit it only ten feet, Fitzpatrick accused him of losing the bet for him and snarled, "You're gonna get it, Daniel, you just wait! You're gonna get it!"

A few nights later, after study hall, I went to the showers, and there in the middle of the room, white-tiled and Spartan as a hospital, under a glaring yellow bulb, crouched my friend Daniel. Jamie Fitzpatrick was holding him down while two other seniors, their pants unzipped, urinated on him. In hor-ror I watched as the rivulets ran over his head and down his back. I rushed forward and grabbed Fitzpatrick's arm. He shoved me aside. "Landau, things are going to be rough on you around here." Finished, they zipped up their pants.

An officer of the school appeared in the doorway. "Hey, what's going on in here?"

"Oh, we were just horsing around," said Fitzpatrick. Daniel and I said nothing. The officer left.

The sun continued to rise and set, the grounds were mowed and flowers continued to bloom, but something in me had changed.

I asked my mother to send me food. When Velveeta cheese and a box of Hershey bars arrived, Jamie Fitzpatrick confiscated them and put them in his top drawer. I continued to shine shoes and stand at attention, but a cold rage had begun to burn within me.

It was soon afterward that we learned officials were coming from Washington for a week of reviewing. Buildings were scrubbed, lawns manicured, brass polished, every cadet shined. Even the air had a brusqueness about it. We were inspected twice a day instead of once, went through extra drills. On the third day of inspection, General Baker, the commandant of the school, three student officers, and a Captain Johnston from Washington came up to me when we were standing in ranks.

"Soldier, how do you find The Fortress?" the captain asked.

"I decline to answer, sir."

"Speak up, speak up, Private."

"I'd rather not, sir."

"At ease. Now, tell me, what is your name?"

"Landau, sir. Private Landau."

"Private Landau, you can talk to me man to man, shoulder to shoulder, eye to eye. How do you find The Fortress?"

"Not to be rude, but I don't like talking about it, sir. I'm not here of my own wishes."

"What are you trying to tell me, Private Landau?"

"Sir, this is really not a very good place."

"What is it that you don't like about it, soldier?"

"Other than the food, the thing that bothers me most is that there is just no dignity here, sir. I'm no more than a caddy, and to make matters worse, they did it to my best friend and there was nothing I could do about it."

"They did what?"

"You know, what they do in a bathroom."

"You mean the latrine?"

"Yes, sir, the latrine."

"What did they do?"

"Well, you know, sir . . . upperclassmen pissed on him."

68

Captain Johnston turned to Baker. "Is that what you do here?"

Captain Johnston dismissed us. I was surrounded by freshmen clapping me on the back, congratulating me. But my hero status was short-lived. When the officials returned to Washington, I was called into the office of General Baker. He sat behind a mahogany desk, the United States flag in one corner, the Army flag in another, a portrait of Robert E. Lee behind him.

"Landau, you have disgraced yourself as a soldier, and you have disgraced this school, but more than that, you have betrayed it. You are a traitor!"

"No, sir, I have not disgraced the school. The boys who pissed on Daniel betrayed the school."

"There has been an investigation by Washington, and as a result, after 122 years of wearing the honor star of accreditation, we have lost that privilege." He leaned across the desk and ripped the star from my sleeve. I flinched.

"Every star on every uniform in this academy will be removed. You have destroyed 122 years of honor." The vein in his temple throbbed. "You are now under martial law, Landau. To be guarded at all times. You will do three hundred hours in the bullring, and that's no bullshit." The bullring was a square area inside four surrounding buildings which made up the quadrangle. The procedure for working off hours was to march in full uniform, carrying a rifle.

He pressed a buzzer, and an upperclassman stood at attention in the doorway. "Escort Cadet Landau to his quarters and post a guard around the clock. Dismissed!"

I was guarded at meals, in the showers, in the classroom. I was not allowed to speak, nor was anyone allowed to speak to me. But all hazing stopped. And I became the subject of every first-year cadet's conversation with his girlfriend and of every letter home.

Within two weeks I knew I could not stay on at The Fortress. I wanted to call my mother, but I knew she would only become hysterical. My father was in the Pacific. Uncle Laurence . . . There was no help. I wished I knew Andrew's new address, but he was on the road.

I could speak now, but inside me was muted rage that had

started in childhood when I couldn't express myself or be understood. I was laughed at, picked on, frightened; I couldn't even eat properly. Food and drink got lost in the empty roof of my mouth. Through a thousand separate feelings, it never seemed fair, and now I could protest not only in word but also in action, now I refused to be captive. When I was little, when I was smaller, there were few places I could go, and I had to return home. This time I came home on my own terms, a simple protest against hazing and meanness. I was mad and I was determined and defiant; I would not be part of the system that supported pissing on another human being. I'd overcome my handicap and now I started to vent my feelings with action rather than words.

Every Sunday, the only time the gates opened, the military band played "Three Cheers for the Red, White, and Blue," and we marched through town to the parade grounds and passed in review. Before I fell into place, I went to Fitzpatrick's room for my food. The cheese was gone, but I put the last three Hershey bars in my inside breast pocket and left.

At attention outside the barracks, the battalion commander yelled, "Battalion," echoed by the company commander, "Company!"

"Forward, 'arch," and forward we marched. The honor guard unfurled its flags. Cymbals clanged and trombones blared against the booming of the bass drum.

"Yer left, yer left, yer left, right left." We marched down the center of the cobblestone street. There weren't many viewers—mostly small boys, a few dogs, and assorted Legionnaires whose dim eyes watered in the October sun and in memory of their own long-lost Army days.

"Column left," shouted the battalion commander.
"Column left," shouted the company commander.
"Column left," shouted the platoon leader.
Column left, we marched onto the parade grounds.
"Sound off, one, two. Sound off, three, four."
We stood in formation at attention, ready to execute the manual of arms.

"Right shoulder, *arms*."
"Left shoulder, *arms*." The slapping of wood echoed in the air.

70

"Present *arms.*"

"Parade *rest!*"

"Atten . . . *tion.*"

The band played "Three Cheers for the Red, White, and Blue" again. It was on the second chorus that I broke ranks and began to march forward alone. It was either courage or just defiance, but I marched smartly. Behind me three companies stood at attention. They couldn't move. I approached the three visiting generals who had come to review the troops. They watched with General Baker on the stand.

Eyes right, I saluted smartly and marched past.

They hesitated, then returned my salute. The drum continued to sound as I marched off the parade ground, up an embankment, and across to the highway, where I stuck out my thumb. I was lucky. The first car stopped—a gray Packard.

"Hop in, soldier. Where are you going?"

"Augusta."

"That's where I'm headed. You from The Fortress?"

"Yes, sir."

"I dropped my son off an hour ago. He was on leave. Sorry I couldn't stay for the parade, but I've got business in Charleston. Fine school, The Fortress."

"Yes, indeed, sir."

"I've known General Baker all my life. We were in the war together. Fine man. Kind of man the Army needs more of. General Baker is all-American. Believes in the fundamentals that have kept this country the backbone of the world."

"I'm proud to be a cadet there, sir."

"How long have you been at The Fortress?"

"Three weeks, sir."

"What is your name?"

"Landau, sir."

"Are you Dr. Landau's son?"

"Yes, sir, I am."

"I've heard of your father. Perhaps you know my boy, Dennis Sugarman?"

"No, sir, I don't, not personally. You see, I'm a plebe."

"That's the start of making a man out of you, Landau. It'll toughen you up. You can't be too tough for the Army."

"With your permission, sir, I'd like to relax."

"Go right ahead. You're not at attention here, ha-ha." He pulled a cigarette out of a Lucky Strike green package. "Say, isn't it odd for you to be hitchhiking?"

"It is indeed, sir. Very odd. Not acceptable at all. But you see, I have to get home quickly—illness in the family. I couldn't get a plane. It's a desperate situation."

"I'm sorry, Landau. Not your father, I hope."

"No, sir. He's in the Pacific." The martial music was still ringing in my head. I was humming the tune under my breath.

"That's a stirring song, now, isn't it?" He began whistling. I wanted to pound the dashboard with my fist to match the drumbeat. But I didn't. Instead, I reached into my breast pocket. "Would you care for some chocolate, sir . . . soft chocolate?" I opened the package, and the squares had run together.

He looked down at the dark pool of chocolate. "No, thank you."

We sped down the highway to Augusta and to freedom.

"Mr. Sugarman, I do appreciate this, sir. Thank you for taking me to my door. I hope it's not far out of your way."

"Give my regards to your father. I hope all will be well at home."

When I walked in the front door, I heard my mother on the phone. "Of course he's not at home, General Baker. Why would he be . . . ?" She looked up, and her eyes went wide. "Yes, he is, General Baker." She handed me the phone.

"Landau, you are AWOL."

"Yes, sir, I know."

"You come back here and take your punishment like a man."

"What would that be, sir?"

"One thousand hours in the bullring and on bounds for the rest of the year."

"I don't think so, sir." I put down the phone quietly.

My mother didn't know what to do. So she didn't do anything. And she decided, as usual, to pretend that *nothing* had happened.

8

The next day I asked my mother to drop me off at a driving range several miles from my house. She didn't think to inquire why I wanted to go there. But if it kept me out of trouble, it was all right. It was run by a retired golfer named Kip Tyler who had been in the money for many years until arthritis set in and it became too painful for him to play anymore. I went there every day for the next month. He saw me struggling to hit the balls—one after another—and soon came over and asked if he could give me some pointers. He said I was making the same mistakes over and over, but that with my height, I could create an arch and develop a hell of a drive if I applied myself. I did—with a vengeance.

He started with the basics: First relax, then address the ball, slow backswing, left arm straight, glide the club as you pull it back, slowly, a slight pause at the top of the swing, then bring the club down, throwing your hips into the ball, keeping your head down and your eye on the tee, lock and snap your wrists, and follow through with an arch and a slow backswing. Day after day Kip coached me as if it were a personal achievement to see me take the driver and start hitting the ball well. Buckets of balls became a thousand swings.

"Why are you so determined?" Kip asked me finally. "Hour after hour, day after day. Why?"

I told him what had happened to me at The Fortress. I told him I wanted to hit the ball farther than anyone else, especially Jamie Fitzpatrick.

Swack! And again, *swack!* It seemed at first as if I'd never learn, but then one day I began to get the feel of it. I began to hit the ball solidly and with consistency, farther every day. Fifty yards, 100 yards, 150 yards, 175 yards, then 200. By the end of two weeks I was averaging 225 yards. Once my swing

73

was in the groove, it became easier and easier. Then one day I hit a perfect ball—it all came together perfectly, form following pattern—and the ball soared 250 yards. Kip was impressed.

"Can I hit it longer?" I asked.

"Longer?"

"I've got to." I knew that Jamie Fitzpatrick averaged 225 yards, and I knew that he'd be competing in the yearly driving contest that was coming up at the club. I intended to beat him.

Kip told me that he could make me a special driver with a weight in the club head. It wasn't entirely legal, but it wasn't exactly illegal, either. A little longer shaft, a heavier head with lead inserts, and with my height, he thought I could handle the weight as long as I had the control in my wrist and glided into the ball with my hips. The extra weight threw me off completely at first, but in time I was able to drive the ball an incredible 300 yards.

Several weeks later my mother announced that my father was coming home on leave. I waited by the window until I heard tires on the gravel, and the next thing I knew I was on the front porch hugging him as hard as I could.

I had practically memorized his letter by now, and I was beside myself with excitement because I knew he was going to begin talking to me and listening to me at last. But the man who wrote that letter to me wasn't the man who came home on leave.

"Well, Cricket," he said, stiffening at the intensity of my embrace, "what are we going to do about your education?" Mother must have told him on the telephone that I had left The Fortress.

I didn't answer, but I dropped my eyes and my arms and felt foolish, stricken, and ashamed. He didn't wait for a reply and walked into the house with his arm around my mother. I spent the next few days in my room, but he never came to see me. And he never spoke to me—ever again—as he had written to me in his letter.

He did, however, make a number of phone calls on my behalf and finally found a school for me in Connecticut: Avon Old Farms. Among its many distinctions was the fact that it accepted boys who had been expelled from other schools. He made an appointment for an interview with the headmaster, Donald Pierpont, and the next day we took the train for Farmington.

"I have found," Pierpont told my father gravely, "that the best-quality boys come from the ranks of the expelled. Our boys come to us from Andover, Exeter, Deerfield. Some may have used bad judgment now and again, but the true measure of a man is that he learns from his mistakes. Give me a colossal failure and I'll show you colossal growth. I understand, Landau, that it was you who was responsible for The Fortress' losing its honor rating after 122 years. Extraordinary." He looked at my father. "Commander, Jonathan sounds like our kind of boy. We'll be pleased to have him."

I would be moving into Avon the following Sunday. That left me four days at home. On Thursday I was on the veranda reading *The Moon and Sixpence* when I heard my parents talking in the living room.

"I think our being asked to join the club is a bit of tokenism," my father said.

"But I have some good friends there," my mother said.

"No doubt, but the committee turned down Eberhart, who is not only a brilliant scientist but a crack golfer. And Rosen has a better chance at the Nobel Prize than he has of membership in the club."

Were they talking about the National?

I blundered into the room. "The club asked us to join?" I asked disbelievingly.

"Yes, but we are going to turn them down," my father said.

"Why?"

"It would be wrong for us to join when they've turned down two of our friends."

"But it would be good for Jonathan," said my mother, on my side for a change, or so it seemed to me at the time.

"There are certain principles that go beyond social status, and this is one of them," said my father sternly.

"What do you mean?" I asked.

"We would be the only Jewish family that belonged to the club, and I feel that would not be right."

I knew what my father meant, but I felt that the club would

make life better. It could make me feel accepted, give me something to belong to. And give me the chance to enter the driving contest.

But he would not be swerved. I called Lady and told her of my father's decision.

"Oh, Jonathan, come to the dance Saturday night anyway, as my guest. It'll be loads of fun."

I accepted without hesitation. The driving contest was going to be held immediately before the dance.

On Saturday at five, her parents picked me up. I had my golf club with me.

"What is that?" asked Mr. Ashley.

"That's my golf club, sir. I'm planning to enter the driving contest before the dance tonight."

Mr. Ashley coughed. He thought that was funny.

"I didn't know you played golf," Lady said.

"I don't. Still, I want to enter the driving contest, if that's all right with you, sir," I said, looking at Mr. Ashley.

"Of course it's okay," Lady broke in. "But you may look silly."

It was a ten-minute drive through winding tree-lined streets, and when we turned at the sign, "The National," I entered at last a world I had dreamed of becoming part of since my first long walk from home to the iron fence that had always seemed an embodiment of the invisible barrier that had made me feel like an outsider at the gates of life.

The car stopped under the porte cochere of the clubhouse, and Lady's mother stepped out and swept up the stairs. From inside I could hear laughter, the tinkling of ice, the sound of a band tuning up. Silver cups engraved with the names of Bobby Jones, Sammy Snead, Byron Nelson, Gene Littler, Gene Sarazan, Tommy Haig, stood in shining rows in the clubhouse lobby. The Ashleys headed for the bar near the eighteenth hole, and I followed Lady toward a table. The room was white and crystal—silver bowls holding azaleas, camellias, and gardenias; wineglasses; and chandeliers. Black waiters in green livery waited ready to serve at the flick of an eye. People stood in small groups laughing and talking, knowing they belonged.

Lady slipped her arm through mine, and we went outside,

where twenty or more golfers were lined up at the driving range.

"Well, look who's here! If it isn't An-na-hun, my old caddy," said Jamie Fitzpatrick.

"Say something funny for us," David Phillips said, talking through his nose. A waiter approached.

"Two Coca-Colas," I said.

"Hey," Jamie said, laughing and clapping his hands. "Two oka-olas."

Five golfers took their places in individual lanes. "Well, An-na-hun." Fitzpatrick said, "why don't you enter the contest?" I shook my head no. "Oh, come on, show us that Jerusalem Jewish swing of yours." I knew Lady was embarrassed by his comments, but he was the best golfer around, and his comments went noticed but unprotested.

The contest was the best of three balls. The first wave of golfers all hit beyond 200 yards. The second wave included Jamie, who averaged 265 on his three drives. I then put my name on the list and teed up three balls in a row.

Fitzpatrick cried out with David Phillips, "There he is— any bets on Landau? I betcha he can hit it fifteen feet." Lady hushed him as I stepped up to the tee. Slow backswing . . . head down . . . glide the club . . . pause . . . pull down . . . lead with the hips . . . unlock the wrist . . . *swack!*—260 yards. *Swack!*—305 yards. Swack!—290 yards.

"Jesus Christ!" said Fitzpatrick.

I walked off the tee. Lady was excited. Everyone was amazed. I had beaten the club record. I looked at Fitzpatrick and tossed him a ball. "Only practicing," I said, and took Lady's hand and walked back inside the club.

We sat down at a round table with a reserved sign: "Ashley." We were alone at the table. I felt elated. I belonged. There were four couples on the dance floor. I asked Lady to dance, and we got up to join them. We started to dance, and I overheard passing conversation. "That's the Landau boy. Wasn't he expelled from The Fort?" "What the hell! He just broke the club record." "His family's from the North— Yankees from Canada." I pretended not to hear. As we danced, I thought about Fred Astaire and Ginger Rogers, my eyes half-closed. Lady and I were just like them, impossibly well-matched. I followed with my feet, keeping a certain elegance, as the orchestra played "A Fine Romance." I swung Lady out and we did a little tap step and she swirled back into my arms.

When we finished, a few people clapped. Mrs. Ashley reached out and touched my arm. "You dance very well, Jonathan."

"Thank you."

I followed Lady through the crowded room toward the veranda.

"If people kept their place," said one member, "we wouldn't be in trouble today. Roosevelt and Jews have ruined this country."

"I'm with Lindbergh," said another. "Let the Germans do things their way. And we Georgians will do things our way."

I wasn't sure I wanted to stay at the club any longer.

We ran into Butch McCoy coming in from the porch. I hadn't seen him since school with the Jesuits. "Hey, it's good to see you," he said. "You broke the club record. That's great, just great. But I heard my parents say that your father turned down membership."

"Yeah."

"I don't blame you. It's not that good around here."

"I'll be at school anyway."

Lady tightened her arm. "I'll invite you here anytime you want to come. Every day in summer. We can swim, and go—"

"Thanks, but it's not the same as belonging."

"Why isn't your family joining?"

"Because the committee turned down two of my father's friends."

"What does that have to do with you?"

"He feels that we were a token."

"I don't understand—a token of what? Of appreciation. Of affection."

"Just a token," I said.

The Ashleys' pleasure turned to aloofness when I thanked them for a pleasant hour and said I couldn't stay for the evening.

When Lady picked up her jacket to go, Mrs. Ashley said, "I'm afraid we'll have to insist that Meredith stay with us."

"Mother, I don't want to stay."

"The evening will continue as planned."

"I'm going with Jonathan," she said.

"Meredith, you will sit down," Mr. Ashley said.

I touched her shoulder and threaded my way alone out between the tables. I knew the Ashleys would never really accept me, no matter how well I danced or what records I broke. I was Jewish. Unlike some Southerners—mostly Baptists—they didn't hold me personally responsible for Christ's death. The Episcopalian Ashleys looked at my Jewishness more as an unfortunate social disadvantage. Another ten seconds and I would be out the door.

I filled my lungs with air and started down the hill. It seemed I was always having to run away—from the speech camp, from The Fortress, now from the National. Would I ever be able to stop? I felt bad that Lady wasn't with me, but I couldn't blame her. We'd see each other tomorrow. I heard a singer with the band crooning, "You'll never know just how much I love you . . ."

Several blocks from the golf course and behind the country club I pulled out Andrew's postcard that had come that afternoon and read it by the light of a neon sign that flashed "Louise's Snack and Chat" "Dear Cricket, We're still on the road and singing and dancing our way with Glenn Miller. Now we're back calling ourselves the Red Caps. Riding the Chattanooga Choo Choo—it's all aboard for California. I'll be waiting for you. Love, Andrew."

The next morning I called Lady, but her mother said she was out. The tone of her voice meant she was in, but not to me.

9

I arrived at Avon with crew-neck sweaters, sneakers, khakis, button-down shirts, and gray flannel suits from Brooks Brothers. There was a leisurely formality about the buildings with their gray slate roofs and green lawns bordered by boxwood hedges. A perfect replica of a seventeenth-century village, Avon had been built in 1927 at a cost of fifty million dollars by an eccentric woman from Philadelphia, Eugenia Riddle. There was not a nail in the school—only pegs. Every stone and sheet of slate had been quarried in England, and even the red clay which was packed on the outlying roads had been imported from abroad. The history of the school was as remarkable as its students. In the early thirties, they had all been exemplary scholars from the Four Hundred—Rockefellers, Vanderbilts, Morgans—who dressed for dinner, played polo, and had tutors. Then, during the war, the school closed and became a research center for scientists to develop a precision bomb sight, headed by a man named Norden. Some said that Einstein visited frequently and the school had also become part of the Manhattan Project, which developed the atom bomb. In any case, when the school reopened after the war, it had a difficult time reestablishing itself.

When Donald Pierpont became provost, he adopted a sensible new policy of accepting anyone who was reasonably qualified. Most of them turned out to have been expelled from other schools. But only the best schools—Phillips, Andover, Groton, Choate, The Fortress. Avon become known as "The Last Chance Café."

Pierpont had initiated another sensible policy—in view of the recalcitrant nature of the student body: He let them run the school. Any student could "take the bar" and, being admitted, could represent other students in a "court" staffed by appointed and elected student "judges." If a student accumulated a number of demerits for infractions, he would go to court for a hearing, and if it was found that he had broken the Avonian code, he could select a number of activities in which he could pay off his debt: tutoring in a subject he knew best, increasing his study time, working in the kitchen, giving a sermon in chapel. The school imparted a sense of responsibility at a very early age.

But Avon was acutely class-conscious. Who you were and where you lived held currency. Darien and Greenwich, Connecticut, headed the list of towns in which to live. Horses and cotillions and sailing and Easter vacations in Bermuda—all were considered important criteria. Main-line Avonians always talked at the top of their palates, words formed and projected with a broad A. A bit English, but still very American. As a result of all this, I still felt like an outsider. In addition to being Jewish, I was tall for my age, already pushing six feet. I went to J. Press and bought the same Shetland tweeds to wear on weekends so I could look the same, but I still didn't feel part of the circle.

One student, however, Fritz Shearer, became a good friend of mine. He was a freckled redhead and had lived in Connecticut all his life and knew the ropes. The first day I arrived, he was assigned to show me around and help me get settled. I was awkward and scared and Fritz took me by the arm and showed me the mail room, the study hall, the chapel, the library, the stables, the cross-country course, and the Tin Forest. The Tin Forest was in the woods, where students went and drank beer. Everyone knew that you couldn't drink at Avon, even though there were illicit cocktail parties in the afternoons. So Pierpont had designated a special spot in the forest three miles away from campus. "If you must drink," he would say, "then do it in the Tin Forest." It was far enough away not to disturb anyone, and it was such a long walk back that he figured you'd be sober by the time you returned. The Tin Forest opened in the fall and lasted through winter. By the time the snow melted in the spring, you could hardly see the forest for the cans.

Fritz, I soon learned, was too busy most of the time to be a regular visitor to the Tin Forest. He always had a cause. In time it would be Nagasaki and Hiroshima and the victims of radioactivity. He passed out agonizing pamphlets about war. He came from a rich family, and often he and his father gave me a ride into New Haven in their Packard and dropped me off at the Shubert, where I sat alone and watched the openings of pre-Broadway plays. After the 3 P.M. matinee, if I were lucky, I would catch the 5:30 train back to Hartford, take the bus to Farmington, and then walk several miles back to school.

My dormitory smelled of fireplaces that had burned every winter for decades, and the leaded-glass windows reminded me of Montreal. I read O'Neill, Dorothy Parker, Tennessee Williams, Lillian Hellman, Moss Hart. I was impressed that Truman Capote was twenty-two when his first book was published, and I wondered what I'd be doing at twenty-two.

Pierpont took advantage of my military training and initiated an ROTC, of which I became commander. He also appointed me a student judge. All boys with a record of expulsion from other schools did a stint as judge. Often there were more judges than offenders.

One Saturday a month, both judges and offenders jitterbugged in the refectory with girls from Miss Porter's and Ethel Walker's, and the student band played "Old Buttermilk Sky" and "Chattanooga Choo Choo."

Just before the dance, a freshman yelled, "Landau, Jonathan Landau, phone call for Jonathan Landau."

I ran down the hall.

"Hello, Mr. Landau, Mr. Jonathan Landau . . . Hollywood, California is calling you." I heard four voices together. "HmmHmHmmmmmmm—Hollywood is calling," they sang. I laughed. "Pardon me, boys, is this the Chattanooga Choo Choo on Track 29, calling you on this line." The chorus stopped.

It was Andrew.

"Cricket, we sold a million copies. Mr. Miller has a gold record—the first one ever! We wanted to tell you the good news!" I couldn't stop smiling.

"Everybody plays your song here," I said. "I hear it all the time."

"How are you doing, Cricket? I'm getting things all set up. In a few years you'll be coming out."

"I know it, I know it. How are you doing, Andrew?"

"Fine. Andrew is just doing right and fine."

"How'd you get so lucky?"

"You can't go chasing luck. You got to let it come to you," Andrew said. "It just comes."

10

The summer I was fifteen I had extraordinary luck. It just seemed to come to me. I went with my father to Cuba and watched him receive an honorary doctorate from the University of Havana. We went to Camagüey, to a sugar plantation owned by Alfredo de Santos. The house had its own airfield, and fountains shaded by large-leafed palms, and beyond stretched five thousand acres of sugarcane and banana jungle.

There were about a dozen people at the plantation, and one of them was Ernest Hemingway. The rest were doctors and engineers and their wives, all with a mixture of accents. Hemingway, three of the men, and I went guinea-hen hunting one day on horseback. On the way back, a doctor who had bagged twenty hens said, "I'll bet no one can hit a bottle cap on that barbed-wire fence."

"You're on," someone said. Five caps were placed on the fence a distance of about two hundred feet away.

There was laughter and joking and no one seemed to take the bet seriously. Each man raised his rifle and each missed. When I was up, I aimed, pulled the trigger, and a bottle cap flew into the air. I was surprised.

"My God!" the doctor roared. "Did you see that! He did it."

The engineer, whose mustache gave him a dour look, said, "Beginner's luck. He couldn't do it again."

Hemingway said, "It's all luck. The whole goddamned world is luck. I'll bet you he can do it again. How much?"

"Three hundred," the engineer said.

"I'll double it," said the doctor.

The cap was replaced. I was uncomfortable with all this attention on me but tried not to think about it. I raised my rifle and shot again. All five caps flew into the air. "I've never seen anything like it," the doctor said.

I had hit the cap in such a way that it jarred the wire and knocked the others off.

"It defies all statstics," the engineer said.

"Of course it does—it's luck," Hemingway said. "Luck comes in many forms. I would accept it in any form, and pay what they asked. It took me a while," he said, "to find out about luck: that it's uncontrollable, unpredictable . . . and purposeless."

In my room, changing clothes, it came to me—that it's nothing more than luck that determines whether one child shall talk and another one shall not.

That afternoon I went into town with Eduardo, the son of one of the doctors. Siesta was coming to an end. Big double doors opened everywhere, shutters banged into terra-cotta walls, and stores reopened for business. We sat on a bench in the square having our shoes shined. The air was strong with the pungent freshness of washed streets and filled with the shouts of vendors selling fried bananas, mangoes, and lottery tickets.

Eduardo leaned over and said, "Would you like some *puta?*"

I said, "What's that?"

"You know, *puta, puta.*" He gestured with his hands.

I thought it was something to eat. "Sure," I said.

After the shoeshine, I followed Eduardo through the streets and we stopped in front of high mahogany doors. He pulled on the brass bell, and I stepped into a courtyard filled with girls—and into my first whorehouse.

The foyer smelled of fresh fruit, jasmine, and starched sheets. Army officers were laughing and drinking banana daiquiris. A guitar player sang. I began to realize where I was. Girls were smiling at us; two came up and talked. I was too shy to ask the blond, whom I liked most. I guess that was luck, too. The brunette led me upstairs. I followed her through a hallway of doors and she opened one. I tried not to show my inexperience or embarrassment. It was the first time.

It was a large room with tiles, a fan overhead, windows overlooking another courtyard and gardens that were beautiful in the late-afternoon light. It was exciting. My head felt light—almost paralyzed. I wasn't thinking. Her pleated dress dropped into a pool of clothes—panties, slip, bra—and as they came off, she mamboed around them and sang in the most beautiful Spanish:

Pero yo quisiera estar
En el Diván
con Juan
En el Colchón
con Ramón
En el canapé
con José
En el suelo
con el que yo quiero.

She looked at me and smiled. Christ, she was beautiful! I had forgotten about the blond and I felt her warm hands undo my belt and drop my pants. I took off my shirt, and we both looked at each other. She was about five-feet-three and full-breasted, had green eyes made larger by dark mascara. Her hair was long and brown and she spoke mostly in Spanish but sometimes in English. Her voice was soft and knowing and easy. Her face was porcelain—fine and pretty—and her name was Analita.

She led me to a washbowl near the bed and I stood while she examined me. Her hands were soft, and it was the first time anyone had touched me. Slowly she looked closer and inspected me. She looked and smiled. I felt very experienced —as if I had been with a hundred women—and now I demanded close examination to make sure I was without infection. I looked up, and over the bed there was a large cross, and I felt it was all right. Heaven had stopped for a moment. She bathed me in warm water, then laid me down on the bed and rubbed warm lotion over me. She smelled of lavender, rich and exotic. The fans slowly turned overhead. I lay on top of her, not knowing quite what to do, but heavy and flushed with pleasure. I held her close and her legs parted and I felt her wetness and my mind and soul were both inside her— dark and warm and good. She was naked, melon-ripe; chestnut hair flowed across her creamy breasts. Desirable beyond utterance, importuning me with words and rolling r's. She cried out and then her voice softened into murmurs. *"Traí-*

86

game toallas limpias y nuevas y muy calientes," she said sweetly when we were finished.

"*Sí*," I said, not knowing what she meant. "Would you explain?" I asked.

"Nothing," she said.

"Say it again." It is such lovely poetry, I thought, her lilting sound.

"Tráigame toallas limpias y nuevas y muy calientes."

"What does it mean?"

"It is something very important," she whispered, kissing me on the ear.

And too quickly, too softly, too wonderfully, it was all over for me. This moment had brought me into the ranks of experience. The first time, like the last time, you never forget.

I was back at school a week later. I went to the library and read García Lorca's poetry. I had discovered something very important and had to share this with Lady. I suggested we meet that Saturday in New York, where I made a reservation at the Biltmore.

"Lady, meet me under the clock. I must see you."

"All right, Jonathan, I'll be there Saturday afternoon at three."

I got permission from Pierpont and went down to the city. I could think of only one thing.

"Hi, Lady."

"Hi, Jonathan. I'm really happy to see you."

"Drink?"

"Jonathan, you don't drink."

"I do now."

A waiter came over. "A Cuba Libre," I said. "Two Cuba Libres."

"Are you old enough to drink?" he asked. "Any I.D.?"

"A Cuba Libre," I said. "Are *you* old enough to know what that is?"

"Well, I think so." The waiter went over and conferred with the bartender and returned with two drinks.

"Cuba Libres," Lady said excitedly.

I was suave and debonair. "They are very popular in Havana."

"How *was* Havana?" Lady asked. "I heard you went hunting with Hemingway. I bet it was great."

87

"It was nice," I said to Lady. "But I learned something important in Cuba—very important."

"Like?"

"I learned about life and about women."

"Yes?" Lady said.

"*'Hasta las verdes barandas. Barandales de la luna por donde retumba el agua.'* That's García Lorca!" I said.

"But of course," she replied. "He's the most moving of all the Spanish poets."

I had finished my drink too quickly.

"I'd like another Cuba Libre," I said to the waiter.

"Life is fulfillment and pleasure," I said to Lady. "In the afternoon it gives birth to a renewal of spirit, to a meeting of the soul." Just then the towering clock at the Biltmore chimed five o'clock. "Ah, I hear the distant echoing tintinnabulation."

"Jonathan!"

I pulled Lady close to me very warmly and kissed her.

"*A las cinco de la tarde*, the afternoon—remember the afternoon, for you shall never forget. Come with me."

And up, up, up in the elevator we went into my room. I called room service. *"Soy el Señor Landau. Dos Cuba Libres, por favor."* I pulled Lady close to me and kissed her again.

After befuddled preliminaries, she took off her dress. I explored her warm body, taut and hard, and down toward her secret.

"Oh, Jonathan," she said, "we can't do this. We have to wait. Oh, Jonathan, it's not right."

My mind could think of nothing but a wanton nymph with a moist, wet mouth and damp desire.

"Are you sure, Jonathan?"

I thought about Analita and the beautiful poetry she recited in my ear. I said softly, *"Tráigame toallas limpias y nuevas y muy calientes."*

"What?" Lady said.

"Tráigame toallas limpias y nuevas y muy calientes."

"Jonathan," Lady screamed, "why are you asking for hot towels?"

"I did? When?"

"Just now."

I kissed her again, trying to cover up my blunder. She was breathing hard and I had a full erection.

"Do you respect me, Jonathan?"

"Of course I respect you, Lady, and I love you."

"And I think I love you, Jonathan, but we can't, we can't."

I held her closer and kissed her peach-ripe breasts. I wanted to fuck her to a frazzle.

"I want you, but we have to wait."

Oh, no, I thought. My demented fantasies fell into quietude along with my erection. We lay in bed and I played with her until she quivered and came on her thighs. I thought I'd better do some research, and between fall and Christmas vacation I read G. Lombard Kelley's *Sex Manual* every night on foreplay and afterplay, position, cunnilingus, fellatio. Such wonderful words, I thought.

That Christmas when I was home for vacation, I learned to drive in my mother's Buick. This time, behind the wheel, I drove once again past the two-story houses with the ladies in cream-colored slips sitting on balconies, past the cottages with the wash on the line, past tires swinging from the trees and children lolling on sofas discarded in the weeds. There are some things that don't seem to change.

I saw more of Lady that Christmas. She asked me to go to the club on New Year's Eve, but we decided that we'd stay home and spend it at my house. Just the two of us. With a bottle of champagne to drink to the future.

"Jonathan," she said, "I missed my period."

"But we never went all the way, Lady."

"I think I'm pregnant."

"Lady, they don't go around riding on bicycles."

At midnight I kissed her and we talked about love and I sat close, looking into the fire, thinking how I could get her into bed again. But she wouldn't go.

By the end of the holidays, I was in the terminal stages of frustration. I went back to Avon, and Lady was at Vassar, three hours away. Finally I called her. "If I can get out, where can you meet me? I'll be there in two hours."

"Where shall I meet you?"

"Where's the library?" I wrote down directions. "See you at eleven-thirty."

I grabbed a jacket and headed for the garage. The school station wagon had "Old Farms" painted on the side and a stallion dashing ahead on the radiator. To keep myself calm, I pretended I was doing an errand for Pierpont—out to get him some ice cream at 9:30 P.M. I almost believed it. The key was where it always was—in the ignition. Pierpont said he couldn't lose it that way. God! Big cars make noise. I backed it around and drove slowly down the driveway. Not much traffic on the street. Air clean and crisp, stars shining through. A night to remember. I settled down to an easy sixty-five on the Merritt Parkway and marveled at my bravado.

Following Lady's instructions, I arrived on the library steps at Vassar at exactly 11:30. There she was, standing with her hands in the pockets of her trench coat. My God! She looked like Ingrid Bergman waiting on a foggy bridge. Why hadn't I worn *my* trench coat, like Bogie? What can you do with a tweed jacket with patchees on the elbows?

"Here I am," I said.

"You came."

"Sure did. I'd do anything for you."

"Climb a mountain?" she asked.

"Yes."

"Swim an ocean?"

"Yep."

"Cross a desert?"

"Yes. I'd do anything but steal the headmaster's car."

"You didn't!"

"I did." I knew she admired my courage, but I felt guilty about taking advantage of the trust Pierpont had placed in me. I rationalized that he would think it wonderful that I had driven all this way to see Lady. We spent the entire night kissing—not saying too much, but not doing anything more, either. I wanted her so much my insides ached as I drove home.

On the way back, I watched for an open gas station in case Pierpont looked at his gauge, but there was none, and when I pulled back into the garage, it was 4:30.

Barrett, my roommate, turned over when I crept in. "Where you been?"

"Up to Vassar to see Lady."

"Hey! Really!" He was wide-awake and sitting up. "Next time, can I go with you? Sally's at Trinity. It's on the way."

That was the start of what came to be known as the Poughkeepsie run. Twice a week on Monday and Thursday after study hall at nine o'clock, I'd drive Pierpont's station wagon to Vassar to spend two hours with Lady, dropping Barrett off at Trinity and picking him up on the way back. At first it was only Barrett. Then Winslow Phillips asked if, on the way, I could drop him at the University of Connecticut to see his girlfriend. Then Ron MacAffrey wanted to see *his* girl at Miss Porter's, and finally there was Camden Adams, who got off at Ethel Walker, the first stop.

Frankly, my thoughts were of crotch, belly button, and ass. With the delectable anticipation of my approaching tryst, I drove across the cold and isolated mores of conventional standards to a warm and receptive climate.

A half-hour up the Merritt, I would slow the car, Camden jumped out, and we'd speed away. There was no time to lose. The system worked. We estimated on the way up how long the round trip would take and filled the tank accordingly. On the way back our timing was flawless. Everyone was always waiting to be picked up and we made it back before daylight.

Lady and I would meet on the steps of the library. We'd kiss there until we could stand it no more, and then we'd go inside to the stacks in the library. The stalls in the back of the library were narrow and empty. Each week it was different. Some weeks we necked with the English poets, others with the French novelists. But even with the French she wouldn't let me go all the way.

"Someday, Jonathan, I promise. Someday. We have to wait."

Each time, we brought each other to an incredible pitch of excitement. I'd kiss her, taste her, rub her, play with her. And every night I would explode in her hands just before the library closed at twelve o'clock. Each time we'd straighten ourselves and return to the front desk, where we casually checked out a few books. Then back to the parkway.

The Poughkeepsie run had been successful for close to three months. Then, one Thursday night, on the way home, I slowed to pick up Camden Adams. He wasn't on his usual corner. Jesus! He'd had practically all night with his girlfriend, longer than all of us. You'd think he could be on time. The motor idled as we waited at the roadside. Early-morning mist sifted through the streetlight that glared yellow across the hood. Quarter to five.

"You don't think something's happened, do you?" Barrett asked.

"What could happen?" I snapped. "I feel like leaving without him."

We sat in silence until five.

"How much longer do we give him?" I said.

At 5:20 I saw a blurred figure—like a ghost—hurrying through the mist. I opened the door.

"Jesus!" he whispered as I roared back onto the highway. "Tonight was the night. Jesus! I finally made it. I forgot about the time."

"We can't get out if we don't get back in time," I said. But I was impressed with his reason for being late. I wanted to ask him about it, but I was too busy pushing on the accelerator. We were up to sixty-five . . . seventy. There were patches of ice on the road. The Avon turnoff loomed ahead. I braked too fast and we skidded, spun, and the back tires slid into a shallow ditch.

"What did you do *that* for?" Barrett said. I jumped out and looked at the ditch, then climbed behind the wheel and pressed the accelerator. The wheels spun, churning bits of dried grass into the glowing taillight.

Everybody got out. MacAffrey, Phillips, and Barrett pushed from behind. Adams from his side, me from mine. Nothing.

"Let's try rocking it up and back," Barrett said. Up, back . . . up, back . . . up, back—we got a rhythm going. "Forward!" Barrett yelled. We shoved up, up, up—almost. "Keep going!" The wheels fell back.

Finally a truck pulled to a stop. "You boys need some help?"

A man in bib overalls joined in the pushing from the rear. Again we tried. Again and again. Then a mechanic whom I recognized from the station where I'd often gotten gas stopped and pushed from Adams' side. Again we pushed. "Once more!" the man in overalls yelled. "One, two, three, push! Up . . . up . . . up, we've got it! Keep going! Jump in. Brake, for God's sake!" We all jumped in, waved out our thanks, and maneuvered onto the Avon turnoff.

The sun cast a pink glow in the sky as we passed the

administration building. The organ sounded from the chapel, and the choir was singing "Blessed Trinity. Bless the Lord God Almighty." The doors opened and students in gray flannel suits came down the steps and spread out before us on the road. I inched the car through the procession. Somebody stopped in front to talk. I tapped the horn. We hunched down, squeezing our necks into our shoulders. "Hey, Landau, where you been?" someone yelled. I felt like I was driving a hearse.

"And there's Barrett and Adams, and MacAffrey!" In the rearview mirror I saw Pierpont standing on the chapel steps. He was looking in our direction.

"Couldn't have picked a worse time," Camden said as we reached the courtyard.

I wanted to yell at him, but I didn't. I parked the car in the garage, left the keys in the ignition, and walked silently into the office to wait for Pierpont. The others followed. Suddenly I felt they were making me their leader. Dammit! We were all in it together, and I wasn't going to get manipulated into taking responsibility for them.

The door opened. It was hard to tell what Pierpont was thinking. Sitting behind his desk, he looked at us in silence for what seemed to be five minutes. "MacAffrey," he said finally, "you were thrown out of Exeter. Phillips, you had many choices, but you came because you *chose* Avon. Landau disgraced The Fortress. Adams, no one would take you but us, because of your grades. Barrett, you transferred because Choate was giving you a hard time. I took you in. With the exception of Phillips, not one of you came highly recommended. But I took you in. Do you know what my colleagues said to me? 'Donald, how are you going to build a great school by taking in the delinquents—a man who was caught screwing a girl in his room, a man who was responsible for The Fortess losing 122 years of accredited rating, a man who drank in class, a man who didn't study. Why, you'll have mutiny every day.' Could my judgment have been so wrong in deciding to take you in?"

"No, sir."

"Then would you mind telling me where you've been?"

"Ethel Walker to see my girl," Adams said.

"Trinity College to see my girl," Barrett said.

"University of Connecticut to see my girl," Phillips said.

"Miss Porter's to see my girl," MacAffrey said.

"Vassar, sir, to see my girl," I said.

"How did you manage to work it out for everyone on the same night?" he asked in amazement.

"We've been doing it for three months, sir."

"I've got five sex maniacs on my hands. I would suspend you all, but it would reflect badly on my judgment in admitting you to the school."

"Throw me out, sir. I deserve it," I said.

"I can't do that," Pierpont said. "My colleagues would nod their heads and say, 'We warned you.' Landau, how would you handle this? *You're* a judge."

"Well, sir, I'd like to make a contribution to the school. I'd be happy to chop wood for the fireplaces here, and the cars need polishing every week."

"That seems like a fair and honest approach," Pierpont said. "MacAffrey, what about you?"

"Well, sir, I can stock the fish pond and sweep up the quadrangle."

"I'd like to raise money for a scholarship fund, and you know, sir, I'd like to make better marks," Phillips said.

Adams said, "I've noticed how dirty the windows in the refectory are, and I'd like to clean them. Also in the chapel. And I'd like to help in the kitchen the rest of the year."

Barrett said, "Sir, the walks need sweeping at least twice a day. That's the very least I could do."

Pierpont nodded. "That seems reasonable, gentlemen. And in the spring, perhaps we can figure out a way for you to invite your friends down for the weekend."

"Thank you, sir." We filed out, knowing that the Poughkeepsie run had come to an end.

11

Summers were always hot, humid, and lazy in Georgia. Everyone told me I was lucky to have a job as a lifeguard at the Bon Air Hotel. There were a lot of girls splashing in their Catalinas and Jantzens, but I thought only of Lady. She was vacationing with her family in Wyoming and I felt the distance was coming between us. I would not see her until September, when we would meet again at the Biltmore. She was in her second year at Vassar and I was finishing my last year at Avon. I thought about our romantic reunion all summer. My spermatozoa were manufactured under optimum conditions those sunny days, working overtime into the night shifts, hoping for the day when they would pass quality control and be shipped special delivery to Lady. In just a few weeks I would toss her my lascivious lariat.

In September, I rode into the big city. My uncles had bought a town house in New York at Three Beekman Place. The bank had grown and Uncle Laurence needed to be in New York a great deal of the time. I was always welcome to stay there. It was a pretty house—brick facade with a small gate and a brass bell. Inside, the rooms were narrow and high with large windows that opened onto a lawn that swept down to the East River. I had the house to myself except for the English housekeeper. My uncles retained a limousine service, so I called for a car to take me to the Biltmore to meet Lady. I walked back and forth to the corner, waiting for the car. Fall had arrived and New York was crisp. Benny Goodman tunes played over a radio from a stationery store in the middle of the block.

What would she be like? I wondered, enthralled with anticipation. What would she wear? I was wearing the regulation gray flannel suit, and my loafers and fingernails were polished.

A blue-and-red-striped tie. Romantic but sincere. I was pushing six feet, four inches now and was still tan from summer. Where was the limousine? I might be late. We just had time for lunch before the matinee. I planned to bring her back to the town house for cocktails after the theater. That's when I would ask Lady to come to the Avon dance three weeks away. Just wait till my friends met her.

At last, the long black Cadillac appeared. I jumped in, and in minutes I was at the Biltmore. There she was, under the clock—a season older, pretty, always so pretty. She was wearing a new perfume, and I was going to take her to a new musical called *Guys and Dolls*. Everyone was talking about the show. It was New York's current hit. Tickets were hard to come by, but I was rich. After all, I had $250 in my pocket saved from my job, and I had paid the scalper's price of $25 for the best tickets in the house.

My friend Fritz from school knew Vincent Sardi, and he told me to call Jimmy, the maître d', if I ever needed a table at Sardi's. Jimmy obliged, and there I was in the number-one spot on the left, having lunch with Lady. I felt good. Maybe it was the black limousine, or being welcomed at Sardi's, or the niceness of the day.

Now, Lady's soft voice was close to my ear. "Jonathan," she said, "I met someone from Yale when I was in Wyoming —and I like him very much."

"What do you mean?"

Then came the clincher!

"I'm in love. It just happened. His name is Derek."

"Derek?" I said.

"Yes, Derek. He's captain of the polo team. D. J. Jones. Maybe you have heard of him?"

"No, I haven't heard of him."

"His father is head of the New York Stock Exchange and he lives in Bermuda. Imagine. He's just super."

"Super," I said.

"He's invited me to the New York Cotillion."

"What about the dance at Avon?"

"What dance?" Lady asked. "Derek and I are serious. But we will always be friends, Jonathan. I adore you."

I love you, Lady, I thought.

She had to leave right after lunch to meet her Derek at the

Tavern on the Green. I didn't know what I was going to do. I couldn't believe it. Lady with someone else, his arm around her, kissing, laughing. I knew when I picked Lady up that she was different. Maybe it was the rouge or the new lipstick color or the perfumes. She seemed older, more worldly. I felt empty and lonely. I didn't go to the musical that afternoon. And that night I drank all the cocktails by myself. Lady? Jesus Christ, it hurt. She had held so much meaning for me. I thought: But you're my girl. You've always been my girl! You promised. Someday. All those trips up to Poughkeepsie and the library.

The pain comes when you least expect it. You are never ready for it. There is a numbness which goes into nausea, and then into depression.

All I could think about was the illusion of what was and what might have been.

This was it. She didn't love me. A part of me went with Lady. I remember making a note to myself. I should have known that it would always be this way. No one would ever really love me.

I returned to Avon and spent my time studying—mastering history, literature, mathematics. I was determined to become a good student. I became the best. Uncle Laurence thought that I should apply to his old college—Trinity at Oxford. It seemed like a good idea, and I mailed my application. It was accepted in short time. All my other friends were applying to Harvard and Yale and Princeton. The Ivy League held nothing for me.

The September dance came and went. I didn't have a date. I didn't know anyone to ask. I thought about Lady a lot. My friends advised, "Keep busy." "Find another girlfriend." But it didn't work. I kept hoping for a letter from her saying that she had made a mistake—the hell with Yale, it's Avon forever —or a phone call telling me that she really loved me. It never came.

Something else did. A notice for a preinduction physical. The country was at war in Korea, and even though I had been born in Canada, I had lived all my life in the United States. I had to report. It was a simple-enough afternoon—filling out forms and forms to be filed: Name—stamp; address—stamp; health—stamp; classification—stamp; 1A—stamp. I asked for a deferment to continue my education. I was assured by those who were in a position to know that my draft board would be very considerate.

I went horseback riding every day down at the school stables. Pete Kilborn, my classmate, played polo and kept a string of ponies there, even though Avon Old Farms didn't engage in competitive sports. Football, track, basketball, were all intramural. Traditional rivalry did not fit in with the elitism of the school. The exception was polo, and Avon was the only prep school in the country with a team. They played clubs in Westbury, and Southampton, and Yale.

"Why don't you learn polo, Jonathan?" Pete asked me one day. "The way you ride, and with your long arms, you'd be a natural."

"I was hoping you'd say that, but I don't have any ponies."

"Use mine, Jonathan. Christ, I have twelve. George Walker has a few more. Boswick has five, and then there are the Whitney ponies." Jock Whitney was one of the finest polo players in the country, and he kept his horses at Avon. "Give it a chance, try it out," Pete urged.

I thought about Derek Jones. "D.J.," they called him. He was co-captain of the Yale team. Maybe, just maybe, we could beat Yale, if I were on the team. I thought about that a hundred times. Lady will be watching. She'll see. I'm just as good as D.J. Maybe that's what Lady wanted—a polo player. I thought D.J. must be dashingly bold and brash. I'll be like him. We'll beat Yale, and Lady will have second thoughts. Everyone loves a winner.

My polo-playing days began. As with any sport, you go into training. Strong wrists and arms are important, legs equally so. You learn to ride holding with the pressure of your knees and inner thighs. And by balance you guide the pony. Polo is fast, always at a canter or gallop. Back and forth along fields that are two hundred by three hundred yards. It's a bit like soccer. You try for a goal by hitting a four-inch wooden ball with a specially made four-foot-long flexible stem mallet, but there are only four players on each team.

At practice I fell three times before Pete tied my arms in front of me and made me gallop and control the pony with my weight. Each morning I started with push-ups until I worked up to one hundred. I went down to Kaufman's and was fitted with a specially made brimmed helmet, white jodhpurs, high black boots. Avon wore blue shirts. I was given number four. I practiced every day, galloping back and forth over the fields, fighting blisters. Hot showers at night, mentholated lotions. My body was sore and the smell of horses never left me. Back to the grounds, warming up, cantering in figure eights, faster, slower, cutting across, riding off, swinging the mallet, advancing the ball, judging distance, timing a hit, learning plays, retrieving, hitting, forward, backward, holding the mallet high, and in one perfect motion swinging over my head and down—*clack!* Followed by rumbling groups of ponies coming together and breaking away, turning to give chase. You hear the clumping. Who is behind you? Get to the ball, cut across. Strategy, teamwork, and total concentration.

I got better. There were long hours of practice just hitting the ball, winding up, and, *clack*, over and over again. First, at a slow, deliberate pace. Then, finally, full out in a straight-out gallop, leaning forward and standing in my stirrups, advancing the ball with full force.

The first three games I was just held in reserve. Then George Walker took a fall and was out for several weeks with a broken ankle. Next weekend, Yale. Oh, shit, I thought. I hope I can play well. I told Pete that I was nervous.

"Hell, Jonathan," he said, "you've been playing terrific. We'll beat Yale. Except for Jones and Hickcock, they've got no team."

It was Sunday, a cold fall afternoon. The leaves were in colorful arrays of yellows, crimsons, greens, and reds, forming different patterns that were on the ground of the playing field at New Haven. Most people parked their cars in sequential rows behind the safety area along the grassy sidelines. An hour before a match, trunks opened to wicker picnic baskets and woolen blankets. Chilled wine was uncorked and brandy sipped from silver flasks.

The teams had arrived on the field early that morning. The horses had been trucked to the stables in New Haven the night before. Nine groomsmen were engaged to saddle the ponies and bandage their legs in white cotton. Two or three horses were sometimes ridden in one chukker. In between, horses walked, and cooled. I warmed up, cantered a bit, hit a few practice balls.

"Where is D.J.?" I asked Peter.

"He's number six over there."

I spotted him right away. And there at his side was Lady. I had known it would be like this. Oh, Christ. More anxiety. Seeing Meredith made me just as uneasy as playing polo. With studied ease I dismounted, walked across the field, and said hello to her.

"Hi, Lady."

"Jonathan!" She threw her arms around me. "It's been months. Oh, Jonathan Landau, meet Derek Jones."

He was square-jawed, blue-eyed. Black hair, white teeth. Well-proportioned, rich, and confident. I didn't like him. He took off his glove and offered me his hand. "Lady talks a lot about you. Are you playing today?"

"Yes, I am." He's a good-looking son of a bitch, I thought. I affected his same nonchalant poise.

"We will be seeing a lot of each other. Nice to know you, Landau."

Meredith smiled at me. She was wrapped in the camel's-hair coat she had worn the afternoon she left me sitting at Sardi's, alone. "I didn't know you played polo."

"Of course I play."

"Watch him, Derek. I'll tell you right now, he's good. Jonathan, did you know—"

A whistle blew over the loudspeaker, announcing the team and introducing the players.

"I have to run along, Meredith. See you later."

At each end of the field there are goals which are ten feet high and twenty-four feet wide. The play is directed toward hitting the ball to the opposite goal. There are two umpires who ride alongside to check for dangerous riding fouls, carrying the ball, or the illegal use of the mallet.

We mounted our horses and waited. The whistle blew again and the game began. Back and forth across the field we rode. Without much effort we made two goals in the first chukker. Yale made two in the second. The game's early, slow rhythm picked up then in furious competition. Riders galloped to one position, cutting sharply. Bump your opponent. Ride him off. Get the ball. Go for the goal.

I scored once, which was astounding. What do you think of that, Lady! Most of the time I played defensively and passed the ball to Pete whenever I could. D.J. and a fellow named Hickcock were stars. They had played in Argentina. Kilborn and Boswick from Avon were just as good. They qualified for the Challenge Cup team. The match was eight periods, lasting 7½ minutes each. There were no substitutions except for injuries. In the seventh chukker we were leading by one goal. In the eighth period the game became rougher and tempers flared. The afternoon tired and the end of the game approached. Several times sportsmanship gave way to anger, elbowing, shoving. D.J. and I clashed, riding hard side by side; our ponies pounded for the right-of-way to hit the ball. Avon was going to win this game, I thought. There was no question in my mind now. We would win.

Yale tied it up with a stunning goal by Hickcock. There were two minutes to go. The horses were high-strung. A white foam of sweat eased around the saddle. Kilborn gave way to Boswick, who clacked the ball two-thirds down the center. I was just twenty yards away in perfect position. There was no one close enough to interfere. I saw Lady on the sidelines, just a blur as I galloped by. This is the moment. The ball was lying there, dead ahead, shiny and white on the green turf. It was all mine. I heard excited applause. He's going to do it. They knew it and I knew it. I rode with my eyes on the ball, positioned myself, raised my mallet. Closer and closer. At the precise moment, I swung with everything I had and watched for the advancing ball to *clack* past me and score. I missed. I lost the game.

D.J. rode across the field behind me and delivered the ball to Hitch, who controlled the ball to a half-open field and the winning score.

Yale five, Avon four. I couldn't look toward D.J. or Lady. I felt outside again. I just did not want to see them. Pete and Boswick were very decent about it. We cantered off the field slowly.

"Too bad, Jonathan," Pete offered. "But you played damned well. Congratulations."

I decided that my polo-playing days were over.

THE
FIFTIES

We rocked around the clock into the fifties. Bill Haley and the Comets ushered in the Disneyland decade. It was a time when Colonel Sanders gave away S&H Green Stamps and, "good grief," we discovered Charlie Brown. We drove in Studebakers, and Coca-Cola became a national symbol.

The Brink's job was pulled in Boston. Diners Club credited New York, and Le Drug Store gave Paris its first ice-cream soda.

MacArthur was recalled as an old soldier and Americans took notice of the wild and ruthless accusations of a senator from Wisconsin, Joe McCarthy.

President Truman defended his daughter's singing and Kellogg sugared corn flakes were introduced.

Salk vaccinated our kids. The first tranquilizer calmed the nation. Eddie Arcaro won the Derby. Sugar Ray won the crown. Arnold Palmer won the Masters and the Dodgers left Brooklyn for Los Angeles. We stood tall at High Noon, *floated* Around the World in Eighty Days, *and opened our umbrellas and splashed and danced and found ourselves* Singin' in the Rain. *We remembered* Hiroshima, Mon Amour. *Every preppie read* Catcher in the Rye *and the* Caine Mutiny *went on trial.* Auntie Mame *was turned down by ten publishers before becoming a best-seller.*

North Korea continued its fight in the South, and British paratroopers landed in Port Said to protect their interest in Suez. There were 4,300 deaths in London after a four-day smog alert. Khrushchev took off his shoes and announced he would bury us.

And along with frozen TV dinners and Minute Maid orange juice, America decided she liked Ike.

12

"Greetings. You are requested to appear for your induction into the United States Army at the courthouse, Augusta, Georgia." Fuck. Some consideration! Korea for two years. There was nothing for me to do but fly home.

Not much had changed. There was more ivy on the walls, the trees were taller, sheltering the house and casting shadows of afternoon light.

My father still called me "Cricket." I asked about Andrew. No one had heard from him. My mother announced to everyone that I had graduated with honors from Avon and that I was going to Oxford. That was an important emblem for her. She told all her friends how pleased she was, but she never told me. I had worked very hard for this achievement and I wanted her to say to me, "I'm so proud of you, Jonathan," or even, "Not bad, Jonathan," but she didn't. She never did, and she never would, and that made me feel very sad.

I had always hoped that she would give me a bit of praise, but in this moment was the awful realization that even if she did, it wouldn't matter anymore. It was too late, and I felt nauseated.

I made an appointment to see my draft board. I still hoped for a deferment. Then an extraordinary thing happened. I received a phone call from my childhood friend, Butch McCoy.

"Jonathan," he said, "come to the Club."

I did. And when I saw him, he was as tall as I. "Christ, Butch! You grew up, too."

"What are you doing home, Jonathan?" he asked.

"I've been drafted."

"But that's impossible," Butch said. "You're not eligible."

106

"What?"

"That's right. There's a height restriction in the Army. That's what kept me out. I'm just over six-foot-four. And the thing that pissed me off—listen to this—I was in the Air Force ROTC. Came time for graduation, and they told me there's a six-foot-four height restriction. 'You won't fit in a cockpit,' they said. Then I tried the Navy. Shit! A six-foot-two height restriction. 'You won't fit in a boat.' Then the Marines. Fuck! 'You won't fit in a foxhole.' So I was stuck with Uncle Sam's infantry. Who in Christ's name wants to go to Korea? I thought if the Navy and the Air Force and the Marines had height restrictions, what about the Army? I called the Library of Congress in Washington, D.C., and got the medical regulations."

"What did they say?" I asked.

"Volume IV, *Medical Regulations,* 61: 'If you're over six-foot-four, you're not eligible and if you're under five feet, you're not either.' "

I was overwhelmed with such good fortune. "Why didn't you tell me!"

"Tell you? I haven't seen you for ten years! How did I know that you would grow up to be so fucking tall?"

I went over to Butch's house and borrowed his book of Army medical regulations. I talked to my father, who arranged for me to see three physicians at the medical college. I had myself measured the following morning. Six-foot-four in the morning; six-three-and-a-half that afternoon; almost six-foot-three at the end of the day. Why the fluctuation? One of the doctors who measured me explained. "Everybody is taller in the morning than in the evening. During the day you walk around and as your body settles—a fraction here and a fraction there—you become shorter. When you rest, the body relaxes. After a good night's sleep, you can be more than half an inch taller. It's in proportion to your height."

Armed with this information, I went immediately to the draft board. A name tag that read "Becker" looked over the papers and pulled out my file.

"It says here, Landau, that you are five-foot-nine."

"That does not seem to be correct, sir."

"Have you grown nine or ten inches in the last few months?"

"No, sir, I haven't. I haven't grown since I took the preinduction physical."

"But it says here you're five-foot-nine."

"That's right, sir. But they didn't measure me. It's a mistake."

He looked up at me sharply. "Mistake? Well, I admit you don't look five-foot-nine, but still . . ."

"It's obvious I'm not five-foot-nine."

"It says here you are, Mr. Landau, and if it says in this record that you are five-foot-nine, then you are. We can't change the record. It's out of our jurisdiction."

"Oh, fuck."

"You're going to make a fine soldier, Landau. Now that you've graduated, you're 1A."

"Sir, I have the Army *Medical Regulations* and notarized statements by three physicians. I am six-foot-four-and-a-half."

"Sorry, Landau, there's nothing I can do."

"Can I enlist?"

"Yeah, you can enlist. There's a call tomorrow morning. Be in front of the courthouse at six o'clock. Landau, you've just been inducted into Uncle Sam's Army."

I went home and packed my bags and the next morning I was on a bus to Fort Sumter, South Carolina, with a few blacks and a couple of boys who remembered me from The Fortress. Fort Sumter was a large Army complex with barracks and barbed-wire fences. All Army camps look the same. Long slender one-story buildings with rows of square screened windows in perfect symmetry. The buildings at the fort all had green trim. Green lawns bordered each building. Intermittently platoons, squads, and companies walked down streets without names, identified only by a letter or number. "Hut, hut two, three . . ." barked through the camp with even cadence. Name, rank, and serial number—the emphasis always on the latter. It was a nightmare version of The Fortress. I wanted no part. I would go crazy within this structured regimen. I had enough as a kid of not being able to talk back. To move, to fight, to kill in Korea made no sense to me. This was another "conflict." I asked myself, "What for?" and examined the patriotic tenets of honor. For Sumter was a basic training ground for a wasted effort. "The Yanks are coming" held no meaning anymore.

We passed through the gates as an M.P. saluted us. The morning was spent with vocation and education tests. In the afternoon we walked around naked in a huge hall, waiting our turns for physical exams. Doctors took blood pressure, heart rate; inspected eyes, ears, nose, throat; checked for hernia. I leaned down, stood up, smiled, had shots, moving quickly from one area to the next. It was getting late in the afternoon. I was worried about getting shorter. The last procedure was to be measured. I stepped on a scale.

"Okay, get your uniform," the sergeant ordered.

"Excuse me, Sergeant, but I have letters here from three doctors. Could you tell me what I measure?"

"Exactly six-four, soldier."

"Well, I'm afraid that your scale is wrong, sir. I'm six-four-and-a-half."

"Hear that, Lieutenant? Our scale is wrong. Landau, is there anything wrong?"

"Well, I just want to point out to you that there is a discrepancy. On the record, they listed my height at five-nine. Now you're measuring me differently, and I wish to point that out to you, sir. If you'd just look at these letters . . ."

"Lieutenant, you want to step over here? We have a difficult case here." It was obvious to the sergeant and the lieutenant that I had no intention of serving for two years. And it was obvious to me that they had every intention of making sure that I would.

"I'm afraid our scale is right, Landau," the lieutenant pronounced with finality.

"The scale is wrong, Lieutenant, and your blood tests are wrong. I have low blood pressure and your medical officer says it's high."

"Get your uniform, Landau!" the sergeant yelled.

"No, sir, I will not," I yelled back. The others standing in line behind me warmed to my rebellion: "Yeah, I don't feel so good," grumbled one of the inductees at the rear of the line, and another cried out, "I feel something murmuring right here," as he clutched his heart. It was the start of a mutiny. And the lieutenant knew it. "Landau, get the hell out of here and report to Colonel Ostrow in the infirmary at seven-thirty tomorrow morning."

I explained my height problem to my new friends. They all

109

wanted to get out of the Army, and I now represented freedom to the entire company. I knew I'd be taller in the morning. That evening several of the boys pulled my legs and my arms and others pulled me from the shoulders. At the sound of reveille, they found a jeep and drove me to the rear of the barracks and carried me over to the infirmary, not letting me walk a foot of the way. "We're counting on you, Landau," they said. "Go to it. Give it to 'em. Win one for our side."

The infirmary was a green quonset hut. And Colonel Ostrow was the camp psychiatrist. He was a round, chubby man who perspired a lot. He seemed nervous, like he was in fear of losing his job or something.

"Sounds like we have a problem, Private Landoo."

Private? Oh, shit! "Yes, sir, a slight problem—about half an inch, sir."

"Sit down, Landoo . . ."

"It's Landau, sir." I saw a couch. "May I lie, sir?"

"Lie?"

"Lie on the couch?"

"Suit yourself, Landau. I've been asked to see you and interview you."

"Why, thank you, sir."

"Would you mind if we did a little word-association test?"

"Be glad to, sir." I had heard about those tests. I'll just act crazy.

"Say the first thing that comes into your mind, Landoo."

"Landau, sir!"

"Lan*dau*?"

"Yes, sir."

He said, "Father."

I answered, "Doctor."

"Right."

"Wrong."

"Mother."

"Father."

"Army."

"Duty."

"Good."

"Thank you."

"Thank you, Landau?"

"You're welcome."

110

"Day."

"Dream."

"Hot."

"Cold."

"Sex."

"Lady."

"Thank you."

"You're welcome."

"Landau, you're perfectly all right."

"But you don't understand, sir. I really am not."

"In my opinion you are."

"But, sir, how can I be all right when the Army says I'm five-foot-nine and I am in fact six-foot-four-and-a-half? I really wish you would measure me, sir."

"I'll make a deal with you, Landau. We'll measure you, and this is the last measurement that you're going to get while you're in my Army. If you are seventy-six inches, you are in. If not—out! Okay?"

"Yes, sir."

Two medics were present as witnesses when I stood at my full height and knocked the bar off at over seventy-six inches. I smiled. Colonel Ostrow looked disappointed. I gave the colonel my best feeling-bad look.

He wrote a requisition which I exchanged for a ticket back to Georgia. Back at the barracks the company of inductees cheered and hoorayed. They were genuinely pleased to see me make it out. The whole company escorted me to the front gate of the camp and waved good-bye. "Take care of yourself, Jonathan!" they shouted jubilantly. "Have a good time, you hear?" I turned and saw those poor guys getting ready to go to Korea. How lucky I was, this time, to be taller than everyone else. I picked up my bags and went up to New York.

I was sailing to England.

13

A yellow cab sped across Manhattan, along the West Side Highway. I couldn't be late.

The *Queen Elizabeth* was a good ship. Beautifully appointed and considerately cared for. Fritz, my classmate from Avon, and I met at the Fifty-second Street pier with large wardrobe trunks. It was the fifties, and we tried to push time back to the early thirties. We wanted to believe we were in another era. Instinctively, we had both chosen navy-blue blazers with polished gold buttons and white flannels to wear as we walked up the long mahogany gangplank, inspecting the highly polished brass rails as we ascended. Following the instructions from our purser, we looked for our stateroom and got lost three times trying to find C Deck.

Our steward greeted us with reverent politeness. "Mr. Landau, Mr. Shearer—the captain has invited you to dinner." Ah, this was the good life—the tooting whistles, bellowing foghorns. The harbor made a wider gap between the New York skyline and the gracious *Queen*. We were on our way. We were soon to be wiser and more experienced. Soon to be Yanks at Oxford.

We were the guests of a civilization. The ship had carried a million passengers and held a million memories. It was proud and polished, stately and important. We inspected every corner. Each deck led to the great public rooms, the theater, the dining salons—all built in the tradition of English comfort.

We dressed for dinner that night and introduced ourselves to Captain L. R. Jamison. To my right was a woman whose husband was in the diplomatic service. She was traveling alone. She was Irish and very beautiful, with auburn hair and complementary green eyes. She lived in Dublin. Her name was Sheila McKenzie.

Ireland's most outstanding export must be its people. Sheila was a member of that worldwide secret society dedicated to preserving tradition, family, and language. She was warm and cheerful and charming, but her careful composure masked any emotions other than those she wanted to reveal.

I fell back on my childhood practice of listening intently to the tone of the voice, not the words. Sheila's hyperboles were delivered with guileless inflections, and wondrous events related, wit and whimsy, with hushed admiration. Her language exposed a quick imagination and a single-minded devotion to conversation. Sheila's speech took flights of fancy to the sky, creating a verbal stratosphere. A disarming capacity for opinion and endearing qualities of spoken word and thought intimately bound us together.

Interested in my education, my thoughts, Sheila had an irresistible way of making me feel far more intelligent than I was. When her speech became more clipped and mannered, mine became the same, until we were talking in the same patterns and rhythms.

She was also the sexiest woman I had ever seen. I dallied with noticeable tumescence.

"You're quite handsome, Mr. Landau. You look like a young Eugene O'Neill. Long graceful brown hair, soft brown eyes, oh so tall and slim, and a lovely smile that would warm anyone." Intelligent lady, I thought. "I dare not ask what you do," she continued. "I suspect . . . well, I suspect that you are a successful author."

I looked at her and gulped. "Well, yes, as a matter of fact, I am."

"My husband was going to write. He went into the diplomatic service instead."

Why does she have a husband? I thought.

"He's very talented. You two would get on well."

Never. I hadn't the slightest interest in meeting her husband. I was much too attracted to her. And I was already jealous of him.

"I want to know all about you, Jonathan. Tell me about your books."

My books? I hadn't the foggiest notion what I was going to say. I had never written anything.

If only I could tell stories as Andrew used to do. He could invent the most outrageous tales.

"Have I read your latest book?" she persisted brightly.

"Why, perhaps," I replied. I took a deep breath. What the hell. "It had a modest sell. It was called *Destiny*."

"Why, yes, I did read it. In fact, I have it with me in my cabin. I come from a country of language—Yeats, Joyce, Shaw . . ."

My God, I thought, is there a book called *Destiny*?

"Well, the name of my book is *Destiny II*."

Sheila smiled and responded quickly, "That must be a sequel to *Destiny I*, in which Philip escaped."

I picked up the conversation. "Yes, Vivian had the child and Philip inherited the title and lived on a small stipend in France for a bit."

"But Stephen was her lover."

"Precisely."

We were off. Sheila could improvise as well as I. She had a terrific sense of humor. We built an entire plot for the rest of the trip. Devising ways for Vivian's rendezvous; Stephen's letters to his mistress, Melissa; the crazed and jealous General Warsaw; fighting at all odds, resolving conflict, and Philip finally going to war and dying with honor.

As the trip progressed, we assembled a large cast that found its way into the pages of *Destiny III* while Sheila and I sat in deck chairs steaming through high seas, sipping high teas. We attended costume parties, Monte Carlo Night, bingo, late-morning breakfasts, backgammon, movie intermissions, promenading and following the adventures of titled noblemen and romantic heroines who now entered the plot with a thrust and vengeance, for no apparent reason except that it was amusing to see what we could do with them. Would Stephen seduce the countess? Would he betray the secret? Die for humanity? I didn't care. We were always together.

Every night I thought about Sheila. I made up a plot line. She became Vivian. And I became Stephen, with a spontaneous and exorbitant stiffening.

If only she weren't married, I'd hold her and make beautiful love. I think I would do just that, but, oh, God, what

114

would her husband think? Oh, God, it's just not right; she belongs to another, and I just couldn't do it. It meant something very important.

One day at lunch, Sheila invited me to come to her cabin later for tea. "Why don't you be there around about five, Jonathan," she requested. We usually took tea together on deck, but this was a particularly windy and distressing day. When I arrived I noticed her cabin was much bigger than mine, and rather than upper and lower bunks, it was spacious, with a large bed, a dressing table, and three portholes. She was wearing a long housecoat. Or was it a negligee? I could see through it. "Lemon or cream?"

"Cream," I replied, uncertain for the first time in years of my ability to speak. I thought I should tell Sheila that I could see her nakedness.

"Two lumps or one?"

"Lumps?"

"Sugar," she responded.

"Two," I managed to reply.

"Jonathan," she said with one of her legs arched, revealing a soft and slender thigh, "would you hand me the book on the dressing table? It's for you."

I couldn't stand it. But I couldn't stop looking at her. I had an erection, an intransigent rigidity, and I was very embarrassed. I forced myself to look at the gold wedding band on her finger. If only she weren't married. If only I didn't have this hard-on. She leaned over, showing me her full and gentle bosom. Criminy, I'd like to kiss her and touch her breasts!

"I cannot stand up," I said.

"Why not?" She looked. There was understanding in her eyes, and she smiled.

"Well, because I'm just having my tea."

"Yes, I know," she said very quietly.

Christ, I was nervous. Finally I found the courage to stand, and I sidestepped obliquely across her stateroom and gave her the book. It was a volume of James Joyce. She opened it and read the last page in an exquisite Irish accent:

. . . those handsome Moors all in white and turbans like kings asking you to sit down in their little bit of a shop and Ronda with the old windows of the posadas glancing eyes a

115

lattice hid for her lover to kiss the iron and the wineshops half open at night and the castanets and the night we missed the boat at Algeciras the watchman going about serene with his lamp and O that awful deepdown torrent O and the sea the sea crimson sometimes like fire and the glorious sunsets and the figtrees in the Alameda gardens yes and all the queer little streets and pink and blue and yellow houses and the roesgardens and the jessamine and geraniums and cactuses and Gilbraltar as a girl where I was a Flower of the mountain . . .

Oh, God! I sighted. Oh, God! She got up and walked around me—and then sat closer to me and continued reading softly:

> . . . yes when I put the rose in my hair like the Andalusian girls used or shall I wear a red yes and how he kissed me under the Moorish wall and I thought well as well him as another and then I asked him with my eyes to ask again yes and then he asked me would I yes to say yes my mountain flower and first I put my arms around him yes and drew him down to me so he could feel my breasts all perfume yes and his heart was going like mad and yes I said yes I will Yes.

She finished. There was a pause. I closed my eyes and said, "That is absolutely beautiful." Sheila replied, stroking my hair, "This is the story of every man who comes to understand what is going to be. I thought you would enjoy it."

Oh, God, I did.

"Open your eyes, Jonathan." I couldn't. I felt her standing before me.

"What do you think?" she asked.

I couldn't speak.

"What are you thinking, Jonathan?" she asked huskily.

"That is the language of thought and thought itself."

Sheila walked slowly away. "I'd better dress for dinner now."

"They're having baked Alaska tonight!"

"You'd better leave," she said breathlessly, and helped me to the door too quickly.

I walked back to my stateroom, a deck below. I felt very young—and Sheila was perhaps thirty. I suspected she could love me, but I was too young for her and she was married and belonged to another. I was hopelessly in love with her, but I didn't know what to do.

So I assumed a cloak of tragedy, except sometimes in the evening when Sheila and I danced, and again I stood at the ready with embarrassment. She seemed not to be aware, and hummed along with the ship's orchestra. I danced and broke into a cross step. Another hard-on. I wondered if anyone noticed the irreconcilable discord in my trousers. If only she knew how much I wanted her. If only she wanted me, too.

I didn't see much of Fritz on the crossing. From time to time I saw him talking to groups, usually about serious matters. He spoke about capital punishment. "No life should be taken. Every life should be spared."

I thought it was strange, but I didn't pay much attention to his discussions. Other times he danced gaily in the main salon after dinner.

One evening I stood on B Deck thinking of Sheila and watching the waves roll and subside as the sunset.

"Hello," she said. She just appeared.

"Yes, hello."

"I'm Fiona." Blond hair swept across a broad forehead and generous mouth.

"I'm Jonathan."

"On your way to London?" she asked.

"London? London? I'm supposed to be sailing to Rio de Janeiro. Who ever said anything about London?"

She looked at me incredulously. "This boat is sailing to England." She was English, blond, mysterious.

"This is the *Leonardo da Vinci*."

"Silly, you're on the *Queen Elizabeth*."

"I'm not. I am? I'm not." I paused.

"Yes. Yes, you are."

"Well, what luck. What luck I have."

"Why?"

"I'm supposed to be on my way to Rio de Janeiro, and here I am on my way to London. And I would have never met you."

She laughed. "You caught me for a minute. I thought you were rather reserved and shy when I first saw you."

"Yes, I am, actually. I'm painfully shy. But then I have an

117

outburst every once in a while. It happens every time I get a two-day pass from the clinic. I'd better call matron to get some medication." She laughed. I started to leave. I stopped. "I refuse to do that," I said, turning around.

"Why?" Fiona smiled at me.

"Well, I'm also defiant."

"You're crazy."

"Yes, I am. But when I saw you in the dining room last evening, I got crazier. I wanted to see you and, poof, here you are. You appear." I marveled at my bullshit. I was getting so good at smoozing, I wondered if I could ever stop.

"Well, I do have to go now," Fiona said. "Maybe we can meet again."

"Sure. Same time. Same place. How 'bout tonight, nine o'clock? Here?"

"Okay."

I never learned much about Fiona. Every time we met, it would be just a line, a glimpse, casual moments. Her cousin had married in America, she visited Kentucky, she was going to Greece on holiday that summer. She told me about the debutante season, the social round of introduction and pre-sentations to London society. "It's all gay and amusing. It lasts for eight weeks and is utterly exhausting."

She was social. And, of course, I was dazzled. I wanted to be accepted in London. A nod from Fiona would do it. So, at least, I thought.

She talked in a very low whisper, mysteriously, as if spies were lurking all around. If I got involved with Fiona, perhaps my yearning for Sheila would cease. We met again.

Late one evening on A Deck, we were progressing. It was a night aboard that you have on all crossings. The sea air was salty and almost cold. The stars were in clear abundance. I thought of what it would be like if Sheila were with me. Again a half-forgotten verse came from the ship's orchestra, romantic and distant—"You'll never know just how much I love you . . . You'll never know just how much I care . . ." Christ! How sentimental. But the memory traces were there, "a million or more times."

Fiona kissed me, and I felt the first kiss was an honest kiss. We danced around the top deck, just the two of us, and then all at once—poof!—she vanished. She was off—gone.

It happened several times on several subsequent evenings. I went back to my stateroom and wondered about her disappearances. Fritz came in one evening and we talked about all the activities the day had brought.

"I met a sensational English girl. Christ, she is wild. Incredible!"

Could it be possible?

"What's her name?"

"Fiona," Fritz answered.

"You mean you just left her?"

"Yes."

"But I was with her from nine to twelve."

"Well, thank you very much. I was with her from twelve to three."

"How about last night?"

"The same."

We laughed, but I felt betrayed. Those old feelings. I lay in bed thinking.

I told Shelia about this at lunch on deck the next day.

"You seem disappointed, Jonathan."

"Well, actually, I am. Silly, I felt hurt inside. I liked her— not really, but in a way I did. . . ."

"Oh, Jonathan," she said, "you have so much to learn."

"What do you mean?"

"Someday you'll know what I mean."

Sheila left me with that thought.

That night the boat steamed straight ahead for Southampton, cutting a stirring wake that rose and curled and subsided in the vast, dark, silent waters of the Atlantic.

14

The *Queen* was in port the next morning, attended by a ground patrol, customs agents, dockworkers, baggage masters. I said good-bye to Sheila quickly. Too quickly. There was a certain sadness, because I knew, somehow, I would never see her again. I didn't know then that shipboard romances, no matter how serious, never survive. What happens in a five-day crossing is just a pocket in time, like the last rehearsal, the last drink, the last kiss, the last good-bye. It's over.

I waited in the morning fog with Fritz while his forest-green MG was unloaded from the ship's hold. Then we chucked our overnight luggage in the boot and set out for London. Streaks of sunlight touched translucent misty meadows with pale gold, and I saw horsemen canter the jumpers over the turf. All of England was like a garden, I thought, peaceful and beloved. Castles, churches, and country courtyards. The countryside belonged to a thousand years of appreciation and care. This was southern England—a storybook of white cliffs at Dover, protruding walls of chalk that gave foundation to the undulant towns passing by: Sussex . . . Kent . . . Swans on the River Thames. Dreaming villages with weathered stone surrounded by endless lawns shining in light rain.

All through the afternoon we drove on a high road to London and came to Waterloo Bridge at dusk. The lights and sounds and shapes of the great city were softened and muted in light. London was glowing, and the last deepening twilight reflected Westminster Bridge and the Houses of Parliament on the river. There, hidden in the mist of the gathering darkness, was a storied embankment of a brave and steady civilization that would be my home for the next several years.

Fritz interrupted my thoughts to announce, rather smugly, I thought, "I have plans to meet Fiona at a pub called the Ring and Crown. It's near Marble Arch. See if you can find it on the map." I looked. "What do you say we have a drink there, then go out and find a hotel room."

We drove through London's winding streets. Fritz said to me, "This is a nation of shopkeepers."

"Yes," I replied.

"Perhaps it is London where we should plan world peace."

"I don't understand."

"You will, Jonathan—in time."

When we reached the pub, it was crowded and friendly and smelled of a variety of beers. Friends gathered and passed the time with a Guinness, a pint of bitters, a half-pint of Watneys. We waited for an hour. Fritz was impatient. He couldn't understand where Fiona was. "I better try to call her," he said. Fiona had probably found another. I was secretly delighted when she didn't show.

Perched near the dart board was the prettiest girl in the world. And she was smiling at me. Her teeth were perfect, the smile was genuine, and her eyes sparkled. She spoke. "Are you American?"

"More or less," I said. "I'm Canadian."

"First time in London?"

"Yes."

"Do you like it?"

"Well, I think I do."

"You're very cute, ducky."

"Ducky?"

"Yes, it's an English expression—ducky." I noticed a certain tone in her inflection that wasn't exactly a Mayfair accent. "Would you like a turn around the park?"

I looked at Fritz, who was now engaged in a large phone box negotiating with large English pennies. "A turn around the park?"

"Yes, would you like to see a little bit of London?"

"Well, I suppose I would."

"It'll just take about half an hour."

I motioned to Fritz that I'd be back. We went outside and approached a large Austin cab.

"My name is Molly. My mum wanted to call me Millicent —a bit upper-class for me. And yours?"

"Jonathan."

"Lovely name, that."

The cabbie opened the door. "Good evening, governor."

"Just a turn around the park," Molly said. The cabdriver smiled. "Right you are." And we began our tour. This was nice of Molly. The cabbie kept talking over his shoulder, not really looking at us, just nodding to give visual affirmation that he was speaking to us. "Well, in just a few minutes we'll go from the Tower of London over to Waterloo Bridge to the Abbey. Just over the right there is Number 10 Downing Street, the prime minister's residence, and if it's all the same to you, governor, we'll take the Bayswater Road down to Marble Arch—it's a lovely piece of work, that arch—and then over to the Kensington High."

The cabdriver kept talking, never looking directly at us, chatting away without pause. "There's the Strand, and just there a monument to Lord Nelson himself. Trafalgar Square —and there it is now. That tall, cylindrical tower is Nelson's Column." He continued nonstop. "In the city there's the City of London and the City of Westminster, and in between there's a collection of little villages—Chelsea, Fulham, Shepherd's Bush, Hammersmith, Holland Park, Belgravia." The Austin was high and roomy and comfortable enough to accommodate my long legs.

Just then Molly unzipped my pants. "What are you doing?"

"Oh, luv, this will make it easier for our tour."

"Albert Hall on the left . . ."

"What . . . ? For God's sake, Molly, what are you doing?"

"Fucking you, love. A turn around the park," she said.

"A turn around the park," said the driver, "well . . . we'll turn at Hyde Park right off Knightsbridge."

"We can't do that here," I protested.

"But of course we can."

This is what it means? My God, I thought, I'm in a moving brothel—a mechanized whorehouse—in London! Pretty soon she was on top of me and we were humping away as we went over an old cobblestone street. I felt her sedulously sweet body. Up and down . . . up and down . . . being tossed around the back of the cab.

"Buckingham Palace just on your left, governor. The queen is in residence."

Looking up, I tried to see the lights and the palace and the guards, but Molly held me tighter.

"Are you enjoying this, dear? It's tradition, lovey."

"Tradition," the cabdriver said, "tradition indeed. We're a courageous and steady bunch. That is the British character." The cab made its way to Covent Garden, where I could see John Wren's church. "Now, there's a place I like. For the last three hundred years . . ."

Back and forth, up and down. Molly held me and kissed me and we were both pressing and moving with great force.

"St. Paul's Cathedral—a masterpiece."

"Ahhhhhh."

"Glad you like it, sir. Now, we will head over to Queen Mary's Gardens in Regent's Park and . . . Oh, there's the Royal Festival Hall. Mustn't miss that, sir."

"Ahhhhhh."

"Indeed, sir."

With pleasurable release, I had, in the back of the cab, "the tour."

"Now, wasn't that fun, lovey?"

"Yes." I tried to make myself presentable, looking for my pants.

"Oh, you are so dear."

We got out of the cab and I paid the driver. "Good luck to you, governor."

"Where are you going now?" Molly asked.

"Well, my friend and I were going to find a hotel."

"Well, no need for that. You can stay with me. After all, five quid for a turn around the park—why not throw in bed and breakfast. I quite fancy you, Jonathan."

I found Fritz still in the phone box at the receiver, frustrated and disappointed. His mood brightened when I told him we had been invited to stay at Molly's for the night. We walked back to her flat, which was on Curzon Street just off Hyde Park. Fritz asked her how it was living in a socialist state. "Very social," she replied.

It was a three-floor walk-up. Small, cluttered, smelling of makeup and perfume. Molly made us tea. She took off her makeup and looked much prettier. We were tired and the three of us slipped innocently into her large double bed, with Molly between us. She sang softly, "Just Molly and me, and baby makes three." We laughed. She turned and kissed me. I reached over and turned out a light on the bedstand. "Good night, luvs," she whispered. I lay awake looking through the skylight at the monochrome clouds passing over the moon. Here we were in Britain. A country of character, a city of fashionable fun with properly restrained enthusiasm. I was learning much faster than Sheila would ever imagine. I thought of how nice Molly was to invite us to her house for the night. This was more than romantic love and passion. There was a feeling of friendship and companionship and affection. England is going to be wonderful, I thought.

The light shone brightly through the windows the next morning. Molly was very close to me. I had a very strong hard-on and lay still. She opened her eyes and kissed me. Fritz was on the other side of Molly sleeping. She took my hand and put it on her breast. She breathed warm life into the early-morning chill. We kissed and I took a long time exploring her. Very quietly, I entered her. Slowly, back and forth, I enjoyed the ecstasy. I thought at any moment Fritz would wake up and I would have to stop. With undulating rhythm we made love.

I was on top of her and her thighs were parted, receiving me fully. We turned, and now she was astride me, moving, groaning, and sighing. Fritz turned over. We were quiet. Slowly we started again, moving gently and passionately. Fritz stirred, and we stopped again. Cautiously we began once more. Back and forth, filling each other with love and pleasure. Then Fritz looked up and blinked wide-awake. But we couldn't stop. We were past the point of no return.

"That's all right, dear," Molly soothed Fritz. I could see Fritz was amazed and excited. Molly reached over and patted him. "Just a moment, now, be calm, love," and then Molly and I came in one heaving motion.

I held Molly for moments without speaking; then, patting her round and wonderful ass, I went to the bathroom and showered, toweling myself dry. I heard moaning coming from the bedroom. "Wow!" Fritz kept saying. He was being welcomed officially to London. Afterward the three of us crowded into his MG and went for breakfast. After muffins and eggs and sausages, we sped around London. Fritz and I felt very sophisticated, cosmopolitan, and on top of a cloudless world.

There were still several weeks before term began. Fritz drove to France to see friends. He asked me to come along, but I didn't. I had a letter of introduction from Grandpa Honour to Michael Lansdale. His son, David, was up at Oxford.

The Lansdales lived in a fashionable mews house, just off Cadogan Square in Belgravia, where rows of small houses stand side by side on brick lanes lighted by coach lamps. Part of the time, the family lived in Scotland, where Michael Landsale was chairman of a bank. When he heard that I was coming to England, he insisted I spend a week or two in London before term and meet his son, who wanted to write music for the theater.

"You really should know something about English life," Michael Lansdale told me. "The architecture is not as important as the people. Attitude is not as important as character. Conventional civility is combined with indomitable self-reliance. We will dress for any occasion." The English attach great importance to realities, particularly when it comes to appearances. The width of a lapel, the number of buttons on a waistcoat, the design of a sock, the elaborate attention to detail. And I was to learn they also attach great importance to their club.

At the heart of British society is the word "establishment." And the heart of the English establishment is in the West End of London. Running from the Haymarket toward the Palace of St. James's is a handsome street which houses the old London clubs. Some date back to the late seventeenth century. Here are White's, Brooks's, the Reform, Boodle's, the Savage, the Savile, and the Athenaeum.

There is a club for every sort of gentleman. Michael Lansdale took me, along with his son, to the Reform for dinner. It is reputedly the most intellectual of the London clubs. Among the literary lights who once worked there are Thackeray, Macaulay, Matthew Arnold, and Charles Dickens. The dining

125

room was enormous, with high ceilings and well-spaced round tables.

To be fit for a great London club, one must be nurtured. David knew that in the club there were certain things one can and cannot do. He had been told, specifically, what those things were. Vaguely, he might know that one does not buy a member a drink but does converse engagingly among men. Rather than walking in boldly, as he would at home, or waiting at the door at a headmaster's study, he approached the Reform in broad, reverent steps as if it were a church of a familiar faith. Before entering, he gave a glance of indifference to the distant rumble down the road toward Piccadilly Circus.

The club's atmosphere was not like a home, where you are always a child, nor a school, where you're always a boy. Here we were treated as members.

Some clubs are exclusively for prime ministers and others a garret for actors. But, all in all, the great London clubs are, by contrast, male gathering places dedicated to doing nothing at all. Of course, for a human being to do nothing, absolutely nothing, the same highly specialized training is needed that one might develop in Tibet or the Himalayas. A form of meditation is to be found in the clubs, and a member who merely sits in the same chair, at the same window, in complete silence, and leaves only to eat and answer the call of nature, is much admired and pointed out with pride to the new members. It is an essential part of club life and must be firmly grasped for that life to be understood.

David was impeccably well-bred; the evidence of education, taste, and manners was natural and effortless. He was at ease, the heir of a well-polished tradition. I wanted to be like him: smart, British, comfortable. I tried to affect the same manner. Pretty soon my attitude would be just as nonchalant as the members'. The club: when I arrive, the porter will accept me with respect and grace. "Good evening, Mr. Landau. Nice to have you back." It would be nice to belong, I thought.

Although I didn't know it at the time, the visit to the club presaged the beginning of a grand tour that would take me from English pubs to frontier carabineros in Spain.

David was friendly and agreeable.

I was quiet and shy, full of expectations and curiosity. I mirrored everybody I saw that looked good to me. The dress, the accent, the manner. I didn't feel confident at all, but I acted with steady composure. I hoped that no one would find out how inadequate I felt.

After a brandy in the great hall we crossed St. James's Square, turned up St. Martin's Lane, and entered a pub called the Lamb and Flag. The pub had been preserved through all time. Etched glass, clearly original, illustrated the windows. Writers, poets, and actors presided over the bar. In London there are different pubs for different pastimes.

On other evenings, we went down to the Haymarket in the West End to the theater. The Italians may be the best singers, and the Russians the best dancers. But in London the actor is all.

The actors understand words and they summon all their skills to portray a character; gestures, tricks, expressions, humor, and sheer force of theatrical personality are marshaled. And the English playwright has a unique way of informing, but he always entertains you as well. We entered indifferently to drama with a message that said, "Save the world," and watched plays that raised questions no deeper than those that asked if there were "Anyone for tea?"

Just at the week's end, Fritz called me from southern France. "Jonathan," he said excitedly, "take a plane from London to Bordeaux and I can pick you up. Biarritz is wonderful. There are the most beautiful girls I've ever seen in my life down here."

"Fritz, I've got to go up to Oxford and get settled."

"For Christ's sake, Jonathan, you've got four years to get settled. It's great down here! You can get a flight for thirty pounds. Take a week off." I knew he was right. Term at Oxford wouldn't officially start for a while, and it sounded like a good idea.

I asked David if he would like to come, too, but he was going to Scotland. "I'll see you up at Oxford."

I flew to Bordeaux, where Fritz met me and we drove to Biarritz. It was quiet, off season, and the gambling casino was empty. "Where are the girls?" I asked.

Fritz laughed. "I knew that would get you here. Actually, I

127

haven't found any, but I hear that if we drive across to San Sebastian, there's a place called Hotel de Londres."

"Christ, Fritz, that's in Spain!"

"Jonathan, it's two hours away."

We drove through a small passage to the Pyrenees along a jagged coastline revealing the sea from a series of hairpin turns and toward inspiring aqueducts at the narrow coastal plains.

When we came to the frontier, the man at customs was friendly and suggested that we might change our plans and head down to Logroño, several hundred miles south. "A magnificent trip," he offered enthusiastically. "At this time Logroño is having a fiesta. Every Spanish town," he explained, "has a patron saint, and once a year there is a festival with *corridas* and dancing and a full celebration of life."

It seemed like a better idea. We drove through the vast provinces, remote hills, snowcapped peaks, into lush tropical farmland, through enormous estates called *latifundios*, and forts and castles. Austere and ascetic, the land was like its music: sweet and deeply melancholy.

We arrived in Logroño in the evening. In the center of town was the church. Thousands of multicolored lights were suspended overhead, and vendors were selling *empanadas*. In the square, an orchestra played richly, and Gypsy girls wearing flounced skirts twirled in staccato sweeps.

We checked into the Grand Hotel and headed for the dining room with a relaxed and self-conscious grace. We sat at a square wood table with ladderback chairs and rush seats. Tile floors passed through white arches. Fritz ordered wine for himself. I wanted a mandarin soufflé.

At the next table I heard a man say, "Luck comes in many forms. I would often want it in any form and would pay what they asked." It was Hemingway. In Spain. It was too perfect. I introduced myself, and he remembered the day we had spent together in Camagüey. "Is your luck still with you?" he asked.

"Yes, it is," I told him.

He introduced me to Mary and a young man, A. E. Hotchner, who was writing about him. "Are you enjoying Spain?" he asked.

128

"I've been in Spain for ten hours. We just drove down from France."

"Are you on holiday?"

"I'm up at Oxford, and term doesn't begin for a few weeks." Fritz stood by silently. He did not share my appreciation of Hemingway. I had read almost everything he had written, including all his by-lined articles when he was a correspondent. Those essays that became books:

"The Old Man at the Bridge" was cabled as a news dispatch from Barcelona and later appeared in *Across the River and into the Trees; Men at War* used the same collection of Caporetto passages from *A Farewell to Arms* and the El Sordo sequence in *For Whom the Bell Tolls.* My fantasy was to be like him: to have an ability to tell stories, to write books and live in places where I wished to be. His enthusiasm, his compassion and his imagination, made writing far more than timely stuff.

"Would you like to go to the fights?" He was talking about the bullfights.

"Terrific!" I replied.

Throughout the afternoon the next day, Hemingway talked of life and luck and Spain and matadors. He showed me the golden-crested suit of lights, how to observe the pivot which leads into a *verónica* as a bull thunders by and hooks the red *muleta* with his horns. "The most valued matadors," he said, "are those who stand closest to the path of the horns and make passes smoothly." With each pass, the Spanish were emotional and impossible, priest-ridden and coldly indifferent. They showed their emotionality at the ring that afternoon. Black or white, heaven or hell, agony or ecstasy. They were absorbed in a mysterious religion of the fight, living with the consciousness of death. When the bull was defeated, they responded by being sharply and explosively alive.

This was the first time Hemingway had been back to Spain since he had written *A Farewell to Arms.* "The matador and the bull are together in courage," he said simply. I remembered a piece that he had written: "If there is much courage to this world, the world has to kill or break it. The world breaks everyone and afterwards many are strong at the broken places."

129

When the afternoon ended, Hemingway turned to me and said, "You want to be a writer, don't you, Jonathan?"

"Yes, sir, I do. How did you know?"

"You know what you know. You observe, Jonathan, and you listen." Again he put his arm around me. "Jonathan," he said, "write it down."

15

Oxford is a city designed around the thirty-nine colleges which form the university. Some colleges are older, others newer—Trinity, Magdalen, Oriel—all steeped in tradition, value, and history. From the twelfth century Oxford has been a center for the classics. The spired buildings are ancient and formidable. The education it imparts mirrors an established society whose rich tradition extends from the Anglican Church to graceful leisure. Here the character and privilege of Britain have been nurtured and preserved.

Among pale green vines and crumbling fifteenth-century walls, in last glimpses of summer light, are gardens, tall trees, rivers, and lawns. On most mornings, fog surrounds and pockets the countryside and a procession of bicycles races from the Board to the High, whoosing and whizzing, with students in black gowns breaking the morning gray.

My college was Trinity, one of the oldest colleges, founded by Henry VIII. I was assigned my digs—a large living room with Chippendale sofa and Adam chairs, an old chest, and a fireplace. On the oak floors were worn and faded green rugs. Two brass lamps flanked a square desk. My scout, whose name was Evans, told me that my desk had belonged to Max Beerbohm and E. M. Forster and my Uncle Laurence. The desk was distinguished, and he obviously hoped I would be. Past the foyer there was an old porcelain bathtub that, each morning, Evans filled with hot, steaming water, accompanied by warm towels. In the bedroom was a single bed—Spartan but comfortable. Form clearly followed function.

Evans was part of the Oxonian tradition. Every student had a scout, and Evans' job was to look after me. He selected a bicycle, brought me the morning *Times*, made tea, saw that there was always firewood in the grate, attended to my laundry, and kept my digs clean. Evans represented the last of a British tradition. He was a slight man who wore tortoiseshell glasses, slightly bent, with graying hair and wise eyes. He could have easily been mistaken for a don.

The first day, I bought books and my gown. Traditionally, gowns denote scholastic status. Full-length gowns are worn by graduate students; mid-length shows a prized college scholarship; and undergraduates wear a shorter, sleeveless version.

Evans inquired, "Who's your tutor?"

"Neville Coghill."

"Very good, sir. Coghill is the leading expert on Chaucer," Evans cautioned. "Watch him and don't let him fool you. He may appear dim and slow and may not seem to remember you from one tutorial to the next, but he never forgets anything in literature. One of my boys took a critique by Blake that had been written several hundred years ago by some remote scholar."

"And?"

"He presented it as his paper and started to read it. He wasn't halfway through when Coghill rose from his chair, took a book from the shelf, turned to a page, and began reading right along with him."

"What happened?"

"They just sat there for a while reading together."

"Was he thrown out?"

"No, Coghill just told him that he was more concerned with a student's own thoughts than those of a second-rate critic."

During the next few years I met with Coghill and, indeed, he always demanded original concepts and ideas. Each week I wrote one thousand words, although he would accept just five words, as long as I had done research to support what I had written. My rounds of tutorials each week were a constant preparation of papers on specific subjects. I had to attend schools, a large group of buildings that held more traditional classes with a curriculum of subjects, when Coghill thought I was deficient in a particular area. The tutorial was ceremoniously attended.

Once I forgot to wear my gown. Coghill was vaguely disconsolate. Sententious, but never pompous. "Everyone wears a gown," he informed me.

"Everyone?" I replied.

"Everyone," he said flatly.

From that time on, I dressed in my black gown and sipped sherry with Coghill in his quarters and listened. His magisterial intelligence dealt with small auguries. He asked me what I planned to do with my life. My pause for an answer might be termed as provisional silence. Coghill was an inscrutable mystery. I told him I wanted to write, perhaps journalism or theater. The following week he asked me again.

"I want to write. That is what I would like to do, sir." The weeks passed, another assignment commenced, another tutorial followed. Then, the same question: "What will you do with your life, Landau?" And the same reply. I was never quite sure whether he had forgotten.

I once asked him why he kept asking me. "Oh, did I ask you that before? Sorry." Then again, the next week the same question. I wondered. But he probably knew precisely what he was doing.

Part of the Oxonian education is the several hundred societies fulfilling every interest. Sports, dining, political—a round of English pleasures. Fritz was joining every political society he could find. The Young Conservatives, the East African Society, the English Speaking Union, the Liberal-Socialist Club. I joined the Oxford University Dramatic Society, affectionately known as Ouds. David Lansdale introduced me around.

And that is how I met the Honourable April Huxley. David invited me to a wine-tasting party in college. They were always popular. In between myopic blinks were dons, fatuously overvaluing their own accomplishments, among the crowd of charming, sophisticated, sherry-drinking, literary-thinking guests. The room was cascading in conversation when I instinctively saw her. Blue-eyed, blond, lovely. Lady, Sheila, Fiona.

I asked David Lansdale about her. "That is April Huxley. She's up at Lady Margaret's Hall." LMH was part of the university but exclusively for women. "Smashing girl. I'll introduce you later."

She returned my smile. I was suddenly shy and wordless again and not at all comfortable about speaking to her without an introduction. I would wait for David.

I wandered into a small foyer. There was a piano. I had never really learned to play, although I had studied briefly during my period of fantasizing about conducting an orchestra. I had dreamed of writing songs and arranging the music. When I listened to music, I could hear each instrument clearly, a single note, frills, calls, answers and counterpoints joined together in alternating themes.

For some extraordinary reason I could play one tune on the piano. Andrew had taught me six or eight chords when I was young, and I had perfected a tune, light, French, romantic, which I played pretty well. Sometimes when I found a piano I'd sit and play my tune, with concentration and delicacy. The song reminded me of a carousel and children.

People who heard it always asked me to play other songs. "You play the piano very well." I'd thank them, but I couldn't. That was it. One song. I could mimic a convincing ease at the keys with my long slender fingers, so I would apologize with feigned modesty, "Oh, thank you, sorry, thank you." And back out of the room.

There wasn't anyone around, so I sat down and played my tune. Softly, at first, then with more confidence. I must have played it three times. April sat down beside me without a word and played a countermelody along with me. That was fantastic. Then she played my tune with a variation on the theme.

"That's a pretty melody," she said.

"You are very pretty."

We laughed. "I'm April Huxley. Play something else."

"Oh, well, I'd much rather listen to you."

"No, please. I want you to."

"April, I've never told anyone this before, but it's the only tune I know how to play."

"Really?" she said with obvious delight.

I think it was at that moment that I fell in love with her. What was it—a look, a curious expression, the honest way she talked? I don't know.

"You're from America," she said.

"Yes, Georgia."

"Oh, Georgia. I've read Margaret Mitchell. I like Georgia. In fact, I like Americans and Hershey bars."

"You don't."

"It's delicious chocolate. I do, actually. I really do. Don't you?"

"Well, I prefer Cadbury's." I could not think of anything bright to say. I was lost, stumbling in thickets of syntax. "Are you studying English literature?"

"No, I'm interested in children. I'm interested in child development. In how they grow up. Everything they learn now will follow them for the rest of their lives. Yes, I can't think of anything more worthwhile."

I wanted her to like me. To love me.

I was surprised when I received a note from April the next day inviting me to go with her to the National Gallery for an art exhibit. It didn't seem possible that she could care for me. After all, we had just met. Maybe she was just being hospitable to a visiting Yank. Maybe not. Perhaps this was the way people met and started to care for each other.

The exhibition was Gainsborough, and April looked like an English portrait. Tall, delicate features. Graceful porcelain with gentle awareness. She had long wavy hair that looked like sunshine, and the nicest blue eyes. She wore a taupe silk dress with a high ruffled collar and an antique brooch with an intricate gold pattern. We walked through large halls and empty rooms illuminated with large skylights. All of eighteenth-century England was represented on those walls—country people, a barefoot girl, aristocrat soldiers, squires, *Blue Boy*, the people of home. We walked past woodland scenes, rutted roads, and leafy lanes, lazy moods of childhood. And then we entered rooms with lords and lovely ladies, the fair faces of England.

"Gainsborough thought," April explained, "the first part of a picture should be like a tune. And you should try to guess what follows, like a melodic line running through music. It might submerge or disappear, but it always returns."

God, she is bright, I thought. I wished I'd known that.

The last picture in the exhibition was a portrait of a country man caught beneath a darkening and thunderous sky, with his eyes heavenward. "That was the last picture Gainsborough painted before he died." I congratulated myself on an intelligent observation. Finally.

135

Outside, we crossed the road and had tea, cucumber sandwiches, and crumpets in a small restaurant with old curved chairs and Wedgwood china.

"You want to write. Why do you want to write?"

"Maybe I have something to say. It was hard for me to say it as a kid."

"What do you mean?"

"Nothing, really."

"Writers are romantic figures," she said.

"A life of deep suffering is part of the tradition." I laughed.

"Jonathan! Seriously."

"Well, it's a creative refuge."

"But when you were a child?"

"I was one of the few who had a happy childhood."

"Tell me about that."

"It was just a childhood."

"You won't talk about yourself, will you? I really want to know all about you." About me? She was so direct.

I tried to be amusing. "That's a great song title," I said.

About me? My feelings were rumbling inside. I did what I had always done, I just pretended and affected a calm and easy manner.

We all wear a ring of silence around us; it surrounds our very personal thoughts and feelings that we don't reveal too easily. Inside the ring was a private world that only I knew. I could be amusing and fun. That covered my shyness—and it covered my real feelings.

"I'd like to know more about you," I said, begging the question.

"I had a nanny, a routine growing-up, dolls and make-believe."

"Do we ever grow up?"

"I don't think so."

"But your interest in children?"

"They're young and I love them."

"Me, too."

"I guess we're interested in the same things," she said. "We both observe. Patterns and feelings."

"You're more than a pretty face."

136

She talked about her work. It was important to her. "Why don't you come around to the clinic sometime?"

Once I did go over to pick up April. I watched her across the playground. I was almost envious that she felt with such ease. I wished I could do the same. It was as if she had always done exactly what she was doing . . . perfectly orchestrated with the children. She moved silently. Slow to answer, wise to judge, with a voice of reason and an expression of love of who she was. She created new images for children who were happily playing. English children seem better-behaved and well-mannered. They wore gray short pants and school ties and had long hair. And the girls the same shirts and ties but flannel skirts. I watched them play at games. I saw a little boy whose mouth was swollen, and he talked through his nose. He looked at me, not knowing I was once like him. He kicked a soccer ball by himself side to side and it passed my way. I picked it up and returned it to him and smiled. He smiled back at me. He talked to his friends, and they patiently tried to understand him. It made me feel self-conscious. It was too close. I never went back.

"The boy with the busted lip."

"Yes?" April asked. "He had a cleft palate."

"How is he doing?"

"He's doing quite well. He's a loner. He goes to speech therapy every day. Why do you ask?"

"Just interested." I wanted her to think I was perfect. Had always been perfect. And that I would be perfect for her.

David Lansdale called. "There is an Arts Council competition for an original musical play."

"Let's give it a go." If we won, we would receive two hundred pounds.

Every afternoon I walked down a narrow street to the Banbury Road, where David lived. Out came Number 3 Venus-Velvet yellow pencils with matching yellow legal pads whose barrenness was baneful to my eye. We took turns at the typewriter. It was always cold. I put another sweater on and David put another log on the fire. We wrote and drank tea, rewrote with more tea, developing suspense, and resolving conflict. We wrote in terms of sets and scenes.

Back and forth we tossed ideas, playing "what if." We finally hit upon the idea of a revue with ten people who came from different parts of London and meet one Sunday in Hyde Park. Each had his own story. They come together during the course of a day. Chance. Some are misunderstood, but all find meaning in each other, and their lives change just when they thought it could never happen.

In Hyde Park at Speaker's Corner, where colorful characters exchange soapbox views of the world, we used a speaker as the narrator to take us through the show and make occasional comments. His observations bridged the scenes. David had an incredible gift for music. His tunes were beautiful and made my lyrics appear better than they were.

It was a simple format. The sets were designed to change in front of the audience during the performance. We called it *Sunday's People*.

David and I worked for a solid month. I called April, but she'd gone away for several weeks. There was no place I could reach her.

She rang me when she returned. "Where have you been?" I asked. "I've missed you. I couldn't find you."

"Just to London. I'm sorry. I had some important things to do. I guess we've both been busy."

"But I have tried to reach you."

"I am sorry. I did try to call you, too."

"But how can you just leave like that?"

I thought it was odd. Perhaps not. It sounded as if I were being possessive. I didn't want her to mistake that for caring. April came over, and we were together. If was like seeing her for the first time. It was that lovely feeling of aliveness.

Shortly afterward, David received word that *Sunday's People* had won the Arts Council award and the play was actually to be produced in the spring term at the playhouse. We couldn't believe it.

I raced over to Lady Margaret's Hall and found April in her room. "Excuse me. I've come for the festival," I announced.

"The what?"

"The festival. It's a special occasion. Let's make a costume, sing a song, and celebrate. It's a holiday. Which one? Play-day."

"What?"

"David and I just won the Arts Council award. *Sunday's People* won!"

"Jonathan!" she shouted. "That's really good!"

We went to dinner. April suggested a small country inn not far from Oxford. It was warm and nice.

"Can you imagine? We won! We're going to have a play produced."

"Well, now," April said, "you are a writer, after all."

"I guess I am." I smiled. "Now I want to know what you've been doing. How are the children?"

"We're starting a program of activities on creativity at the clinic. There is an interesting new treatment called art therapy."

"How does it work?"

"You paint emotions. Today I gave the children crayons and paper and asked them to paint their feelings."

"What color is love?" I asked.

"The same as gentleness." She smiled. "Pale rose."

"And fear?"

"Dark green."

"And hope?"

"Yellow."

"I think I like pale rose."

"I knew you would."

"How?"

"Because it's my favorite color, too."

I began to court her. Flowers would always be waiting, a book, a Liberty silk scarf, and sometimes a song.

"Why do you keep giving me gifts, Jonathan? You don't have to, but I'm glad you do." The truth was that I was in a constant state of anxiety. I felt more in control if I gave her presents.

We shared the events that crowded the social calendar. Cricket at Lords, picnics at Glyndebourne, Eights Week at Henley, racing at Ascot. We spent long summer evenings driving through the countryside in her dark blue Lagonda convertible. We ate at the Bear at Woodstock and the Bell at Hurley. Small country inns supported our courtship.

We walked through every park in London; the private pleasure grounds of kings became our gardens. A pollenade of wet afternoons, soft evenings, early mornings, surrounded only by lawns and flowers, tall trees and thoughts.

In Kensington Gardens we found a refreshing eighteenth-century pavilion called the Orangery, white treillage surrounded by orange trees. It was a special place.

I was encouraged when April introduced me to her parents, Sir Patrick and Lady Diana Huxley. They were not pretentious, as I had feared they would be. Instead, they were both soft-spoken and warm. Her father was an M.P. and he invited me to come down to the "house" several times.

"Please call me Patrick," he said.

Not to be outdone in the ways of American democracy, Lady Huxley asked if I would call her Diana. There was grace in their every gesture.

Sometimes we went punting. Standing at one end of the punt, I pushed us slowly with a long pole while April, underneath a large straw bonnet, lazily dangled her hand in the water. We flowed through the arbors of graceful trees and gardens at the river's edge. I felt that all of life was just a passing boat ride down the Thames.

Between terms David invited me to his home in the lowlands of Scotland. April was going to be away, so I accepted. The Lansdales had a handsome Georgian estate on thousands of acres, which had belonged to the family for hundreds of years. Old stone walls divided portions of the land.

There was a continual round of guests—statesmen, artists, actors, and bankers. "A curious mix," David would say. Usually there was six to eight weeks of "vac" between terms, at which time I wrote papers and read. Then on one occasion April came up to Dunfreisha. She took the overnight from Victoria Station and David and I met her in the morning. Each day before breakfast we walked the countryside together, warmly synchronated, patterned steps over small and gentle catenated rolling hills, separated by cold streams chuckling over rocks, and once in a while we stumbled upon a piece of sculpture that Henry Moore had appointed to the country.

"Ah, the land of Robert the Bruce. Haggis, Tartans, bagpipes and porridge. For as long as one hundred men of us remain, we shall never submit under any conditions to the domination of the English."

I paused. I turned.

"April, I am yours in this hallowed garden."

"Jonathan, do you always talk the way you write?"

"No. I am just making an impression. Talking comes later."

We walked along sequestered fields. The clouds were low.

"This is really just a rear projection screen for the tourists."

"Jonathan, shouldn't you be studying? What about your writing?"

"I have this automatic typewriter. You just leave a stack of papers there beside it, and whopf, it just writes itself."

"Jonathan, be serious."

I was, but I didn't know how to show it. If I showed me, I might be rejected.

Some days we played golf, and every day we played croquet on the front lawn after lunch.

After one or two games David's father announced that he was going upstairs to write his memoirs. I asked him, from time to time, how his writing was progressing, and with a decided twinkle, he winked. I didn't know why. It was only much later that I found out he was not writing his memoirs at all. This was his way of not letting us know that he was taking his afternoon nap. He often talked of my grandfather with great friendship and respect, and that made me feel proud.

The dinners were formal and exquisitely served, and for hours afterward we talked about "out there"—Australia; "down there"—South Africa; and "over there"—America.

After dinner, and a respectable wait, I quietly tiptoed down the great hall to April's room and into her large lace-curtained canopy bed.

Each evening I made a different entry. I gathered props and improvised costumes with bravura touches. I became the butler turning down the bed. I donned a hunting outfit and marched through the room with a thirty-gauge magnum. With a flashlight I was a constable, and one evening I appeared in a white sheet as the ghost of Dunfreisha. Once I even walked on the outside ledge adjoining the rooms and swept through the window as Douglas Fairbanks.

I thought I had to amuse her to be noticed, in order to be loved. But she accepted me just as I was. And we made love.

She was giving and innocent. Our first time was met with a

painful frown which gave way to a surprised burst of pleasure. I felt her closeness and warmth. Finally I belonged to someone. And she was the first girl that I truly loved. April and I passed the season looking toward tomorrow.

16

"Sir George Dawson-Blake, KBE, invites you to the opening night of *Sunday's People*, Oxford Playhouse," the invitation read.

It was a wonderful evening for us. The important critics came up from London. April's parents came with Michael Lansdale. Christ, I thought this is really happening. If only Andrew could see me now. As soon as I heard the overture, I relaxed. April sat between David and me. Street vendors, politicians, flower vendors and balloon men, buskers and musicians. "Sunday's People" was a production number, sung in rounds. The audience applauded for an encore. The cast came forward on stage and sang. I thought they were singing to April and me.

Later that evening the newspaper reviews told us we had a hit. I was so excited the next day that it was a while before I noticed the note Evans had left on my desk. "There is an emergency meeting at the Union tonight at ten o'clock. Please attend. Fritzie."

I looked at the old Victorian clock on my desk. It was that time now. Still in my gown, I bicycled across the High, in the chilly November wind. In the distance, from the Union, sounds of a demonstration became louder.

In front of the square there was a huge concourse of people. Cards and banners introduced the crowd: "Stop Soviet Aggression," "Free Hungary." Walking through the crush was Fritz, talking frantically and passing out literature. "Hungary is fighting for its life," he said to me breathlessly. The country was entering a bloody revolution. Fighting had already broken out against Russian aggression and dominance. It appeared to be a very small David against an oppressive Goliath, and news was rapidly spreading to the free world.

The torchlight parade illuminated Peter Veres, a representative from the Writer's Association in Hungary. He read a seven-point program calling for an independent national policy and the return of a more democratic way of life. He spoke passionately, yet with control.

Many of the demonstrators carried the red-white-and-green national flag of Hungary from which the symbol of Communist rule, a hammer and an ear of wheat, had been torn out. The crowd marched jubilantly down Beaumont Street to Christ Church, where Fritz organized volunteers and committees to collect food and supplies, medicine and blankets and literature.

Fritz's eyes were wild and delirious. He had a cause, and this time a very major one. A large green army truck with a red cross painted on the side drove up. The crowd cheered. Hungary was in the news. People kept asking: What can we do, what can I give? The next day the students went around collecting donations from the merchants at Oxford. Fritz asked me if I would drive the truck to the Hungarian border with Peter.

"But I can't," I replied.

"Of course you can," said Fritz. "All you have to do is drive it to Vienna. That's all, just drive a truck—as a Red Cross correspondent. You'll be like Hemingway driving an ambulance in Spain."

I called April. I was caught up in the idea. Students at Oxford orchestrated their ideals into causes. It was being a part of life. Yes, I would do it. I went by in the truck to say good-bye to April. I looked at her and almost said: Wait for me. She almost said: Do you have to go? I drove dramatically away with Peter.

He was quiet. I thought we were a lot alike. Peter Veres was slight and tall, brown hair, a softness in his brown eyes, and a fair and warm smile. His politeness softened his sense of urgency. He spoke about his grandfather, a man called Sandro Petrofi, who had been a poet in the latter part of the nineteenth century. "He was part of the 1848 revolution," he said. "My father was killed by the AVH, the Soviet-advised secret police. Sometimes you lose what you love. Nothing is forever."

Revolution was his life, and he was a student just like me.

144

We began a marathon drive. Glimpses I would never forget. Peter and I took alternate turns driving straight through for twenty-eight hours.

The *Express* ran the story the night before, and we were recognized and waved through England with enthusiasm. Student patriots, a Yank at Oxford, and a writer from Budapest —rushing to support a courageous cause.

Across the channel into France. Students at Calais welcomed us and fed us with cassoulet and affection. Here, in a country which has occasionally approached political anarchy, individual expression was indulgently cherished. Glimpse. An old Frenchman was slowly sipping a drink and playing dominoes at a café. He raised his eyebrows and saluted us smartly. An old château from the Renaissance gave background to the jovial countenance of the quiet, unchanging quality of the countryside. In hours we passed through timeless treasures of a lovely land sundered by war. There was a bright-eyed look of a new generation untouched by the horror of the past. It was afternoon in Munich. The city streets alive with traffic. Europe in a hurry. Ladies with packages, men clinging to punctilious hat-raising formality to friends, the bob and bow, standard words of greeting executed at the quickstep. Instinctively disciplined, Germans clustered dutifully at crossings, and officious warning voices were raised at nervous pedestrians crossing against the light at main thoroughfares.

Grandpa Honour used to tell me that he had banks in France and Germany. I wondered how much time he had spent in Germany. There was something in me that would not let me forget Lily and the traits of arrogance and violence of the world war. Grandpa's friends surely had a regard for family, and were, perhaps, poets and philosophers. Where does the strain of violence and aggression come from? Our truck traveled a land where six million Jews went to their deaths in concentration camps a few years before. Now we drove the last frontier between the Western free world and the Iron Curtain.

The country was familiar, and though I had never been in Germany before, some genetic code held memory. Through sloping meadows, dark green forests, and glorious camera-courting mountains. Through the massive chain of Alps, each with supporting spurs, past country inns and hotels tucked

145

away in valleys along watercourses straight out of the elegance of the eighteenth century, which inspired Viennese waltzes and galops and white horses to wheel through their quadrilles at the Spanish Riding School.

In this kiss-on-the-hand, click-of-the-heel culture, we arrived in Austria, where my grandmother had once lived before Vienna had become a city of haunting silence. Nazis, I suspect, had dampened the laughter and warmth that my grandmother had known before she left to escape the war. I wondered if Mahler and Freud, Reinhardt and even Strauss, had seen the same dark clouds.

In Vienna we checked into the Sacher Hotel, a birthday cake of elegance that held memories of halcyon days when ladies from Salzburg with parasols promenaded along balustrades in soft twilight. It was a time of balloon voyages and vertiginous waltzes.

We were tired. We washed up and joined Arthur Saltzman, a rumpled correspondent from the London *Express*, who took us for drinks that evening. He told us that the London *Express* would donate twenty-five thousand pounds for the exclusive rights to the story.

"What story?" I asked. "We just drove from England."

"The story from inside Hungary," Arthur replied patiently.

"Excuse me, but I'm not going inside Hungary. I offered to help drive to Vienna. This is where I get off."

"Come, Jonathan," Peter said, "you can stay with me."

"Why don't you go, Arthur?" I asked.

"It's a bit chancy," he said. "To be truthful, the borders are closed. They are not letting any correspondents in just now—national-security sort of rot. You can get in under the Red Cross. It's important, Jonathan, it really is. The *Express* will give twenty-five thousand pounds to the Writer's Association."

Peter interjected, "That would help us so much, Jonathan."

"But is it safe?" I asked.

"I don't know," said Arthur.

"Yes, it is safe," Peter assured me.

I'm not sure why I said yes, but I did. I wanted Peter to have the funds to support his ideal. Arthur gave me the name and address of Frank Celi, a contact in Budapest, where I would file my stories. He also gave me money for expenses.

"You only need to stay a few days," he said, "report your

impressions, what you see, anything unusual that would make good copy. It's up to you. You'll have the by-line."

No one knew exactly what was happening in Hungary. It was up to me to find out. The lines from the teletype in Budapest would be open between seven and eight each evening.

From Vienna we traveled to the Hungarian border. From England to France to Germany, we had passed easily through customs, but here the security guards, although not unfriendly, were implicit and detailed and searched our vehicle thoroughly. The only thing we had to go on was faith; no passport to protect me now. The slender red steel boom which fell across the border lifted and we rolled across, onto the loneliest roads I would ever see.

East of Vienna the Danube forms the border for about a hundred miles. Clusters of irregularly spaced mountain ranges stretched across the countryside, bearing ruins of ancient forts. In between the villages was a patchwork of green and brown fields. A passing car, a barking dog.

Peter said that Hungary should be rich in antiquities, but the truth is that it had been devastated and destroyed through wars and revolution, and everything of interest was gone. The Communists had established themselves in control of Eastern Europe. They tried to build a Marxist paradise, but it had not worked. The brutality and cynicism that came with the seizure of power had engendered widespread fear.

The Danube is laced with islands where it flows through Budapest. It is a noble, legendary river. Brave history surrounds the city's memorials. I saw kings on horseback, soldiers and saints and statesmen. Nowhere can there be found so many memorials to rebellion. The city abounds with sculptures of the heroes of resistance.

Peter lived with his sister, Anna, near a bridge once lighted by coach lamps. An enormous stone lion marked its entrance. Anna was slim and frail, with deep and sad blue eyes. She was waiting for us in their small apartment, with a few friends who had gathered in a space of books, papers, pamphlets, and slogans bearing a strange language. Peter talked of twenty-five thousand pounds. "This will help us so much," he said over and over again. "This will buy time for the cause."

We left the apartment and drove the ambulance toward a

147

large crowd that gathered near the Duna Hotel. People applauded us and held out flowers. "Are the Americans coming?" they asked me. An old Hungarian man lifted up his son so that he could kiss me. Many were Peter's friends. They spoke in Hungarian and they embraced me in sincere warmth. This was the overground, the visible resistors, the freedom fighters.

That evening in Budapest the yellow streetcars, joined like caterpillars, went raveling by. I saw women conductors and cabdrivers and street-sweepers wearing baggy Russian-style trousers. In the arcades, aged peasant women bent over lace-making frames. Peter told me about former aristocrats who now made their living by making deliveries, and a onetime baron who used to be a big-game hunter now had a job at a zoo.

We passed a little uptown jazz joint where teenagers were twisting madly until a signal from a youth comrade with a red armband prompted the band to switch to a foxtrot. At the big hotels like the Duna, Gypsy orchestras were sparing with their romance. Anna and Peter and I sat in a paneled espresso bar next to young Hungarian men with strong features and hair growing onto their collars. Huddled together, sipping coffee and white wine, discussing and planning the calculated mobility of revolution which causes men to fight and women to weep. At ten o'clock, everybody obediently left the café and the city of two million people became quiet. Peter said to me, "What a wonderful country this would be if we were free."

We went back to Peter's apartment and I thought about my first story. Out came the familiar notepad that had been with me for so long. What would I say? I wanted it to be good. Would the words come easy? Would I be able to express feeling and truth, and still be objective? I placed these demands on myself and started to outline my observations.

The following evening I walked with Peter and Anna to a huge square where we, along with a crowd of six thousand people, stood in the street listening to a loudspeaker. When one of the speakers called for immediate readmission and free elections, the crowd thundered with applause. Peter translated everything. These were serious moments. This was a united cause, and I didn't think about my individual feelings.

I looked at Anna. She was slender and soft, quiet and

gentle. I wasn't thinking about myself now. I was too involved. I was a witness to this time. The applause faded when the speaker announced that the government would also like wholehearted friendship with the Soviet Union. A man next to me said, "The earth is moving."

It was seven o'clock. I went around to the United Press office on Vace Street to see Frank Celi, the teletype operator. He was a stout Hungarian and the United Press office was no more than an eight-by-twelve room with a desk, phone, and teletype. The room was smoky and a yellow cord with a green shade held the light overhead.

"Mr. Celi," I said nervously.

"You are Landau?"

"Yes, I am."

"Come quickly," he urged. "Service is on. They told me, I am seeing you tall. Welcome to Budapest." He smiled and offered me a beer. Then he took the copy that I had written the night before. The line was open, and he started pounding the keys. My first written words, my thoughts, were being transmitted. My God!

> Landau from Budapest. Via Vienna/London *Express*. November 5—When the earth moved. The combination of courage, anger, and desperation that makes men wager their lives for an ideal fired Hungary into revolution this week. Unarmed, unorganized, unaided from the outside. Not even fully aware at first of what might be the consequences of their deeds, the Hungarian people are fighting back the tide of Communism. It is like a carnival day. Thousands of people gathered in Budapest's old cobblestone streets, wearing red-white-and-green boutonnieres, tossing red-white-and-green ribbons into passing cars. The crowd gathers at focal points to express its will and then to march. A Hungarian colonel said to me, "The earth is moving."

I finished filing my story and later that evening Peter and yet more students began to thrill for action. Peter remembered a statue in Budapest that had been put up by the Russians where a church once stood. It was a twenty-five-foot bronze statue of Stalin. There he stood in baggy pants and a handlebar mustache—a symbol of Hungary's servitude. Peter and a group of friends surged down Stalin's Boulevard and mounted the marble base of the statue. They flung ropes around Stalin's neck, but the old dictator stood fast. Then a group of workers appeared, bearing ladders, cables, and torches. Melting through the metal knees, they brought the statue crashing down.

Trucks filled with Hungarian soldiers stood by, and several heavy tanks rumbled into the area around midnight. Soldiers and students and workers fraternized. Cried the Hungarian colonel, standing in an open hatch, "We are unarmed. We came to join you, not to oppose the demonstration." Soon Peter and the students and workers were flourishing tommy guns. "The Army is with us," they shouted. Barricades were built in the street that night. Peter asked me if I wanted a gun. I did not.

Soviet military units moved across the border that night, and Budapest woke early the next morning to the sound of machine-gun fire. A column of eighty Soviet tanks rolled into the city and took up positions covering all bridges, boulevards, and public buildings. Other tank forces ringed the city. At dawn, martial law was imposed on the whole country. Trains and streetcars stopped running. I joined a crowd gathered in front of the huge Parliament Building facing the Danube, intending to present the premier with a petition demanding the withdrawal of all Soviet troops. I was scared, but kept going. Soviet tanks and a platoon of security police blocked all entrances to the building. Then it happened.

Suddenly, trigger-sensitive young Russian tankers became unnerved by the milling crowd around them and began firing indiscriminately at us, a mass of unarmed people. In a few minutes, hundreds of men and women were lying dead and wounded on the ground, while others crouched behind columns for cover or just lay flat on the pavement. Jesus! Oh, no! Oh, Jesus! This can't be real! But it was.

The news that the AVH had opened fire on the crowd reached Peter rapidly. Immediately he joined workers in the armament plants, where they broke open stores of arms and ammunition and brought truckloads of pistols and rifles and submachine guns to the center of the city.

Newly armed citizens occupied the main square, halting cars they suspected of carring AVH personnel. They formed a small squad and ran to the National Theater and the radio building on Sandor Street, where they found the AVH in command. They demanded a list of grievances against the regime be broadcast. The doors of the radio building opened and the AVH began firing into another mass of people.

On this November day, another hundred people were killed, including Peter. Christ, what the fuck is going on? Peter killed? What am I doing? What am I doing here? This is crazy! I wanted to get out and to run away. Then I looked at Anna and I saw her quiet strength and I held her. Oh, Christ, I held her! She was like a deer, a softness so delicate. Moving quietly, she said nothing, she wept. She grieved the loss of her brother.

That evening Radio Budapest called for doctors and supplies of plasma, asking rebels not to fire on ambulances. Anna moved through the streets with me. Close and cautiously we walked together.

In the night, surgical operations were carried out by flashlight. The Hungarians continued to fight. In a radio speech, Premier Nagy promised talks with the Soviet Union on the basis of complete equality. Radio Budapest pleaded, "Tell the youths we have a new leadership. Tell the youths there is no danger." But there was danger.

I saw Soviet tanks firing on all moving objects, and Soviet soldiers were executing Hungarian soldiers and civilian rebels in the streets. People were hanging in rows along the Danube pier, and I counted twenty bodies hanging from flagpoles and streetlights. The Russians had started a horror regime. Suddenly I believed it. All of it. And was right in the middle.

Then the Hungarians retaliated. Roaming bands outside Budapest drove back Soviet units and set up roadblocks. I ran over to the United Press office to file another report. "Is the service open?" I cried to Frank.

"Yes, it is," he said.

"Frank, this is Anna. Her brother was just killed."

Frank spoke to her in Hungarian. In any language it would have sounded the same. Her sorrow, his regret—it was in their voices.

Landau from Budapest:
I saw a column of rioters march with arms outstretched into machine-gun fire. Students were killed en masse by Soviet tanks. Workers fought their way into an arms depot and got themselves machine guns. Others made gasoline bombs out of

wine bottles. Soon Soviet Army cars were burning in the streets. Fierce battles are breaking out for control of Communist-party headquarters. Out of the fog and smoke that obscured the sky, Soviet jet planes are roaring down with cannons blazing. A carnival has become a revolution.

Anna and I went back to her apartment. I held and kissed her all night, until her tears ceased their flow. "You must leave," she whispered. I couldn't leave. I wanted just to stay with her. We passed the night in silence.

The next day, the tide of the battle turned in favor of resistance. There was a general strike throughout the country. The Soviet leaders made a crucial decision. They agreed that Hungary should have a new government in which there would be non-Communists. Communist Radio Budapest broadcast: "Please, please stop! You have won! Your demands will be fulfilled."

For the next few days, Hungary was free. There was great celebration. There was jubilation in the streets as the Hungarians began to realize what they had done. Their faces were lit with a kind of ecstasy. There were vigorous students and tough-looking workers among them, and many seemed pitifully young. I saw a boy who could not have been more than ten years old, holding himself at the ready with a rifle as tall as he was. Under the warm November sun, Budapest was a city ravaged by full-scale war. The streets were choked by rubble and glass. The revolution had not counted its dead, but an estimate put the total at 15,000, including 3,000 Soviet soldiers, and twice as many wounded. Men in white coats moved among corpses sprinkling snow-white lime which transformed the dead into marblelike statues. Peter was among them. I filed my last story:

> The Hungarian people overthrew a government. One of them was Peter Veres, my friend. He took on the Soviet Army. Peter fought well enough and long enough to win at least a pledge that his country would be free of Moscow's one-party dictatorship, but it cost him his life. The Hungarian people have suffered by the thousands and died by the hundreds, and although the strength of their arms was no match for the guns and tanks of their enemy, their strength and their passion for an ideal, for freedom, for good, was enough to defeat a Russian army.

Peter was dead and I was devastated, although I knew him for such a short time. I remembered his courage. We mourned for him.

Additional calls for medical help went out to Vienna and Geneva, and convoys of supplies crossed the borders from Austria. A quiet atmosphere gradually descended upon Budapest. Old women with brooms began sweeping at the doorways of blasted buildings. A man with paint pots went from tank to tank painting over the Soviet red star with the Hungarian republican emblem. What had come over Hungary, without anyone's realizing it, was democracy. The Russians called for a meeting with the provisional government to discuss technical details for the withdrawal of the Russian troops.

Anna and I went to a restaurant that night for a traditional Hungarian meal. Budapest would now hear the violins at night, and be swarmed with well-dressed girls, and warmed by its pride. Anna thanked me for my friendship. "I'll never forget you, Jonathan," she said brokenly.

Just days ago, I had driven with Peter through the border, into this strange and beautiful country. There was distance and emptiness in the lakes and forests. The impact of an ancient humanity was evident in the planting and the villages and the windless folds of hills beneath summits and the stones that showed the mark of man and a balance with nature. The great forests were still in the sun's light, striking at an oblique angle between the regularly spaced rows of trees that gave the impression of a plan for a Gothic cathedral.

Whenever circumstances bring men close to danger, we seem to feel with care. I looked at Anna. She appreciated simple pleasures, an artistic vitality, and an ever-renewing independence of spirit. She smiled and kissed me. I knew I would never see her again. Then, I felt a familiar emptiness. Anna remained in a country of proud soldiers and farmers with an intense sense of belonging to those mountains and monuments where her ancestors have always lived for a better life. I went to Vienna.

I took a train from the border, and when I arrived that evening, I checked into the hotel again. Here there were new reports of Russian movements. The Hungarians had been tricked. Arthur Saltzman pounded on my door. "Come quickly," he said. We ran over to the United Press office in

Vienna. The lonesome shadow of the teletype in the dead of the night told the world of Hungary's return to shadows. Early Sunday morning Frank Celi punched out an urgent teletype message. The circuit between the Budapest United Press and the Vienna London *Express* chattered to life: "SOS SOS SOS."

"Russian gangsters have betrayed us. They are opening fire on all of Budapest. Please inform Europe and the Austrian government. . . . They opened fire on everybody."

There was a pause.

"A few hundred tanks attacked Budapest . . . a thousand. . . . There is heavy fighting. . . . I stay open and continue with the news. . . . We shall inform the world about everything."

The clatter stilled once more, resumed.

"We are under heavy machine-gun fire. Premier Nagy will speak to the people. . . . Have you information you can pass on? Tell me. Urgent, urgent."

I didn't know what to do. "What can we do, Arthur? For Christ's sake, what can we do?"

Pause.

"Long live Hungary and Europe. The Russians are using phosphorous bullets. Any news about help? Quickly, quickly. We have no time to lose. No time to lose. . . . We are quiet, not afraid. Send the news to the world. I don't know how long we can resist. . . . Heavy shells are exploding nearby. . . . I am running over to the window in the next room to shoot, but I will be back. We will hold out to the last drop of blood. . . . What is the United Nations doing? Give us some encouragement. . . . They've just brought a rumor that American troops will be here within one or two hours."

That was the last to be heard from Frank. He composed, as his final message to Vienna, an epitaph: "Good-bye, friends. Good-bye, friends. God save our souls. The Russians are too near."

The line went dead.

"We have to get the news out!"

"The whole world knows," Arthur replied quietly.

17

A winter sun, a disk of pale fire, cut a marble arch through the cold British sky. I had not told April I was coming. I stepped quickly aboard BOAC and into another world. The flight was too long and I was impatient. I thought over and over in my mind how I would surprise her. The crew served a routine dinner, and several hours later, London.

The plane touched down, and at the airport an editor from the *Express* introduced himself to me.

"Well done, Jonathan," he congratulated me. Then he presented me with a check for a thousand pounds, along with a cable from CBS News in New York offering me a job as a news correspondent. It was an open ticket. Would I meet with Richard Shepley, who would be in London the following day?

"Looks like you're on your way, Landau," the editor told me. "We'd like to have you at the *Express* if you don't take the CBS offer."

"Thank you," I said. "Would you let Shepley know I'll be at Claridge's." Luck was with me.

While waiting for my luggage, I read in the papers that the people of Hungary had been watching from rooftops, hoping for U.S. planes to arrive. When they didn't appear, they no longer had any hope. I also read, from dozens of sources, the astonishing news that Hungary, far from lying down under martial law, was alive and kicking. The Red Army had been unable to halt another paralyzing general strike of the incredible Hungarians, who, abandoning street fighting after twenty-five thousand of their countrymen had lost their lives, found another way to resist.

I felt guilty because I had received so much attention and praise for something that began as a lark. I thought I was

Hemingway. But then I saw people fighting and dying for their freedom. They were the heroes. Not me. I wondered if caring for the Hungarians became secondary to carrying the banner for the relief parade. I realized how easy it was to give up the ideal for the idea of something else. It all become a question of motive.

On the way into town I passed Lockes. I stopped and bought a hat. It was a trilby. It wasn't taking me long to affect an English manner. Well, April would like it. She didn't know yet that I was back.

Through the turbulent flow of traffic, I arrived at Claridge's. The manager suggested, "Would you like a small suite on the eighth floor, sir? Your uncles always prefer that one. It looks out onto the garden."

Claridge's has the distinction of being the only hotel in which Queen Victoria ever spent the night. Ever since then it has been the London residence for kings, queens, statesmen, important actors, quiet Americans. Top-hatted doormen welcome you as if you were entering your own home.

I called David.

"Jonathan, you're back. Your reports were incredible. I read them all. Where are you?"

"Claridge's," I said.

"Rather nice," David answered. "April seems to be ill."

I didn't know.

"She came down from Oxford before term ended."

"Anything serious, do you suppose?"

"Of course not."

"I want to surprise her. I thought I'd go and get her a few things."

"Why don't I come around and fetch you?"

David met me in the foyer, next to the concierge. I was dressed in tweeds, and so was he. His car was an expensive, fashionable, vintage Bentley, a saloon, the kind you drive yourself.

We drove up Park Lane to Knightsbridge, past distinguished squares and seasoned shops with "By Appointment to the Queen" discreetly displayed overhead. Down to the Portobello Road, where antiques are housed in stalls and stores.

"I thought I'd get an old Victorian music box. There are some made with long cylinders that can play lovely tunes for

156

thirty minutes in one winding. It's a perfect gift for Christmas."

I found precisely what I was looking for. It was made in the eighteenth century. A brass plate from the maker read, "James Fitzgerald."

Over to the great food hall at Harrods, a vaulted Victorian arcade. Noble game, succulent bird, rural cheeses surrounded the Merrydown cider and summer puddings, steak-and-kidney pies, currants, truffles, and the ritual of many teas. Here was a repository of familiar flavors, gastronomic flourishes that brought nostalgia, and memories heightened with time. I selected petits fours, a cheese quiche, assorted cheeses, French baguettes, a ripe Brie, crème brulée in separate fluted cups, chocolate mousse, oranges and caramel syrup, strawberries with Devonshire cream, and a bottle of '52 Romanèe-Conti.

"Do you think that's enough?"

"Hmm, suppose so," David said with an understated smile.

An elegant large French basket of fresh flowers was sent to precede me.

April was in bed when I arrived that evening with two waiters I borrowed from Claridge's. The housekeeper at Addison Road let me in quietly. I went to the kitchen and prepared a large tray of food and went upstairs. Outside, I turned on the music box. It was a delicate tune by Strauss.

April had fallen asleep while reading. Her light was on and a *Tatler* magazine lay open in her arms.

Her room was painted in a pale rose. There were old Victorian paint prints in gold-leaf frames.

The walls were striated, heavy paint combed in a pale rose and washed over with white. The quilt on the bed was a *toile de Jouy* which matched the curtains. There was a deep-cushioned velvet sofa and chairs, and a built-in window seat. A Wilton carpet was in a lighter shade and in perfect consonance with the colors. Starlight passed through tall French doors adjacent to the terrace.

I saw the fresh flowers on a small table beside April's bed. She was wearing a white gown and her blond hair fell evenly to the side. Her eyes opened. She looked at me.

"I don't believe you're back," she said over and over, softly. I held her for a long time. "I worried when I didn't hear from you."

The waiters arranged dinner and disappeared.

"How are you feeling, April?"

"A bit weak. Some sort of virus. I haven't had much of an appetite, and they're doing all sorts of tests. Sit down, let me look at you." She rang for the housekeeper. "Where are you staying?"

"I'm staying at Claridge's."

"Oh, Jonathan, you must stay here."

The housekeeper appeared. "Yes, ma'am?"

"Would you bring some brown sugar for the strawberries?"

"Sorry, I forgot. I brought you a Hershey bar."

"It's funny; you like Cadbury's and I like Hershey's. Where's the music coming from?" she asked.

I showed her the music box.

"Christmas is early this year." She smiled.

"You know me, I'm impulsive. I can't wait." She looked pretty and, like the room, English rose, original and proud, mannered and soft.

April fell asleep. I was down in the foyer when the Huxleys came in.

"Jonathan, you're back. That was a bit of a mess you were in. Welcome home."

"Is April all right?" I asked.

"Oh, she's under excellent care. Trevor Hopkins is a very fine man. He's over at King's Hospital. Please come in and sit down." Diana left the room for a moment and Patrick and I were alone.

"Have you seen April?"

"Yes, I was just with her."

"Jonathan, I haven't seen you in months," Patrick said. "Have a brandy with me."

We went into the living room. There were light Portuguese rugs in a floral design. Silk damask covered the walls. The room was tastefully appointed—several Turners and a Monet.

"That's a painting of Waterloo Bridge."

"Can you believe he painted it thirty-fours times from his suite at the Savoy? Summer, winter, different times of day. All the same exact perspective. He painted the light. That one's in late afternoon at the beginning of summer. I am glad to see you."

158

"I've been meaning to talk to you. I think April . . . I would like to give April a ring."

"Does that mean an engagement?"

"With your permission. I'd like to marry your daughter."

I had no idea I'd be asking for April's hand that evening. But I did so with reasonable assurance and boldness and without any hesitation.

"Napoleon Cognac or Courvoisier?"

"Courvoisier will be fine."

He poured me a drink and handed it to me without looking. "We like you very much, Jonathan."

"Thank you."

He didn't give me an answer.

Diana returned. "Jonathan, we are so glad you're safe."

"They want to get married," Sir Patrick told her.

Diana looked at me curiously.

They're not quite sure of me, I realized. I'm not titled; I'm American, and still a student. I'm not at all what they had in mind for their daughter.

Then Patrick and I talked well into the night about the revolution.

The next afternoon Shepley was at Claridge's. He was head of CBS News. We met for two hours in the Grill. He looked more like a Madison Avenue advertising executive than a newsman. He had been an aide to Eisenhower, was his press secretary before Jim Hagerty took over, and he was well-connected in Washington.

"I want to build a young, aggressive news-gathering team," he said. "Your story from Hungary is CBS' kind of journalism."

He leaned toward me. "I want to make CBS unique in the minds of our viewers, a cachet of leadership that will present any statistic—*sui generis.*

"I want to combine nostalgia with currency, ideas and men, people with personalities, a cynosure for all eyes."

For a moment, I thought he was on the air.

His enthusiasm was freighted with hype and hope.

"The news as continuum. I want human interest, that's what it's all about. Editorial reminiscing. I want to break the mold and create a video vogue. I'm searching for new ways to establish the facility for flair as well as fact, more than dialect, diction, and glib contrivances. A new CBS news profile, a profile to comprehend a human level of awareness."

"I still have terms to finish before I take my degree."

"Look," he said, "you could do the occasional story for us in Europe. Human interest. Nothing that will take you more than a day or two. It will be good training ground for you, Jonathan. Then, when you come to New York you'll have more experience."

"All right, let's give it a whirl."

He reinforced my metaphor with conscious precision. "I know you can be outstanding."

I joined that legion and tradition of newsmen and journalists, reporting and researching the continuing story called news.

I told April about the CBS meeting. "Don't you feel good?" she asked. I did.

There was a cast on her wrist. I hadn't noticed it before.

"How did that happen?"

"I slipped while you were away. Just a stupid fall."

"Are you up for the Gallery? There is an exhibit on Venetian art."

"Just try to keep me away. I'll be ready in ten minutes."

Diana called from the drawing room, "Will you have dinner with us, Jonathan? When will you be back?"

"Oh, four o'clock, if we're going up to Oxford. Nine o'clock if we fly to Paris. And if we drive to Venice, then maybe in a few days?" We looked at each other and smiled. "Of course, we'll have dinner with you."

April came downstairs.

"A remarkable recovery."

"The Hershey bar cured me."

We walked down the Addison Road.

"I want to write a paper on creativity. Will you help me?"

"I'm not the creative sort. You know me. I'm a businessman. I have the English franchise on Hershey bars."

"Jonathan! Why is one person more creative than another?"

"Interesting question," I said. " I don't know."

"What do you think?" she asked.

"I think creativity takes courage. It's much easier in a profession like medicine, law, business. There are known factors.

You know that you will be able to make a living. But how do you know if you'll succeed acting or writing, designing houses? Everybody is creative. We start as children. It's a refuge for our imagination and loneliness. Perhaps scientists are the most creative of all."

"Why is that?"

"They need scientific data to back up their creativity."

The sky was cloudy. We walked past Westminster, toward Parliament. The Abbey was behind us. In a few minutes we were in Saint James's Park echoing the softness of the surrounding countryside. There was a long lake running through it to a bridge. From here we could take a long look at London, the cupolas, and the Italian palaces of Whitehall blending into a view reminiscent of Italy.

We walked through the park and crossed briefly in front of Buckingham Palace, then over to Piccadilly. On the streets at Knightsbridge, in order to relieve the repetitive regularity of black-painted iron railings at each front door, the householders had set bright windowboxes full of frilly pink petunias. Here were reserved and uniformly wide front doors, painted and varnished and accented by doorknobs and handles that added a touch of individuality, brilliantly polished eighteenth- and nineteenth-century designs.

Across the street, into Green Park, London burst upon us with a roar. There were streets to cross, and in a few minutes we were through this gateway into Hyde Park. In the country again—a great swath of it for miles round. We climbed easy slopes and felt London under our feet, a city built on hills and paths under the shadows of great trees. We saw water and the colored sails, and we crossed yet another bridge, the most graceful in London, and we were still in the country. Here, Kensington Gardens, a more steady perspective and trails wandering across meadows. There was a pond and children sailing boats. And in this same place, England's most inspired child, Shelley, folded his own banknotes to make his own boat and set them sailing.

There ahead of us was our pavilion. The Orangery.

After the Venetian exhibition we returned to the Huxleys' for dinner. There were just the four of us that night, April, her parents, and I. Candlelight, a light salad, chicken, a Pouilly Fuissé, *sorbet* with petits fours. Later, April fell asleep

161

in front of the fire and I took her upstairs and put her to bed.

"I'll see you tomorrow, April."

"Jonathan," she said, "I love every day with you."

Because of my coverage of the Hungarian revolution, I received an invitation for dinner in the House of Lords. Me, at the House of Lords? Four hundred of the country's most politically astute. Lord Boyd-Orr, Trevor Roper, Arnold Toynbee, Peter Thornycroft. I accepted. And immediately asked April if she and Patrick would come with me. I knew he would soon be running again for his seat in the House of Commons. "Of course, we'll come."

It was a stunning dinner. In a large, paneled hall, a tall, imposing majordomo with red tails and medals across his upper breast pocket announced each guest as he entered the room. "Lord David Cecil, the Honourable April Huxley, Sir Philip Hornsby, Lord and Lady McIntire, Mr. Jonathan Landau."

When my name was announced, several people who had read my report from Hungary came over to talk with me, and Lord Boyd-Orr asked if I might like to say a few words later. The thought paralyzed me. Conversation led to cocktails and cocktails to dinner and dinner to a debate in which several speakers, having been introduced, spoke eloquently and critically, decisively and controversially, about Hungary, about Suez.

"My lords, ladies and gentlemen, I give you Foreign Secretary Selwyn Lloyd . . ." He complemented each passing course with philosophic and political thought. Liveried waiters served port, Stilton, and Havanas with great precision. I listened attentively to Lloyd's words about foreign policy. He talked about the Russians, the Aswan Dam, the United Nations. Christ, I thought, how many people know what they are talking about? How easy it is to chat on, and how difficult it is to fight. Lloyd praised Anthony Eden. Then Hugh Gaitskell, the leader of the opposition, responded, "The government and Mr. Eden have committed an act of disastrous folly with tragic consequences we shall regret for years. It will have done irreparable harm to the prestige and reputation of our country. This reckless and foolish decision has just been made

162

when events in Hungary have given the free world its greatest hope and encouragement in ten years."

Events in Hungary? Give the world hope? Fuck—a slaughter! Because his accent was so crisp the speech sounded more intelligent than it actually was. The lack of content was disguised by his authoritative clipped tones.

I leaned toward April and whispered, "Would you like to hear me speak?"

"Of course," she whispered back.

I sent a note to Lord Boyd-Orr, who introduced me. "Mr. Jonathan Landau—Oxford scholar, foreign correspondent, American. . . ."

I knew I had to say something about America, the Communist party, the UN. Thoughts—hundreds of them—raced in my mind. This was it. I could speak and I had something to say. They were just political dilettantes.

I stood to my formidable six-foot-six and waited a moment before saying, "Mr. Secretary, Lord Boyd-Orr, lords, ladies and gentlemen, thank you."

I had planned a give-them-hell, no-nonsense, brass-tacks oration. I was going to take on the whole establishment. What did they know about revolution and humanity? Just then they started to applaud. Christ. It felt good. Well, to be courteous, I'll modulate my speech just a little bit. I quoted Blake: "You become what you behold." More applause. I was surprised. So I adjusted my speech further to a theme of individual responsibility and freedom. I likened Britain to the United States, as father to son, wisdom to impropriety, sagacity to ignorance, strategy to impulsiveness. I wasn't even sure of the continuity. However, it seemed to be a good speech, well received, broken by a "hear, hear" now and again. I realized I couldn't cut through all the bullshit to this august group. They were listening to me. They wanted to know what I had to say. They accepted me. I was part of the club. Did it feel any different? I guess it did at that moment. The applause started again. I liked it. I thought I should talk about Hungary. I suppose that's what they wanted.

I concluded by reading a letter from Anna which I had received that morning:

> It is a month to the day since you were here. It's been a month to the day since the Russians crushed the city by

treachery and murder. We succeeded partly in throwing off a completely Communist regime. Very often I walk by the Danube to the street corner near the radio station where Peter was killed. Today housewives and young girls and black-shawled old women came from shopping arcades and broken buildings and rubble-strewn side streets. There were four thousand of us. We are the widows and sisters of Budapest. We marched for our heroes to honor their memory. We trudged through the rain. Some of us had flowers. Others carried bundles of bread, cabbages, and onions. Threading past the wreckage of our city, we chanted the words of Sando Petrofi, our poet: "When you win a war with your power . . . you have won the war but not the heart. Real victory is to win the heart."

I studied the audience and recalled the quotation from Blake. Blake and Petrofi. Two men, two poets, two visionaries with ideas, both beacons of hope.

"Here we are tonight, shining light on the very things that have made this country great, courage and honor. I know that Britain will always honor those values."

The applause seemed distant now as I remembered Mr. Balmain and his magic machine, and trying to make a telephone call from Travis City, Michigan, being unable to ask Lady to dance. Now I was not only understood, I was acclaimed by lords and ladies and gentlemen. And that felt very good. But now I wondered if I were doing things for effect and for the effect they had on others rather than on me.

18

It was a chilly morning. Not enough heat to keep me warm, so I stayed in a hot bath, boiling water trickling out of old pipes into the oversized tub. I was lathering with lemon soap, in Roman ritual, when Evans knocked and entered with warm towels and a long telegram assigning my first story.

"Get to Munich," the cable said. "Hitler had a mistress." Of course, he had a mistress, I thought. It was Eva Braun. No. "He was cheating on Eva," the cable continued. "Contact Gunther Peis at Reuters."

I left the comforts of my bath, packed an overnight bag, and flew to Munich, where it was even colder.

Gunther met me at the airport and helped me through customs. His long, black cigars smoked up the car as we passed the rural German countryside on the way to town.

"Hitler had a sister," he told me, "Paula Wolf, who casually mentioned last week that a woman, Maria Reiter, is perhaps the only woman her brother ever loved." That was human interest, all right.

Maria turned out to be blond, buxom, and fortish. She lived in the suburbs. The apartment was dark. It smelled of bread and wine and there were dried flowers and little china bric-a-brac animals in the cabinet. An alpine clock hung on the wall in between lace curtains, tablecloths, doilies, and stuffed chairs which accommodated me. On a table beneath a country snow scene of a church and steeple were silver-framed pictures of aunts and uncles, mothers and fathers, brothers and sisters, and Hitler.

Reluctant at first, she finally gave us the long-kept secret of her uneven romance with Hitler from 1929 into the thirties. It was straight soap opera.

"It all began at Berchtesgaden Park," she began.

"What year?" I asked. I started to write.

"In 1926. I was sixteen; Hitler was in his thirties. We met while we were walking our police dogs. He was a struggling young party leader then. Beer?"

"Yes, thank you." She brought a bottle of Lowenbrau.

"I think he liked my . . . , how to you say in English, Nordic charm?"

"Nordic charm," I said.

The wrinkles smiled through her makeup, but when she talked about Hitler, her eyes danced.

"He cut a fine figure with those riding breeches and that riding crop." She looked wistfully at the past.

"One night he invited me to come and listen to him speak. And afterward"—she giggled—"he fed me cake with his fingers."

"It sounds as if it were a serious romance."

Maria was talking freely and openly now. She seemed relieved, finally, to tell her story. And she had a more-than-willing listener.

"But I was a good girl. After we got home from the hall, on our first meeting, he wanted a good-*nachen* kiss."

"What did you do?" I asked.

"Another beer?"

"Yes, thank you."

She left the room.

"Is this woman serious?" I asked Gunther.

"Yes," he whispered. "And she has his letters and photographs to prove it."

Maria returned. Her small schnauzer was at her side. He kept biting my leg at different intervals. "What did the Führer do when you rejected his advances?"

"Well, I didn't reject him. Just not so soon. We had just met. He glowered and stalked out with a good-night *heil*. But soon we were taking rides in his sporty Mercedes. He called me Mimi, and I called him Wolf."

"Nice," I said, writing furiously. The dog kept pulling at my pants leg. I tried to disengage myself from him. Mimi and Wolf.

"The only thing that troubled me was that he never put down that riding crop. But we had golden days. We walked in

166

the meadows and he led me to a tall pine. 'Just stand there as you are.' Then it was our first stormy kiss. I was so happy. And on the way back to the car, Wolf told me that he wanted to marry me and have blond children, but he must save Germany first. After that we met in his apartment in Munich at 4 Lugestrasse. We dreamed. You have a girl?"

"Yes."

"Then you know how you dream and how you feel. But it was not to be. There were rumors; not nice rumors. And he felt I was hurting him politically. I would never do such a thing. But a year later, we broke up. I was devastated, my dear. It took me years before I met someone else."

"A politician?"

"No. He was a hotel keeper in Seefeld."

"Did you ever see Hitler again?"

"One day I got a knock on my door, and of all people, it was Rudolf Hess. 'Hitler sent me,' he said. 'He wants to know if you are happy.' I got the idea, and I ran off to Munich for one breathless *liebesnacht*, a night of love. I let him do what he wanted," she exclaimed. "I was never so happy."

Her schnauzer was eating my pants legs now. I tried to cross my legs to get away from him.

"Hitler told me, 'Mimilein, I am rich now. I can offer everything. Stay with me. I never loved any woman as I love you. I love you.'

"You must understand, I was not married. But I could not. I had heard about Eva. It was sad, but such a life. It was 1938, and we were in for hard times."

"Did you see him after that?"

"No . . . he held me and he kissed me and I asked him if we would see each other. And he looked away distantly. I asked him what we were all thinking. Will there be a war? He shrugged his shoulders and turned away. He paused a moment or two, and then he did a surprising little jig."

"How do you feel about Wolf now?"

"Well, I can't say I trusted him. He was moody. He could never make up his mind."

"I'm sorry," I said.

"*Danke*," she replied wistfully.

Maria was far away with her memories.

The cameraman I had engaged took appropriate shots of Munich, of the interview, and of Maria's apartment. I smiled all the way back to London and filed my first story for CBS News. Several days later I received a cable from Shepley.

"Nice story, Jonathan. Regards to Mimi."

A few weeks later, back at Oxford, there was another demonstration at the Union. Nasser had closed the Suez Canal and broken a long-standing treaty with Great Britain. The students were marching in protest.

I looked for Fritz everywhere but could not find him. I wanted to tell him about Anna and Peter and what had happened to me.

David told me that Fritz had been very upset about the events in Hungary and was passing out more literature. He had stopped the Wednesday-night debate at the Oxford Union, and shouted, calling a halt to arms and saying we must cooperate with the Russians. I went over to St. Edmonds Hall and asked the porter where I could find Fritz. A scout pointed to his room. His door was locked. I knocked.

"Fritz," I cried out. There was no answer. I knocked again.

"It's Jonathan, Fritz." The door opened quickly and shut again almost as fast. Then it opened slowly to reveal walls plastered with posters of Lenin, Marx, and Mao Tse-tung. In the far corner, Fritz had built an altar. I thought this was all very strange.

He looked at me accusingly. "You failed in Hungary." His tone was enraged.

"What in the hell are you talking about, Fritz? I failed in Hungary?"

"You betrayed me," he said. "I trusted you to drive the Red Cross truck for humanity, goddammit, not for violence! Why didn't you stop it?"

I sat down. The room was in complete disarray. It appeared that Fritz had not been out, nor washed, nor eaten for weeks. He reached under his coffee table.

"What are all these candles and pictures, Fritz?"

"It's a memorial. I let you in because I think I can still trust y-- " He picked up a banana from the coffee table and sliced it in half. "You see the markings inside this banana?"

"What markings, Fritz?"

"The markings of Jesus Christ. Can't you see? Jesus Christ is inside this banana!"

Jesus Christ inside a banana? I knew he had gone mad. I couldn't label it. I didn't know much about paranoia, but I knew he had lost touch.

He grabbed me, and gritting his teeth, said, "Don't you understand that it is over? I am sacrificing my life for humanity. It's the only way. We must end war. I am Jesus Christ!"

"Now, calm down, Fritz," I said. "Jesus Christ may be a banana, but you are not."

He pulled out a gun.

"Where did you get the gun, Fritz?"

"This is not a gun. It's a banana."

"Put down the banana, Fritz."

"I'm gonna eat the banana."

With all my force I sprang. I threw him to the floor and held him with my weight. Fritz let out a deafening howl. He was hitting me with the force of a hundred men, tearing at me, biting and growling. I yelled for help. Within seconds other students burst through the old oak door and restrained him.

"Call an ambulance," I said. "He's very sick and he needs help."

Fifteen minutes later an ambulance from the Radcliff Infirmary arrived and two attendants gave him a shot, which I guess was a tranquilizing agent. We half-dragged Fritz to the ambulance. Its high-frequency warning sounded as we sped down the empty streets. Fritz was drowsy from the medication.

"Oh, Jonathan," he managed to say, "it's all right. We'll bring peace to the world. It's all right."

What's wrong with you, Fritz? I thought over and over. The ambulance pulled into a narrow and quiet alley which led to the night emergency room. Fritz was carried through the halls, then strapped down and placed under observation.

I was called the next morning by Dr. Summerhill, who was the attending physician at Northampton Medical Center outside Oxford. He told me that Fritz was mentally ill, suffering from delusions, and suggested electric shock and insulin treatments. Perhaps with therapy he would, in time, recover. He wasn't sure. Like so much in mental health, he explained, there are environmental, genetic, and biochemical determinants, all in different ratios, fitting the pattern of the individual. I would have to have him committed.

I went over to the infirmary. I couldn't believe Fritz was that ill. I looked through the glass to a padded observation room where Fritz was seated, looking to heaven, blessing an imaginary audience, and speaking as if to his Apostles. I signed papers and went to Fritz's college to pick up some things for him. He had given away all his worldly belongings. His scout had been able to retrieve some things, a watch, a suitcase, a suit. I placed a call to his father in Connecticut. The call went through without delay.

"Mr. Shearer," I said, "Fritz is very sick and I suggest that you come over here."

"Well, what's wrong with him?"

"I don't really know, sir. He's just not himself."

"Oh, Fritzie's never been himself." He laughed.

"I'd appreciate it if you came over now, sir. He's in a mental hospital."

"Mental hospital? What is he doing there?"

"Mr. Shearer," I said firmly, "I'm paying for this call and I'm telling you that you and Mrs. Shearer should get over here and look after your son."

"Mrs. Shearer will be there in the morning," he replied after a moment's pause.

I had never met Fritz's mother.

She arrived the next day at Oxford, and I met her at the train station. She was garishly dressed with furs over tweeds and too many diamonds, too much jewelry, and too much makeup, which failed to conceal her age. She stayed at Oxford for several days, visiting Fritz at the hospital.

Usually with electric shock there is a discernible recovery after two or three treatments, but the series of twelve should not be interrupted. Fritz was contained and spoke slowly. His eyes were bloodshot when we sat in a garden at Northampton on a bright and warm winter day. "All I was doing, Momma, was trying to help save the world before it's too late!" Fritz said quietly. He looked at me then and smiled oddly. He's still not well, I thought. He's still on his crusade, but he's being clever just now. Strange thing: Was he crazy? Did he know what he was doing? And why did I not detect some signs of his impending breakdown? Maybe they were always there, but I didn't see them.

Mrs. Shearer smiled serenely. "See how well Fritz is, Jonthan? My Fritzie is so bright. Have you heard his ideas on world peace?" I had. She didn't see the signs either. She took Fritz out of the hospital and away to Majorca. When they returned six weeks later, Fritz packed his few belongings. They were going back to New York. Fritz was quiet and subdued, but he still talked about leadership and God. I knew that this was the residue of the outer reaches of fantasy.

My digs at Oxford had turned into a newsroom. Evans brought in eight papers daily—*Le Monde, der Stern, The New York Times, The Observer, New Statesman* and *Nation*. There was an Associated Press telex at the Oxford Union, and Evans collected news releases for me. I was looking for human interest stories.

Shepley queried me about Victor Footer, a guard at Buckingham Palace. He had been harassed by an American tourist, and he, in return, kicked her. It was an international incident. I went to London to interview him. On the way, I scribbled some notes.

Not since Christopher Robin went down to see the changing of the guard at Buckingham Palace had a sentry's life been so terribly hard. In those days, the rigid young soldiers of the queen, in their scarlet tunics and black bearskins slung high on their shoulders, were symbols of the empire's glory. Englishmen and foreigners alike respectfully held their tongues and kept their distance. But after World War II was won and the war's glamour past, the solemn and expressionless sentries marching mechanically twenty-five paces this way, and twenty-five paces the other, no longer seemed to inspire the same respect. At least, not to tourists, especially Americans.

I thought it would be effective to open the interview with film of the palace guards pacing, marching, standing at attention, executing high-stepping turns.

So into Wellington Barracks, No. 1 Company, Coldstream Guards, I went. The barracks were near Buckingham Palace. I asked for Guardsman Footer.

"Footer, Footer, Footer," echoed down the hall. He would

see me. There were rows of bunk beds in the barracks. Relaxed soldiers sat around their mate during the interview.

"Jonathan Landau—I'm a correspondent for CBS."

"Guardsman Footer, Coldstream Guards. Sit down, sir."

His manners were polite, his face solemn.

"Three hundred years of iron discipline. I guess a break finally came," I began.

"Well, you know, sir. I just lost my head."

"What happened?"

"You must understand, sir, we take a lot of abuse. It was, in fact, a terribly hard summer. The tourists finally got to me. One bloke stuck a toffee apple at the end of my bayonet. And there was nothing I could do."

His mates sympathized and nodded in agreement.

"Then, a few weeks later, I found myself standing at attention and, blimey, my shoelaces had been tied together. Some predicament." His fellow guards murmured agreement. "And this past week has been particularly distressing. They think we're exhibits in the zoo."

Other guardsmen joined in. "We've been stroked, poked, tickled. We've had banana peels set underfoot, ice-cream cups pitched at us, obscene orders shouted."

"Excuse me, Mr. Landau, if I may. But I had one man place French postcards, one after another, naked women, in front of my face, while I stood at attention, no pun intended." The group laughed.

Footer continued, "We all have a breaking point. I guess mine came when this lady—"

"This was the American tourist?"

"I assume so, sir. She started shining my buttons, and it tickled. Out came a can of Brasso, and she polished one after another as I was standing there. I lost all control. You can understand that? What is a soldier to do? I couldn't take it anymore."

All of London was talking about the incident. Footer had, indeed, become a hero.

"It's important that the truth be told. We need protection," he implored. "This is tough duty. I'm ashamed of my irregular conduct while on sentry go. I'm confined to barracks. But one of us has to speak out. Are you with me, mates?"

They were.

172

"I consented to the interview, Mr. Landau, because I hope you will tell the story fairly and honestly."

My story closed with a suggestion that extra bobbies be assigned to guard the guards who guard the palace.

Evans read the piece and commented, "Very good, sir. Very good."

The years passed easily at Oxford. *Sunday's People* was supported by the chic set of the establishment. "A smart Oxonian musical . . . bright and original." It played at Oxford through the summer, and then the playhouse company took it into London, where it ran at the Lyric. I enjoyed a certain celebrity station. In fact, I enjoyed it very much.

My life at Oxford was secure. I wanted to spend more time with April, but we were isolated, each with papers, projects, and pressures as the term neared its end. She had to go away again for a few weeks, and she didn't tell me why.

As often as I could, I took the train to London, just an hour away. On Saturdays I took in a matinee and then another play in the evening. Once I spent a week in London at David Lansdale's mews house and saw ten plays, one each night and matinees Wednesday, Saturday, and sometimes Sunday. It cost me just less than three dollars, a little under a pound. A half-crown was all it cost to sit in the unreserved section of the balcony. The theater's magic was always there for me. It was as potent a high as any drug could be. As long as I was softly ensconced in my seat, I felt warm and enchanted. I observed every detail of each theater. The seats, the proscenium, boxes, fire curtains, the dress circle, stalls, lights, spotlights, speakers, exits. The elements of make-believe.

And luck was with me. The night I invited April and David to the Royal Ballet was a good example. There were just three tickets left. Two in the stalls and one in a box. I suggested that April and David sit together and I took the single. The performance was delayed. I looked around the theater just as the orchestra played "God Save the Queen," and at that moment the queen walked into the royal box, followed by an entourage of ladies-in-waiting and security people. I didn't know what to do. Kneel? Bow? My God. I had gone to the Royal Box by mistake. Finally, I rose with the royal party and struck the pose of a loyal and humble servant. I started to leave but the queen graciously asked me to stay and then the queen waved from her side of the box and I nodded from mine. I knew she had once before attended a performance of *Sunday's People*. I heard how much she had enjoyed it and I wanted to tell her that I wrote it, but somehow I could not. The show remained fresh for me even though I had seen it more than a dozen times. At every opportunity, I walked around to the Lyric to see *Sunday's People* again. A full house always thrilled me. The narrator of the play was an Everyman. I wondered if this had helped its success. So many of us pretend, wear different masks, act and react, never speak our real feelings, are polite when we should be irate, soft when we should be hard, say yes when we should say no. And sometimes, just sometimes, we are not really the people that people think we are. The audience knew this. I liked the score. There were fine songs, and some of them were recorded by popular singers. *Sunday* was especially tuneful, and everybody was humming it. From the front of the house I walked through an exit to an adjacent alley to a stage door. Here was the fantasy behind the fantasy, sets, stagehands, dancers, performers, a carefully charted world of cues. This was my favorite territory. I knew most of the cast and I hoped the show would never close. I stood alone in the wings and watched the lights on the stage soften and create a mood. In a moment I was standing with Andrew in that open field waiting for the dawn and watching all the technicians with their cameras. The magic was just as real now as it was then. In the province of the mind, I could make anything happen. How extraordinary it was to see my thoughts translated to a stage.

Where was Andrew? If only he could see me now. Had he seen me on television? I wondered. Why hadn't he contacted me? When I got back to the States, I would begin to search. And I would find him, if my luck was still with me.

The lights changed and the orchestra played another tune. The performers moved into their places with well-designed precision. Another cue. What was more important—the writing and creating, or the enjoyment and belonging? I knew that I wrote in order to belong.

At the end of term was commencement. I remember a blur of black gowns with crimson and blue silk hoods outlined in soft ermine trim. Students followed scholars following dons in a long honorable procession threading through narrow streets. Undergraduates lined the road, forming a structured bridge that respected our walk down the High into the Broad, where in front of old buildings seasoned and witness to time, I received my degree and joined the fellowship that is part of the Oxonian tradition. The day was fresh. The air effervescent and April was there.

When I returned to Trinity, diploma in hand, Evans told me there had been a call from Mr. Shepley in New York asking when I would be arriving. He would send a car and put me up at the CBS suite at the Dorset until I got settled. I went around and spoke to Coghill. Perhaps I should stay at Oxford and read for a graduate degree. And perhaps I was scared all to hell of Shepley's offer.

"Unless you're going to teach, Jonathan, you must get on with the concerns of your life," Coghill advised.

Just when all the pieces were beginning to take shape and I felt, at last, in place at Oxford and with April, I was being drawn by a sense of fate to get on to what needed attending to. My life is here, I thought. It's comfortable here.

Coghill dusted off a book and turned to me, saying, "But you have as much now as you will ever have. You can stay on for as long as you want, but it won't mean anything. What do you want to do with your life, Jonathan?"

He was asking me again, and I still didn't have the answer.

I stopped by to see April that evening, to ask her to come with me to New York. She looked beautiful, but a little wan, a little pale. Too pale. I would have to convince her she was working too hard.

"I received a grant today, from the Children's Society, to study creativity in children." She was happy.

What rotten timing.

"That's great, April. But I came here to ask you to come with me to New York."

"I want to come." She smiled.

I poured her a bit of sherry. April held the glass, and as I filled it, she dropped the glass.

"Anything wrong?"

"Sorry, that was clumsy of me."

"Are you quite all right?"

175

"Yes, I am, Jonathan."

I looked at her and listened intensely to her reply.

"Really," she assured me. "The CBS job—that's a wonderful opportunity. You'll be just smashing. And we'll be together soon, I promise."

We talked far into the night, but a certain uneasiness stayed with me.

A few weeks later Evans put all my things together.

"You've done well here, sir." Evans spoke in an unmistakably affectionate tone. He said, "I think you've made a good choice, although we shall all miss you."

Later that afternoon I left a place and a time that I had come to love very much.

THE
SIXTIES

Cuba sí, Yanqui no.

We elected a man for all seasons whose station was Camelot. Rocket ships soared from science fiction into reality.

A procession of television game shows, formula comedies, structured violence, private eyes, doctors, and storefront lawyers advanced an endless variety of commercials and cartoons into a vast wasteland.

San Francisco introduced topless bars. We discovered organic foods and the Jolly Green Giant. We stood under McDonald's yellow arches, waiting for another twenty-one billion hamburgers to be served. Avery Fisher sold his hi-fi business for thirty-one million dollars.

John Kennedy said to us, "Ask not what your country can do for you," and Martin Luther King had a dream.

The dream stopped. Both killed. America had a silent spring.

Peace Corps and freedom fighters, Chaney, Schermer, and Goodman gave their lives in Mississippi. Israel fought a heroic six-day war and won.

We heard about hijacking, Blue Cross and Medicare. Zip and area codes divided the land.

Christine Keeler and John Profumo danced to Sergeant Pepper's Lonely Hearts Club Band. *And when America went to Vietnam, we sang with the Beatles, "I Want to Hold Your Hand."*

Calories didn't count. We drank Stillman's water diet, Weight Watchers, and Diet Rite Cola helped America to lighten up. On Saturday mornings we watched Star Trek *and* Sesame Street, *with Mr. Spock and Big Bird. And then one day Neil Armstrong stepped out of Apollo 11 onto the moon, taking a giant small step.*

179

We thought about that. We became part of the Great Society.

Bob Dylan was "Blowing in the Wind." Chubby Checker twisted at the Peppermint Lounge. Andy Warhol painted an oversized Campbell's tomato-soup can. Ken Kesey "flew over the cuckoo's nest." Sonny and Cher "babed" each other. Mario Salvo spoke freely at Berkeley, and America made a pilgrimage to Woodstock.

Bonnie and Clyde played the drive-ins, and Fellini told us something of la dolce vita. *Muhammad Ali became the heavyweight poet of the world, and Nixon announced that we did not have him to kick around anymore.*

The pill was introduced. Another war was escalated. We dined at Maxwell's Plum and drove through Strawberry Fields forever.

19

New York is the city of many lands, a home for all nations and all languages. Ancestral voyages continue to form part of the Manhattan mythology, woven through with legends of hell and purgatory on the high seas, all rooted in tales of terrible persecution and all terribly true. Why did they come? Because of worthlessness, hunger, political oppression, racial and religious persecution. Why did they stay? Often for a simple reason. It was America. Majestic Manhattan. Monolith, minaret, and spire. If their dreams could not come true in this land, there was nowhere else to go. Irish, Italians, Germans, and Jews saturated the city and permeated cultural pockets with music and literature, giving the neighborhoods colloquial speech and ethnic cuisine. The old world fermented with the new, restless, febrile, neurotic, brutal, creative, destructive, bizzare, creating an electrically charged society unique in the world. Irish cops, Italian shopkeepers, Jews and Catholics, slums and penthouses, champagne air in a killing climate of perpetual decay and renewal, in forced-skyward compression. And with this deed of trust I came to New York to take my bite out of the "Big Apple."

One of the buildings reaching upward in the city of dreams was "Black Rock"; its dark windows looked ominously over the city.

Richard Shepley welcomed me to his office. "We thought you were never coming, Jonathan. I'm glad you're here. Let me introduce you around." He led me down a hall bordered by the offices of the legendary newsmen. Cronkite, Wallace, Severeid, Reasoner, Murrow. They were all there. Some in makeup, a few in shirt sleeves, all at typewriters.

"Well, Jonathan, let's go to work."

I watched miles of videotapes, learned to read teleprompters, wrote special stories, and affected a characteristic CBS chattercasting talking-to-you style.

Weeks were spent in the newsroom, where a dozen teletype machines stood as robots, mechanically spewing stories from the Associated Press, United Press, Reuters, and correspondents around the world. The frenetic and frantic activity of Remington-punctuated deadlines. Words became sentences, minutes became seconds, in this dash-and-dazzle open forum of events, chance, and circumstance. Here Shepley directed "the news as continuum."

"You speak with an easy grace, Jonathan. Your Oxford background gives us another slant. And you enunciate with perfection."

Me! The kid who couldn't talk, couldn't be understood, was never accepted. Now I'm a television correspondent and New York will be watching. I wondered if I could pull it off. And I wondered if Andrew would see me. Surely, one day, he would call. He could stay with me as soon as I found an apartment. And he would be "real proud" of me when I introduced him to all the CBS newsmen I now spoke to on a first-name basis. Walter, I'd like you to meet my best friend, Andrew Johnson. Pretty big stuff.

Finally, the time came when I was assigned to be part of Cronkite and Company, an on-the-air special correspondent on Sunday evenings at seven.

The weekly rundown was, as follows:

> Washington feed-in—the president to visit nine nations—
>   Camp David
> New York update
> Kennedy
> Britain asks for nuclear tests
> USSR Lunik III moon photographs
> Van Doren admits quiz hoax
> UN investigates Red aggression
> De Gaulle peace bid
> Commercial
> Station break
> Noel Baker Nobel Prize
> NATO Soviet Berlin request
> Hammarskjöld—Israel—UAR
> Apollo Mission preparation
> Cape Canaveral lead-in

Commercial
Mexican hurricane
Yankees—Milwaukee Braves
Special story—Joe Martin

"Stand by, master control, reel three in the rack. Five, four, three . . . cue telecine . . . two, one . . . sound up, lead in, go!" Music up, graphics. Think of Cronkite. Always relaxed. Hot lights overhead, pressure, speak, clearly, sincerely. But, for God's sake, *speak*.

> This is Jonathan Landau in New York.
> After months on the road, John Fitzgerald Kennedy is the most practiced performer in this season's Democratic road show. Today in Louisiana, Senator Kennedy gave an impressive demonstration of his growing ability to do the right thing, say the right word, pump the right hand, at just the right time. With warring candidates and wary Negroes, with congressmen and Cajuns, with segregationists and rice farmers, he showed a highly honed instinct for the correct thing.
> A Southerner demanded Kennedy's views on segregation, received an answer that offended no one.
> [*Cut to Kennedy*]: "All this was decided in 1954 by the Supreme Court. There is no question about it, nor should there be."
> To top it off, Kennedy brought on his pretty thirty-year-old wife, Jacqueline, who stopped the show before ninety-five thousand French-speaking Cajuns in Crowley with a graceful speech in her best Parisian accent.
> [*Cut to Jackie*]: "*Bonjour, mes amis . . . Je suis d'origine française . . .*"
> This is Jonathan Landau for CBS.

I did it!
Shepley gave me a thumb-up sign of approval from the control booth. Then the red light flashed and I was on camera again, leading the local reporters in and out of their stories.
Cronkite followed with the network news, then a story on Joe Martin, beloved speaker of the house, who had just been defeated. I watched and listened to Walter's easy and brilliant style.

> They called him Old Joe. They loved the man in the blue serge suit and the box-toe, ankle-high shoes, the teetotaling bachelor with the cowlick and the beetle-browed scowl that

183

could vanish in a smile of quick warmth. They delighted in such malaprops as "gilded muscle" for "guided missile" and "the chair recognizes the gentleman from Rayburn, Mr. Texas." They marveled at his instinct for the House that was his home.

The president said, "I can't understand how he knows what's going to happen in the House months before it happens. It's uncanny."

For years, then, Old Joe was a term of respect and affection. But some of his fondest followers had recently come to admit that Joseph William Martin, Jr., seventy-four, of North Attleboro, Massachusetts, two-time speaker of the House, really was Old Joe—too old. Last week the Republican members of the House of Representatives voted Old Joe out of the leadership post he had held for twenty years.

Beaten in the balloting, Joe Martin returned to his office and sat down sadly at his desk. All week long, he had been awaiting a telephone call from President Eisenhower. Now— too late—it came.

"How are you, Joe?" asked the president. "I'm sorry that two good friends got in a fight." Ike suggested that Martin keep on coming to the weekly White House legislative conferences.

"No, that I can't do," replied Martin. He hung up, dropped his head between his arms on his desk, and, as visitors turned silently away, Old Joe Martin wept.

Walter was the best. And he spent a lot of time with me. He translated his years as a commentator into professional advice. Knowledge replaced experience. I took every shortcut to a practiced performance until I was pretty good.

At News, over mugs of steaming coffee, Eric Severeid told me of an apartment overlooking Central Park.

"It's a beautiful little duplex, Jonathan. I was going to take it, but I've been transferred. Would you like to take a look? It's rent-controlled, and every room overlooks the park."

I took it without seeing it. Severeid also told me about Terry Smith, a new set designer who was doing the Como show.

"He's ingenious and tasteful. I'll give him a ring and see if he'd like to help you with the apartment."

Terry Smith was the brightest set designer at the network, and for a small fee he assigned carpenters and painters right out of the network's construction department. They were professionals who worked on their own time. Terry sketched the layout for my approval and then his crew arrived. Walls were paneled, floors tiled, windows framed, and the dining room expanded into a country kitchen that accommodated twenty people.

The two-story living room graciously accommodated the art and some large-scale antiques I had gradually collected in England with my royalties from *Sunday's People*. Each morning, sun silhouetted the New York skyline in oranges and reds and yellows, and the evening sunset drenched the city's architecture with a stirring haze of sunlight dust until it became evening blue.

Manhattan lights illustrated night into another day. In between the high and mighty towers of zigzagged, sharp-edged forms, dazzling in arrestingly beautiful patterns of light and shadow, was the small duplex that I called my home.

The Centry was thirties-built, deco-decorated. There were only two apartments on each floor. I was high on twenty. Each morning, uniformly polite elevator operators and amicable doormen met me and dispatched current bulletins:

"New neighbor on fifteen."

"The Fishers got robbed."

"The mail is late."

"Cabs are on strike."

"The window cleaner is here."

"The tow truck is out front."

"The Yankees won."

I was waiting for the elevator one morning when a little fellow came out. He was on a crutch, wearing a brace. He had an artificial leg and his name was Max. He was always trying to move faster than he could, hobbling around the apartment, down halls, even the fire escapes. And once I saw him in the park trying to run.

"Why do you run so much? Are you trying to lose weight?"

"I'm in training," he said. "I'm going to run a mile in the New York field-and-track trials this spring."

"Are you going to win?"

"Yes," he said. "No one will catch me. But I think I need a coach."

He tried to skip, hopelessly out of step, at my side as I

185

walked through Central Park over to my office near Rocke-feller Center.

"Will you be my coach? Do you know anything about track?"

"Well, a little."

"Could ya learn?"

"Why?"

"I need someone to help me win the track meet. All the schools are entering. But I really need a coach."

"I'd like to be your coach, Max, but I'm just starting a new job, and I'll be traveling a lot. I won't be around."

"What do you do?"

"I give the news at CBS."

"Can I watch?"

"Every night at seven."

"No, I mean at the studio."

"Well, I don't know. Sure, come with me. I'll see if I can arrange a tour for you."

"That'd be great, Jonathan."

"They do game shows in the morning. You can see them."

Over at CBS I went to the tour desk and arranged a guide to show Max the productions.

"Then come up to my office. I'll see you at noon; we can have a sandwich."

"Thanks, Jonathan."

All morning I read news reports. There was a story about a court-martial down in Virginia that looked like an outrageous piece of human interest. The court-martial of Andrew God, Jr., who refused to peel potatoes, according to Army regula-tions, while on KP. Under the new Uniform Code of Military Justice, he demanded a court-martial and got one. The trial had all the trimmings of a traditional military tribunal, even a heavily worded bill of specifications:

> Private Andrew God, twenty-five, having knowledge of the lawful order to peel and eye potatoes as directed, an order which it was his duty to obey, did fail to obey same. He did, without proper authority, willfully suffer potatoes, of some value, military property of the United States, to be destroyed by improper peeling.

The prosecution's case was clear enough. The mess sergeant testified that Private God, knife in hand, had removed the eyes in gouged chunks and sliced off random slabs instead of peeling them delicately with the swift wrist motion appropriate to the task. Then the mess sergeant, armed with a potato and peeler, earnestly reenacted the whole business, mimicking God's offense, slashing ruthlessly away until the potato looked like a candidate for shoestring fries.

The case for the defense was even stronger. A mess sergeant from another company earnestly testified that Private God's peelings were quite normal, considering that the accused had only a knife to work with instead of a potato peeler.

That did it! The trial lasted two hours. Andrew God got off scot-free. The whole thing seemed ridiculous. "Only God knew" how the wheels of justice turned.

Shepley okayed the story; the news was continuing!

Max was late, so I went down to Production to find him in Special Effects, where they were making bubbles for a commercial. I stopped and watched for a moment. Large airborne bubbles reflected rainbow colors. I asked if I could have some. "Sure, why not?"

Max and I went back up to my office and opened the window high above New York. We blew soap bubbles and floated them into westerly winds where undulating currents took them far away. They then descended and sailed across Manhattan, disappearing over the canyons to the Hudson River.

This was an Andrew adventure. The bubbles caused me to think of him. I had searched for him everywhere. The Red Caps? Sure, they were with Glenn Miller. One story crossed another, leads, all dead ends. At one point I heard he was in Los Angeles. I checked with agents.

"Yes, the Red Caps were there, but they broke up some time ago." They had never heard of Andrew.

Another impersonal telephone voice told me he knew a black man from the South. He thought his name was Andrew and he had gone to San Diego to work as a gardener, but he didn't know exactly where. I wondered if Andrew had ever been in Hollywood with the Red Caps, or had he been spinning another fantasy for me?

I just wanted to find him. He was important to me and I wanted him to know that. I thought about all the reasons I had loved him and the magical and mystical way he appeared that August in Augusta, Georgia, for a short time and helped me with my life. Then, like the bubbles, he disappeared. I had to face it. I might never find him.

20

Sunday. The telephone rang.

"Hello, Jonathan? Jonathan Landau? This is Lady. Lady Meredith. Do you remember me?"

"Hello, Lady. Of course I do."

A thousand memories. Her voice was slow and Southern. "I've been watching you on the news, Jonathan."

"Really. Well, I'm happy to hear from you."

"I want to see you, Jonathan. I was just wondering . . . the last time I saw you, it was at Yale—"

"How is your polo player?" I interrupted.

Lady laughed. "Oh, Jonathan!"

She always had the most enchanting way of saying "Oh, Jonathan." It was never "Jonathan," but just like it was all one name, O-h-j-o-n-a-t-h-a-n. And she could say it in so many ways: "Ohjonathan!" with shock and surprise; "Ohjonathan" with excitement and anticipation.

"I've thought of you. There you were with a perfect shot at the goal, and—"

"I remember, Lady." I settled back into my leather chair, feet up on the desk. The lights were changing. I looked out to the East River. Boats were chugging away. "I remember. I missed."

"That was so funny."

"I didn't think so at the time."

"You tried so hard. I felt so badly for you."

"I was just trying to win you. I thought if I won the game that would do it."

She laughed again and said, "How are your parents?"

"Fine."

189

"Jonathan, I have an art gallery now and there's an opening Thursday night. Then I'm having a few people over for dinner. Will you come?"

"What time?"

"The opening is at six, and dinner is at nine."

"I'm afraid that I can't make the gallery, but dinner would be fine."

"That's wonderful, Jonathan. I'm at four-eleven Park at Fifty-second Street, across from Delmonico's. Nine o'clock. Black tie."

"Black tie. I'll be there." Click.

Thursday evening came quickly. I was still reading the local news on Channel 2 News but Shepley had also given me a national spot with Cronkite. I was becoming more of a personality than a writer. I had learned to affect a six-o'clock news attitude and speak in a newscaster lilt. No one ever spoke that way in conversation. It was just for the news.

"And now," pause, "the news. Washington," pause, "on Capitol Hill this evening," pause. London, the queen; the president; events; eyewitness reports; disasters—all held equal currency. I watched Cronkite and Ed Murrow, their studied composure. It was all in the attitude. Shepley told me, "You're young. That's a good contrast for the audience we're reaching. You have an innocent credibility." It was the image CBS wanted to establish that year.

I arrived at Lady's apartment the obligatory few minutes after nine. The doorman rang Ashley. The apartment was modern, spacious, stark, and chromed. The colors were subdued, shades of beige and white, to accent a collection of modern art that gallerized the walls. Extravagantly understated. Obviously expensive. Intellectually pretentious. A studied ease. Black-tie people counterpointed the decor.

Lady was beautiful, dressed in black chiffon, very bare. Her breasts were full. Once they had been olives, then peaches, now free-floating melons. I had watched and followed her ripening progression. Her butter-blond hair was darker, not quite as bright. Her eyes were just as blue and her smile Ipana perfect.

190

"Ohjonathan," Lady sighed. She kissed me and introduced me around the room to ten or so guests. "Philip, this is Jonathan Landau. Marissa, Jonathan."

"How do you do?"

"Hello."

"Enjoy you on the news."

"Very established."

I thought: What?

"Thank you."

"Missy, Missy Pulitzer, Jonathan Landau."

Lady was actually showing me off to young brokers and lawyers who spent leisure hours at their profession, and ladies who lunched. New York's finest. Café society. It was the Avon group talking in that pitched, clipped, up-front, top-of-the-palate style. This was the summer-in-Southampton, lunch-at-21, cocktails-at-River House, squash-at the-Racquet Club, dancing-at-El Morocco, East Side, shop-at-Bloomingdale's set. I followed the rules and played just as easily as they. As long as you knew the vocabulary you could work the territory. Passwords like "Republican," "amusing," "really," "bullish," "Yale," "*Mayflower*," "Piping Rock," "Eddie Condon's," all held value.

At dinner the conversation focused around Senator Kennedy, Catholicism, and Cuba. I was expected to comment. I did. I talked at great length. I was held in esteem and I knew this. Everyone wanted to know my views. They accepted anything I said. I performed for them.

"Jonathan and I have known each other since we were seven. Can you imagine? And now here he is, doing the news on television, and he couldn't even talk when he was a little boy," Lady exclaimed in a soft flow of Southern honey.

"Why is that?" Missy asked, looking at me with courtesy rather than interest.

"I just didn't talk much. I was always a better listener."

Lady changed the conversation to her field and spoke authoritatively about art. Her prestigious gallery was inconsistent with the programmed intelligence of her guests.

The dinner was light and acceptable: vichyssoise, Bibb-lettuce-and-watercress-salad, chicken in a Mornay sauce,

191

braised asparagus, chocolate soufflé, followed by a Château d'Yquem.

All evening Lady gave me revealing little squeezes with her hand. We were alone only when I was leaving. We were standing at the door.

"Jonathan, my friends just adored you. Won't you stay for a brandy? We could talk like we used to and"—she paused—"everything."

"I'd really love to, Lady, but I have an early assignment. I'll call you."

"That would be nice, Jonathan. But are you sure you can't stay?" Her tone was easy.

"Maybe we'll go dancing one night. The Pierre has an intimate orchestra, very danceable." I spoke the jargon fluently.

She kissed me good night. Her kiss asked and demanded a deeper response than I could give.

"It's been lovely seeing you, Lady. Thank you for asking me."

"I want to see you again, Jonathan. I hope it will be very soon."

In the paneled elevator, riding down, the uniformed operator, sixtyish and distinguished, looked more like a tenant of the building. Good for Lady's image. She was always part of an exclusive club. At the National. And at home.

"Are you Jonathan . . . CBS . . . ?"

"Yes."

"That story on the court-martial was very funny. I like seeing the human side of the news."

Apparently, I appeared to be successful. Life had changed but I had not. Seeing Lady, I still felt like the same kid who didn't belong. All the recognition and acclaim should have meant more to me. But I was feeling phony. A terrific phony. Fooling everybody—I'm a fraud, I thought. I should have felt wonderful and terrific, and I began to wonder why I didn't. I didn't know that night, but I found out later, I wasn't being me.

"Good night, sir," said the elevator man.

"Good night."

Outside, the doorman had a cab waiting for me, and the car

sped through empty New York streets, our progress orchestrated by traffic lights changing to red and green and yellow.

I saw Lady several times after that, and we did go dancing one evening at the Pierre Grill. Occasionally people would recognize me, and Lady seemed to like that.

I wrote long letters to April, different sizes, different styles, different shapes. One letter was written on a large scroll over 150 feet long. Another was two feet by three feet. The post office said they couldn't send a letter that size.

"Why not?"

"We have nothing in our postal regulations to cover it."

"Well, send it as a package." They did.

I made a small envelope twice the size of a stamp. I wrote under a magnifying glass. The post office wouldn't accept that either. So I attached a large tag and off it went. Some days I carried a tape machine with me and recorded the music of a favorite song, a thought.

I sent pictures of the apartment to April. And I photographed a day from sunrise to sunset, the same angle, same view. Some of the photographs showed a yellow sky with amber clouds, others with ribbons of pink melding into oranges and reds. I attached a note to Patrick: "Too bad Monet didn't have a camera."

April's letters started out filled with sentiment and feeling. Gradually they became shorter and shorter, diminished by distance, just chronicling her activities. I looked at the salutation first.

"I love you," "I think of you," "Kisses," "Love and kisses," "Must go now," "I'll write again," "I'll write again soon."

"I'll write again soon" was never soon enough. No matter how close you are, it seems how close you were. It's like standing on a beach and watching a piece of driftwood floating out to sea. The waves bring it back a few times, and each time it goes farther away until it is no more. I felt helpless.

Christmas was just a few weeks away. There was a letter from David telling me that April was not well and had again come down from Oxford.

The operator put me through.

"I'd better bring you a box of Hershey bars."

"Jonathan, it's just this silly virus again."

"I'll try to come over."

"That would be wonderful. I'm sure I just have a case of missing you too much."

"It's contagious. It's reached epidemic proportions over here. I'll be there for Christmas."

I felt better knowing I would see her in a few weeks.

21

A few mornings later Max appeared at my door. "I came to borrow something for my mom."

"Sure, come on in. What do you need to borrow?"

"I forgot."

"Well, ask your mom."

"She forgot, too. I just wanted to see you, I guess."

"That's nice. Do you like pie?"

"Yeah."

"Come on in and borrow a piece of pie, then. It's lemon meringue."

"It's my favorite," Max said. "Thanks," he managed with a mouth full of pie. "Jonathan, I really need a favor."

"What is it, Max?"

"I need someone to help me train for the track meet, like I was telling you."

"I'm still busy, Max. Maybe in a few weeks." I didn't know how to tell him. How could he compete in a track meet with just one leg? "Yeah, I'll see what I can do."

"Thanks, Jonathan."

I walked over to CBS News. Max was enough to break your heart. He was a fighter. Imagine, that kid had enough guts to want to run track. I couldn't get him out of my mind.

I was checking out a new space-program presentation from NASA when Shepley called me into his office.

"Landau, you're going to Cuba. The story is Castro. I'd like you to be in Havana just after Christmas."

"Any trouble getting in?"

"No, Castro is an ally. Batista is out. Fidel has won the revolution. It's a good story, your kind of story. Should be a

195

lot happening the first of the year. Take a few days off. Do your homework."

I pulled out the file on Fidel Castro.

He is the first hero to appear in Cuba in modern times. Born on his father's sugar plantation, August 13, 1926, in Oriente, a province which had been the cradle of Cuban revolutionary activity. His radical tendencies were born in the 1940's, when he was a student in Havana. He combines physical bigness and physical strength, has a reputation for intellect, and a gift for oratory. He projected his role as man of the people by affecting military clothes, beard and cigar, and was known to give five-hour speeches. He made efforts to launch a revolution in 1953. He failed and was jailed, but was granted freedom in Batista's amnesty of 1955. He spent a year and a half in Mexico preparing the next move. He obtained money from Cuban exiles in New York and Florida, trained a military cadre, and maintained contacts with revolutionaries at home and Cuba. . . .

Another invasion took place at Oriente Beach, December 1956. It was a disaster. Castro's men were captured by government troops almost immediately after landing. Out of eighty-two of the invaders, only Castro and eleven others escaped to reach the Sierra Maestra mountains. He was believed dead until Herbert Mathews of the New York *Times* made a journey to Castro's hideout in the remote mountains and wrote a series of articles about the dedicated revolution and its followers.

Things broke fast around News. It was a contest of deadlines, with pressure on content. I was the odd man out, anytime an important story was breaking, I was sent to pick up the human-interest angles. I wasn't a *Times*-trained journalist with fast-breaking writing ability, facts hard-checked by editors. I saw the world in a different way, another perspective. That is what Shepley wanted.

"Dick, I'd like to take a few days off before Havana. I want to go to London."

"No problem, as long as you're in Havana by New Year's."

I was on my way to London when Shepley intercepted me at Pan Am. "Reroute yourself to Turkey. One of our planes was just shot down in a Russian vector. We have the transmission tapes in Ankara now being translated. It will just delay your trip a day or so. Do you mind, Jonathan? It's a hot story."

When I arrived in Istanbul I went straight to SAC headquarters. Colonel Arthur Henry had translated the tapes. They were remarkable. I took a camera crew up to the border. Along the way, I received information about the flight. I put the facts down and waited to hear when we would have satellite transmission.

Three hours later the telephone rang, "We have it in fifteen minutes. Three o'clock your time. You have a story, you're on live."

This is Jonathan Landau in Turkey, looking across the border to Soviet Armenia.

There is a huge plume of smoke rising from the Communist territory. Yesterday, just minutes before the smoke rose, Allied radio monitors around the southern ring of the USSR taped their quota of Russian radio talk and recorded the grim conversation of five Soviet jet-fighter pilots. The jets had scrambled into the sky for a look at an intruder inside Russia's southern border. It was, in fact, an unarmed four-engine U.S. Air Force C-130 transport, carrying seventeen men and flying a course from Trabzon to Van, Turkey, in high winds and bad weather. The C-130 strayed over the Turkish fence into Communist territory, possibly confused by high-strength directional signals from Soviet radio stations. Following the vectors from their own ground radar stations, the Russians sped toward the target area, barking pilot's comeback chatter over the radio. The monitors caught virtually every word. This is what they said:

"582, I see the target to the right. It's altitude is 100 hectometers."

"I am 201. I see the target. Attack! Attack! Attack, 218, attack!"

"The target is burning. There is a hit."

"The target is banking. Open fire!"

"The tail assembly is falling off the target. Look at him. He will not get away. He is already falling."

"Yes, he is falling. I will finish him off, boys. I will finish him off on the run."

"The target has lost control and is going down. The target has turned over. Ah, ha. You see? He is falling."

"Yes, form up. Go home."

After U.S. protest, the Soviets have denied any knowledge of the plane.

Today, the wreckage has been found and the Soviets have announced that they have no information about the seventeen airmen who are missing. Somewhere in the Soviet territory are those men, all of them, perhaps, dead. And if it is any consolation to the United States, it lies in the fact that the free world now knows how they died.

This is Jonathan Landau in Turkey.

I wrapped the story and headed for London.

David met me at the airport. I wore a dark pin-striped suit.

"Very English," David commented, "like the suit."

"Me, English?"

"Jonathan, you look more English than any Englishman."

It was true. A lot of people were surprised that I was not. As soon as they heard my accent, which was more Canadian than American, they'd say, "But, you're not English." They'd hold on to the Englishhhhh.

"*Sunday's People* is still doing well. You have royalties in account at Barclays Bank."

"I know."

"We should write another sometime, partner," David said, trying to sound American. "But you're going off to Cuba, giving up the theater, hey?"

We moved carefully through traffic.

"How is April?"

"I'm not quite sure. She's just not herself. It doesn't make sense. It could be mononucleosis."

"If it is, you better get a shot of gamma globulin."

"Who's her doctor?"

"A man by the name of Trevor Hopkins—I think that's it."

"Trevor Hopkins at King's Hospital?" David turned to me and said quietly, "He's a cancer specialist."

It couldn't be possible. "David, would you stop at that call box?"

"Of course."

I jumped out of the car before it reached the curb, looked through the directory inquiries and found Trevor Hopkins. His receptionist told me that if I'd like to drop over, he would see me. I got back in the car.

"David, would you drop me off in Harley Street?"

"Of course. When I said he was a specialist in cancer, I didn't mean to scare you. He's really a very fine internist."

"Oh, I understand. I would just like to see him."

Harley Street was narrow, lined with old houses, three- and four-story brownstones, with long flights of steps leading to the first floors.

His receptionist showed me into the doctor's office without delay. Outside, in a reception hall, there were four or five people waiting to see him. One man looked dully into the distance; the others read old magazines. There was a large, square desk in the center of the office. It was a campaign desk with drawers on all four sides. One wall was covered with colored prints of physicians in their gowns, sixteenth-, seventeenth-, and eighteenth-century doctors. On the other wall were autographed pictures of famous physicians. A microscope was on a side table. It reminded me of my father's office. There was a box with assorted bandages and implements, needles and medicine. The double door opened, and a tall, distinguished man in a dark suit and polka-dot tie walked in. His hair was gray and rather long.

"Good afternoon, Mr. Landau. I'm Trevor Hopkins."

"How do you do, sir. I like your desk."

"Yes, thank you. India. It was originally a campaign desk out there. Please sit down. Tea?"

"Yes, thank you."

"You want to know about April?"

"Yes, in fact, I just flew over to see her."

"Then you know. She's very ill. But she has an even chance."

The words echoed dissonantly, "an even chance."

"No, sir," I whispered. "I didn't know she was so sick."

"I'm sorry," the physician said. "I first suspected something ten years ago when April broke her arm and it wouldn't heal after the cast was removed. It was hard to diagnose. I thought it could be bone cancer, or leukemia, or a severe calcium disorder.

"I suspected a disease called hyperplasia of the parathyroid —but I couldn't find a tumor.

"Her symptoms were extreme fatigue, some anemia. Then her bone healed. Strange.

"I even thought it could be neuromuscular. She also had the symptoms of autoimmune disease. That is why her illness was so difficult to diagnose. I did a biopsy.

"I suspect April had a disease called multiple myeloma. It is related to leukemia and it often goes into remission.

"The disease affects the myeloid tissue, which produces white blood cells.

"If her immune system is active and functioning, then her own system will fight and tolerate the disease."

"But will she live?" I asked. Everything was dissonant and confused.

"As I said, an even chance."

An even chance—"even chance" echoed over and over.

"There's a conservative estimate. Every day, she is getting better. But you must remember, it's an absolutely hellish disease. Not much is known."

"Can it be fatal?" I was sick inside. It was a feeling of a terrible hurt. I kept seeing her in different places, across summer lawns into winter rooms.

"Yes. She could take a turn for the worst. But she has been making good progress. The transfusions seem to be helping. The medication eases pain, which is considerable. And I am hoping for a complete breakthrough in time."

That's where she was, I thought to myself, when she was away for weeks at a time "doing research."

"How does she look?"

"She looks well. A little tired. There might be some weight loss. She might fall down and bruise herself. Her resistance is low. I'm doing the best I can."

"Does she know?"

"Yes, she knows."

"Her parents know?"

"Yes."

I couldn't believe she was seriously ill. April would get better. I'd call my father. Surely he'd know the latest advancements.

I went around to the clinic and waited across the street. Then the children broke onto the playground. They flooded recess, thrusting with all their energy. Out the doors they came, slowly followed by April. She was on crutches. I watched her.

200

I wanted to shout: April, I'm here! I'm here. Everything is going to be all right.

There she was, brave and alone. She had been quiet all these years, never mentioning any pain, any fear. I had no idea. The times when she had disappeared for several weeks—Christ, she had been going for treatments.

There was an unbearable aching in me. I watched her with the children. She's going to make it. With that spirit she will. She has an even chance. There will be a breakthrough. Luck is with us.

That afternoon I talked to Patrick while I waited for April to come home. "We must get another opinion."

"We have, Jonathan. We all have great hope, and I want you to have it, too."

"Why didn't you tell me?"

"I promised April, Jonathan. She's determined to beat this thing. You remember the evening you asked for her hand?"

"You never answered me."

"Now you know why. We couldn't bring ourselves to tell you. Jonathan, I want you to know, your being here brings a lot of happiness to us all."

"I'm very touched by that."

"We're touched by you. We heard about the dinner and the presents you gave to April when you were last here."

"And I didn't even know."

"I guess you love April very much."

We were interrupted by the sound of a door and splashing rain when April came in the front hall.

"Jonathan, not a word, please. She doesn't want you to know."

I hid in the kitchen. I wanted to surprise her.

I rang her room from the house phone in the pantry. She answered. "Hi. Remember me? This is Jonathan Landau. Tall American, downy brown eyes, winning smile, intelligent."

"Jonathan, where are you?"

"I'm in the kitchen trying to fit into the dumbwaiter so I can come up and see you."

"Jonathan! It's not big enough. It won't hold you."

It was about two feet wide and about four feet high.

"Jonathan!"

I folded myself thin and shut the door. "All right," I

shouted, "I'm coming up." There was a muffled shout. "Ring for me."

April pushed the buzzer in her room. Straining, the lift slowly ascended to the second floor. April opened the door, smiling. I unfolded myself out.

"Welcome to London," she said.

"Here, have a Hershey bar."

I was self-conscious. I went to the extreme, small talk, my trip, the weather, New York. I stumbled through conversation.

"Let's have some tea." We went downstairs to the library, and high tea was brought to us. Overcompensating, I was too attentive. I kept looking at her to see if I could visually detect any illness. She looked wonderful, a little tired.

"You haven't asked about the crutches."

"Oh. Crutches. Yes. I noticed. You seem to be on crutches. I guess you broke a leg or something."

"I fell and bruised my hip."

"Broken arm, broken hip."

"I just hurt it."

"You're accident-prone." I couldn't look at her.

Everything I was saying was wrong. I couldn't get my thoughts together.

She knows that I know. I faltered.

"I have to tell you, I met this young kid, Max, who lives next door to me. He just knocked on my door and asked me to be his coach. He only has one leg, a brace, and he wants to enter a track meet. Can you imagine that? He wants to enter a track meet and run the four hundred."

"You'll make a good coach," April said. "You've got to help him."

"But he can't win. He can't run," I said.

"Yes, he can." There was a long pause. "You did."

"I did."

I thought to myself: Yeah, I had a handicap. And it left emotional scars. You never feel you're really all right. You have to be on guard against setting yourself up to be rejected, because that feeling is so familiar it becomes comfortable. You feel you're always wearing the wrong suit at the wrong party at the wrong time.

202

You can't be understood, so you fight it, and you finally get on top of it. You become obsessed with language and possessed with the ability to communicate. Talk, talk fluidly, words and thoughts and poetry, language, the importance of words, big words, kind words, little words, small words.

There was a time when words didn't mean anything to me. There was a communication beyond words, as it was with Lily, something you couldn't put into words, that you put into feelings, an expression, a thought, a look. Now when I wanted words to count and mean something wonderful and good and comforting, they wouldn't come. I reached for them and they weren't there. For the first time in many years, I reached to break the silence.

Finally, it just came out.

"I used to be on crutches once. I never told anyone. I couldn't talk."

"I know," she said.

April took a piece of paper and wrote, "I love you, Jonathan." It was then that I knew that she knew not so much where I was going as where I was coming from. It reminded me of all those years when I was a child when I had written down my thoughts on a piece of paper.

At that moment, we developed a bond, a feeling, a knowing, a coming together. Like Hemingway, I thought. "You know what you know." We knew, both of us, about each other.

I held April, and without looking up, she reached for my cheek and brushed away my tears.

"I didn't want you to know. I'm sorry."

I held her and thought about all she meant to me. I *could not* lose her. We belong to each other. For the first time in my life I didn't feel alone. I was comfortable. I *belonged* with April. I stayed with her until she fell asleep.

The next morning, I went down to the medical library at St. George's Hospital and read everything I could on multiple myeloma and also on autoimmune disease. A section on catastrophic illness in a medical textbook read:

> *Multiple Myeloma* is a *plasma cell* neoplasm (tumor growth) belonging to the disorders associated with *hypergammaglobulinemia*.

The onset and early courses are usually insidious:
1. weakness
2. anorexia (loss of appetite)
3. weight loss (in more advanced cases)
4. bone involvement (pathologic fractures, osteolytic lesions, collapsed vertebrae)
5. *anemia*
6. renal insufficiency (protein in urine)
7. neurologic deficits (pain, palsies, paresthesias)
8. repeated bacterial infections

Hypercalcemia is frequently encountered (hypercalcemia occurs in hyperparathyroidism and this disease must be differentiated from it).

Although multiple myeloma advances with varying degrees of rapidity, it may remain static for prolonged periods.

Management:
1. Supportive treatment of bone pain, refractory anemia, skeletal defects, renal insufficiency and bacterial infections.
2. Myelomatous tumors are moderately radiosensitive (i.e., X-ray treatment). Callus formation is commonly observed at the site of pathologic fractures.
3. The alkylating agents (L-phenylalanine mustard) and cytotoxan have been reported to induce partial remissions in 25–30%.
4. Cortisone may also produce similar remissions but its main use is to ameliorate hypercalcemia, hemolytic anemia, and bleeding tendencies.
5. Some investigators use a combination of cortisone, testosterone, and an alkylating agent as the basic systemic treatment.

Then I read in *Lancet* about an experiment that had brought about remission and then a cure.

The study stated a new technique for fractinating human blood and separating out the immune globulin components and suggested new treatment modalities. Immune globulins assisted the body's defense mechanism in supportable control studies at the Karolinska Clinic in Stockholm. It was still in its experimental stages and thirty case histories reported good results. I called Trevor Hopkins and asked him about it.

"We're trying that just now, Jonathan. I know about Hansen's work. Thank you for calling me. And, Jonathan, did you ever think about going into medicine? You would make a fine doctor."

We celebrated Christmas. The table was set with roast turkey and pheasant, a Christmas goose, stuffing and sauces, nuts and raisins, and plum pudding.

Patrick stood up. "I know that you will be leaving tomorrow, Jonathan, and we have a tradition in our family to read a passage from the sixteenth century at Christmas each year. I'd like to share it with you now, as part of our family.

"I salute you. There is nothing I can give you which you have not; there is much, that, which I cannot give, you can take.

"No heaven can come to us unless our hearts find rest in it today.

"Take heaven. No peace lies in the future which is not hidden in the present instant. Take peace.

"The gloom of the world is but a shadow; behind it, yet, within our reach, is joy. Take joy.

"And so, at this Christmastime, I greet you, with the prayer that, for you, now and forever, the day will break and the shadows will flee away."

There was quiet. In this spirit of Christmastide a fire blazed and pine cones crackled. It was a lovely moment.

Later in the evening we exchanged presents. April gave me a lovely desk, a small table from Asprey's. I gave her a Picasso lithograph of children dancing. And a simple ring from Cartier.

It was wrapped in a small box.

"Open it up, April."

"What is it?"

"It's a house."

She looked up at me and smiled. She knew what it was.

"It's a beautiful ring, Jonathan. Does this mean we're engaged?"

"Absolutely committed," I said. "I know an eighteenth-century pavilion with orange trees. It's a nice place to get married."

"Just can't let a good thing pass by, aye, Jonathan?"

"Seems to be the thing to do this season. Do you mind if I support you in a style to which you are unaccustomed?"

"Unaccustomed?"

"Yes, I can't afford the finer things in life."

"In that case, you'd better get back to work, because I want a very long honeymoon."

"How long?"

"Six months at least."

"How 'bout sunny Havana? Come with me, we'll make love through a revolution. We'll revolutionize lovemaking. A little mambo, a little cha-cha-cha. It's the Latin in me. I'm hot-blooded."

"Jonathan."

"Yes?"

"I love it."

"The Hotel Nacional, a warm temperate climate, we'll drive through the palm trees, we'll dance at the Tropicana. 'Hasta las verdes barandas. Barandales, de la luna por donde retumba el agua.' That's García Lorca."

"What does it mean?" said April.

"I haven't a clue. But doesn't it sound good? Barandales . . . retumba . . ." Suddenly I said, "I don't want to leave. I really don't."

"Jonathan, you must, and you'd better make some money. I have expensive tastes."

"Why didn't you tell me you've been so sick?"

"I didn't want to worry you. I'm going to be fine. You believe me, don't you? I'll come to New York in a few months."

"Promise?"

"Of course, I promise. We'll walk through America together."

I left for Havana the following morning.

22

The BOAC from London flew directly to Miami. Ninety miles from Key West to Cuba. The Cubana Airways flight to Havana was empty. From the airport, the driver speeded along the Malicón, past colonial buildings painted in pastels, past memories of a time when Cuba was alive with cruise ships and luxury hotels, gambling casinos and brothels, and rum and Coca-Cola competing for the Yankee dollar.

The first tourist to the balmy island went ashore, sword in one hand, cross in the other. The gentle Siboney Indians left their hammocks and met Christopher Columbus crying, "Peace, we are friends." The Spanish slid into Havana harbor with black slaves, and the Pearl of the Antilles was formed and forged into a elegant sugar-based society of stately mansions, which gave way to arrogant functionaries and grafting politicians gathering fortunes from gambling, prostitution, and a leaky public till.

Now, in disgust and shame, a small band of guerrillas started a civil war that cost a hundred million dollars and took eight thousand lives.

All of Havana had massed to greet its hero. Intermittent motorcades with riflemen passed before us, waiting for Castro, the towering thirty-one-year-old lawyer and intellectual, Cuba's new Robin Hood. With eighty-two seasick rebels he had invaded the southern coast in 1956 to fight the military dictatorship of Batista. While one thousand ragged, rugged rebels ruled the jungle-patched mountains of the Sierra Maestra, calling themselves Fidelistas.

The movement was known as the "Twenty-sixth of July," after Castro's first abortive attempt at a revolution. Whether he had eighty-two men at the start or twelve at the worst, or the ten thousand he had now, at the end Castro fought a classically frugal guerrilla war.

All week long, the rebel leaders blared victory, reporting their forces sweeping town after town in Oriente and Las Villas provinces, rooting out small garrisons, taking over civil authority. There was little question that the rebels were on the move and that dictator Batista's army had retreated.

Castro was a man of ideals, a visionary who cared for his people. A restoration of democracy, elections, a congress, court justice. He promised all. I had never liked Batista. Not since the *St. Louis*, when pervading corruption sent Lily and seven hundred passengers to their deaths.

And now, Havana waited. The celebration was on. Thousands of girls paraded about dressed in red and black, the rebel colors. I passed cheering students roaming through Havana University. Amiable Cubans dancing in the street, chanting *Cuba sí, Yanqui no,"* in a mambo beat. *"Fidel Castro es tu papa, Eisenhower ha ha ha."* Still, they were open and friendly.

The revolution seemed to be run for and by Cubans no older than thirty.

In the harbor were Russian ships with their red stars displayed against the tropical sky. At the Hotel Nacional, there was a new type of tourist. I tripped over exotic types—Russian and Czech technicians in square-toed shoes and terrible haircuts; British newsmen privately tickled that the United States had its own bloody Suez-Nasser mess; imported Mexican oil experts; Bolivian female labor leaders in derbies.

People in the lobby were speaking in many languages. A Yugoslav saw in Fidel a Latin Tito using Russian aid to arrest independence from the United States, as Tito used U.S. aid to pry loose from the hug of the Bear.

When I registered, the manager looked up. "You Americans are crazy. You keep pushing Castro into the arms of the Soviets. This revolution is a blow to you."

I checked into my room. The Nacional did not hold its former elegance. It had weathered with misuse. I went swimming in the pool with members of the Peking Opera Company. They were solemn, frightened Chinese, and when they saw I was American, they paddled away.

Down from the eastern hills, where he had forged his victory, Fidel Castro marched in tumultuous triumph through towns and villages of post-Batista Cuba. He came, not as a dutifully honored conqueror, but as a man ecstatically acclaimed by the people he had liberated. All of Havana was lined on the boulevards, teeming crowds had waited deep in the night to get a glimpse of him. They screamed *Viva!* with thunderous applause and flung torrents of flowers when Castro and the Barbudos appeared.

A new *guaracha* was playing. "Fidel has arrived, Fidel has arrived. Now we Cubans are free."

Across the country, workers responded to Castro's appeal for funds to buy arms abroad. Around-the-clock Havana television stations paraded donors. Unions set up a ten-percent deduction from salaries. Four hundred people pledged to stop smoking for two days and sent in the twenty cents saved. Castro was going to get the arms and missiles and jets he wanted, if not from the U.S., from Russia. My intepreter told me that Castro would not become premier, and free elections would be held for all of Cuba.

It was New Year's Eve. The mood was a combination of jubilation and bloody revenge. The palace in Havana was lit with spotlights, and on the balcony were three men in green fatigues; Fidel, his brother Raul, and Ché Guevara stood monumentally insolent. They smiled and waved to the crowd. From the hoarse throats of 500,000 Cubans jammed before the presidential palace rose the cry, "Fi-del! Fi-del! Fi-del! Fi-del!" Fidel stood on the balcony and told them about his dream. He would purify Cuba.

"I want to go back to the Sierra Maestra," he said, "and build roads and hospitals and schools. We must have teachers. We must have a heroine in every classroom. A plot of land for every Cuban, and a people's army built to protect the people.

"There will be free elections," Castro shouted. "Those who have no land must have some. The land should belong to those who work it. We must win our economic freedom and cease being ruled by U.S. ambassadors who have been running our country for fifty years."

Then a bad thing happened in the midst of a great thing. Castro told how he had talked to two old women who had requested that their murdered sons be avenged. "It is because of people like you," said Castro, "that I'm determined to show no mercy. We must kill the traitors who stand in the way of a free people." The crowd again shouted and applauded, for eight solid minutes.

All over Cuba, crackpot patriots squared minor accounts, filled black notebooks with the names of candidates for rebel justice.

From kangaroo courts, Castro took judgment in his own hands. Nineteen pilots, ten gunners, sixteen mechanics from the Air Force went on trial for war crimes and were ordered shot.

"Fi-del, Fi-del," the crowd chanted again and again. From the balcony, Fidel Castro estimated that no fewer than 450 would be shot. His younger brother, Raul, bragged that as many as a thousand may die. This seemed to be nothing new to history. No Cuban voices rose in protest. Instead a chilling cry: *Paredón!* To the wall, to the firing squad.

Fidel sought mob approval for drumhead justice that was to put to death hundreds of Cubans accused as supporters of ex-dictator Batista. Raul Castro excited the crowd further. "None of our prisoners are tortured," he cried. "But when necessary, we execute them."

The crowd of peasants and union members that had been trucked in from outlying provinces for the New Year's Eve show screamed with delight. "*Paredón! Paredón!* To the wall! To the firing squad," was shouted over and over. "People of Cuba!" cried Castro. His shirt was gaping open to his pot-belly, his eyes were rolling. "Life is not important. All that is important is the destiny of the nation. All those in accord with the establishment of revolutionary tribunals raise their hands." Instantly, half a million hands shot up. Machetes clinked in the air, and again came the chant, "*Paredón!*"

They were not only supporters of Castro, but defectors as well. Castro shouted the name of one candidate for the wall: Major Matos, a revolutionary hero who had quit the Army a fortnight ago, charging Communist infiltration and, for his troubles, wound up in prison, along with thirty-eight of Castro's officers.

Castro's voice hardly died that night when the nation rushed to do his bidding. Over the next few days, executioners' rifles cracked across Havana. The cheering for a new democracy fell still. The only man who could silence the firing squad was Fidel, and he was in no mood for mercy. "They are criminals," he said. "Everybody knows that. Mothers come in and say, 'This man killed my son.'"

One morning I went to Fort Santiago to visit San Juan Hill, where Teddy Roosevelt led the charge. There, a bulldozer ripped out a trench 140 feet long, 15 feet wide, and 10 feet deep. Nearby, at Boniato prison, six priests listened to confessions. At dawn buses rolled out to the range where condemned men dismounted, hundreds of them, their hands tied, faces drawn. Some pleaded that they had been rebel sympathizers all along. Some were weeping. Most stood silent.

Priests led the prisoners into the glare of truck headlights to the edge of the trench, then stepped back. Fifty rebel executioners fired a fusillade of hot bullets. Bodies jackknifed backward into the grave. More prisoners stepped forward, and the grave slowly filled.

On a hill overlooking the range, a crowd gathered and cheered as each volley rang out. "Kill them, kill them, *paredón!*" the spectators bellowed as the death toll continued relentlessly.

Then there was a Lieutenant Henrique Despaigne, who had been charged with defection. He was a young, innocent man. He was singled out and allowed to write a note to his son, smoke a final cigarette, and show his scorn and nerve by shouting the order for his own execution.

It was horrible. I was sick. I left Cuba. I could not witness this for our time. A new democracy had fallen still.

Castro had betrayed Cuban hopes for democracy. He was assuming the role of dictator and demagogue and his vision had given way to terror.

23

London, Madrid, Paris. Stories coming in, teletypes clacking furiously in the New York newsroom. I filed my story and Shepley handed me the copy for the six-o'clock news.

"Welcome home, Jonathan. *Como está?*"

"Dick, I must talk to you."

"Let's go over the copy and edit," Shepley said hurriedly.

I started to read:

> This is Jonathan Landau. Not many Americans gave Cuba's Fidel Castro much of a chance when CBS reported on his rebel movement a year ago. He was a Robin Hood in the hills, a bearded bandit to some, a political messiah to others. Now, he is Cuba. His was a clean and disciplined revolution. It was an uprising of decent people against indecency . . .

"Dick, you're not serious? Whose fantasy is this?"

Shepley interrupted, "Christ, we supported a dictator who was morally bankrupt. His badges were corruptions and graft and terror."

"That might be, but this was not a clean revolution."

"Jonathan, Castro is what deGaulle was to France in 1944, when he could do no wrong. He's a man of the people."

I continued reading the copy:

> Technically, Castro is not a political leader, but only chief of the revolutionary army. The government is in the hands of his Cuban supporters.

"Christ, Dick, the government is in the hands of Ché, a Marxist."

> And when the long victory celebration subsides, new political parties will take shape. The predominant group will be Castro's Twenty-sixth of July movement. His program will be

modeled after Roosevelt's New Deal. The Communists are trying to get aboard Castro's bandwagon. But he's assured the United States that he has no use for them. Elections will be held in two years, and whether or not Castro runs for office, he now plans to keep control of the new army, as a kind of watchdog to make sure the government doesn't betray the goals of the revolution. The Castro mandate is social and economic reform and the end of graft and corruption.

"Bullshit. How about killing, and torture, and murder? Where did you get this report?"

"Bill Sherwood of *Look* has confirmed the copy. He was just down there."

"So was I. You know what is going on right now? They're killing five thousand men without a trial. I saw hundreds of men executed and piled in a ditch."

"Calm down, Jonathan. Come in the booth."

I got up from the news desk and walked in.

We were alone.

"Dick, I'm not reading this."

"You're losing your objectivity. You're being emotional, Jonathan."

"You bet your ass, I'm emotional. I was just fucking there. That egomaniac who is running Cuba has passed a point of no return. He's crazy, Dick!"

"This country is behind him," Dick warned, "behind Castro to restore Cuban democracy."

"But he's murdering, just as Machado and Batista did before him. He's betraying his own people. He's a goddamned tinhorn terror tyrant. This is no banana revolution."

Shepley almost exploded. Then, with control, he explained, "The American business community can now get used to dealing with officials who won't demand bribes and charge for special favors. And with police officers who can't be put on company payrolls in case of labor troubles. Now, listen to me, Jonathan. You have some lessons to learn. Now, sit down. The first lesson is that we always end up on the losing side, and Castro is a winner! Cuba, in this popular uprising, is a fight for all the ideals we claim to stand for. Castro cares for his people."

"You don't execute people you care for," I pointed out. "Castro is a Marxist and he's anti-American."

"You're wrong," Shepley replied vehemently. "I'm news director of this network. And the policy of this network and this government is pro-Castro. Got it, kid?"

"Yeah, I got it. And, if that is the view of this network, then it is completely out of focus."

"You'd better back off, Jonathan."

"I am, Dick." That was my last day. I had clearly failed to fit the CBS News profile.

24

I walked up Madison Avenue, and down Fifth, in a confused cycle of rejection. Everyone I wanted to see was busy. I was not sure what they were all doing. If they weren't busy they were out to lunch, out of the office, out of town, out of the country. Armies of receptionists and secretaries kept guard. You're overqualified, underqualified, check with me in a few days. We'll call you. Who is calling, please? What is this in reference to? He's in a meeting. Is there something I can help you with?

No replies. Word was around. Landau is difficult. Shepley was having the last word. I walked the streets, knocked on doors, wrote letters.

As the weeks passed, I wondered how I was going to continue paying the rent for my apartment. I had saved some money, but not enough to last very long without a job. I went around to Time-Life and saw one of the editors, Tom Birmingham, who liked my report from Hungary and some of my television stuff.

"I like your style, Jonathan, but nothing now. Wait awhile, I think we'll have an opening for you here."

We talked a bit. Birmingham was one of the few who agreed with me on Castro.

Finally I received a call from Michael Mann, head of programming at CBS. This was my chance to write television drama, I thought. Even produce. What a break! I arrived fifteen minutes early and waited in the outer office. All the offices were designed as modules. While I was waiting, the mail boy asked the receptionist about an office that had been there the day before.

"Oh, Mr. Weintraub is no longer here," she replied casually. "He left yesterday."

When an executive left, panels came down and desks went out. No more office, no more job. That's how it worked. Corporate humanity. They had no idea they had been fired, and only found out upon their return. Bewildered and lost, they could not find their offices because they no longer existed.

Mann appeared at his door. "You see that lad?" he asked, nodding as he shook my hand. "He'll be the next president around here."

The mail boy smiled, Mann winked. "Keep those cards and letters coming."

Michael Mann was an executive Napoleon, with a fierce determination to win at any cost. His smooth, unruffled voice exuded confidence. If there had been an earthquake at that moment, Michael Mann would have stood amidst the debris of charts and graphs in his office in studied composure. His empire was two suites and a corner office. That was important in the managerial hierarchy. Windows were yet another power symbol, along with sculpture, paintings, and a stand-up desk.

Two speakers stood on either side of his office. I thought it was stereo, but I soon found out it was two radios. He played them both at once. Different stations.

"I heard what happened over at News," Mann began. "You're a fighter. I like that. I can preempt those bastards anytime I want. They don't bring in any revenue, but the FCC says I gotta keep 'em. You got style, Landau, but no street sense. You'll get sliced up around here. That's why I'm sending you out there."

"Where do you want to send me?"

"Shubert Alley. I want you to spend every night seeing the shows. Every show. Give me a critique, and during the day read these proposals," he said, pointing to four boxes of scripts. "Give me criticism, give me vision. I'm so fucking tied up, I've lost my creativity. Tell me what you like, what kind of shows we should be doing."

He reached into a large drawer where there were hundreds of marbles and scooped out a handful. "You see these? These are the ratings. Nielsen hyping bullshit. Jesus! He uses less than a thousand marbles for seventy million sets. Fucking ass. Nielsen says, 'If I pick out ten marbles, one will be orange.' It's ratings. It's marbles. You gotta have the marbles in your

216

head. That's what its all about. When you're number one, you're in. When you're number two, you're out."

Just then the telephone rang. He talked for a moment and then whispered to me, "It's Johnny Frankenheimer, he's directing *For Whom the Bell Tolls* over at Studio 51," he said, his hand over the mouthpiece. "Hi, John. About Armando driving the motorcycle? Who's Armando? I thought we hired a stunt man. Your barber. Oh, your lucky charm. Well, can he drive a cycle? Well, how much do we have to pay him? Five hundred dollars more. John, if he gives you a better show, hire your barber. Just bring it in on time. By the way" —Mann looked at me—"have you seen *For Whom the Bell Tolls?*"

"No. Just read the book."

"You might want to go over to Studio 51 and see Frankenheimer shoot. John, I'm sending an associate of mine over. He's working for me. Jonathan Landau. Make him comfortable. Good-bye." Michael Mann hung up the phone.

"Lucky charm, shit. I want a lucky marble. This is what the business is all about. Marbles. And If I don't get 'em, I'll be out looking for a job."

"I'll do good work for you, Mike."

I went from Emmy winner and star producer to a script reader in ten minutes flat. Well, it was a job. Good-bye, pride. Hello, survival.

I walked over to Studio 51 and took a seat in the control room. They were taping the bombing of Madrid. From the opening scenes, the Madrid of the thirties had been recreated with colorful flats. Buildings, vendors, flower stalls, cobblestone streets, atmosphere, actors, a monastery, all surrounding a square. Special-effects men stood on rafters above, dispensing smoke and directing explosions.

"I'm John Frankenheimer."

"Jonathan Landau."

"This is my friend Armando. He'll be riding the motorcycle. He's my lucky charm." He stood by a vintage motorcycle with a sidecar.

They shot the first take. The bombing started. Special-effects men threw down debris and smoke, and bombs exploded all over the studio. The extras were cued and ran through the streets. Taking cover.

"Cue the motorcycle," Frankenheimer yelled.

Armando, dressed as a dispatching officer, zoomed across the stage. The motorcycle went out of control. Frankenheimer shouted for the cameraman to follow the motorcycle, which careened wildly, smashing through four sets. Collapsed. The studio was demolished.

"Goddammit!" Frankenheimer cursed.

No wonder Michael Mann kept two radios on simultaneously in his office. It was the only way he could keep his sanity.

The timing was good, and when Max knocked on my door, I said, "I've been expecting you."

"Why?"

"I thought you needed a coach."

"But the man said I had a brace and I couldn't enter the competition."

"What man?"

"Mr. Carmichael. He's the athletic director. You know, for all the public schools."

"You stay here."

"Where are you going?"

"To work some magic. I'll see you later." I went around to the park, where a sign on the door announced, "New York Trials, Track and Field Competition, Junior Division."

"Are you Carmichael?"

"Yes, I am."

"How does one enter?"

"Well, anyone can enter," Mr. Carmichael said. "Any kid in public school, that is."

"A friend of mine told me he couldn't enter."

"Well, if he's healthy and lives in New York, he certainly can. Is he in a New York public school?"

"Yes. He's over at the Center for Special Education."

"Then he's handicapped."

"So are horses. What does that mean?"

"Well, he has some sort of impediment. Those kids, you know, are mute, deaf and dumb. Please don't think I'm difficult. Your name again?"

"Jonathan Landau. And we are going to enter the trials."

"But this event, Mr. Landau, is not for handicapped children." He spoke with insensate authority. "It's really too tough on them. Why humiliate the kids? They have a hard-enough time."

"Surely a man of your background and character can make an exception."

"It is impossible. I'm sorry."

He had no use for my charm, no tolerance for my cause, no reception for my concern.

I gave up. "I see your point."

"I'm glad you do."

"And I'd like for you to see mine."

"Of course."

"Fuck off."

In the morning, April. Reading scripts, April. In the park, April. At the theater, April. At dinner, April. At night, April. I thought about her constantly. She had been taken to St. George's Hospital for the new treatment. I called her. She was well. There was new medication and she was in remission. She sounded bright and good. Even the nurse told me how well she was doing.

She was so spontaneous, laughing, interested. It was like winning a prize. The phone rings and, congratulations, you've won! It was like seeing the most beautiful girl you ever saw in your life. You daydream about her, you feel butterflies. You don't dare speak. All of a sudden she comes over to you and says, "I want to be with you. I've always wanted to be with someone like you." Or, the phone rings, "We've been watching you. With your talent and hard work, we're making you president of the company. You deserve it." That's what it was like. April was getting well. I was happy and alive.

"How is your job?" she asked.

What could I say? "The news has been discontinued"? "I have a fabulous new job"? Christ! New job. Should I say: "April, I have an exciting new demotion—I've been fired"?

"Everything is great."

"How are the children?"

The children? Fuck! What can I say about the children? About Carmichael?

"Well, I had a little difficulty in signing Max up."

"What do you mean?"

219

"Well, they made it tough. But Jonathan Landau did it. He'll be running."

There was a pause.

"When?"

"In just a few weeks. We're in training. Coach Landau is training everybody." I was lying beyond belief. Shit!

"Jonathan," April said, "I love you for what you're doing. It's really important. I love you, I really do. Even if Max just runs a few feet, it's a shining accomplishment. It's like your first few words."

"I love you, April."

"I wish I could be there for the meet."

"I wish I could be there right now. Good night, April. I miss you terribly."

I put down the phone. How can Max run? Carmichael was right. They have rules and regulations. The kid would make a fool out of himself. He has a handicap. I went to bed, thinking. I thought about handicaps. About being so fucking alone with it, how you hurt and sometimes you don't know how to express the feelings. "Hey, nanny goat, nanny goat." Back to Augusta, Georgia, and the kids at school, talking through their noses, mocking me. I pushed it down so far, so far away, that it was hard now to remember what it was like at the dawn of difference. Escaping into fantasy and make-believe, then being reminded that I wasn't all right at all. But I was.

How many people can't speak or hear or walk? There are options. I couldn't talk, so I learned to listen. A deaf person can't listen, but he can see. The blind can't see, but they can feel and speak and understand. We move in unknown territory, silent, alone.

Some people are physically handicapped, some have a financial handicap. How many people are emotionally handicapped? Those who lose their feelings, their humanity, that's the greatest handicap of all. It's not the handicap that matters. We're all handicapped in some way. It's what we do about it that counts. April did it. Goddammit, she did it! Imagine that!

It's a wonderful accomplishment to just get better. And Max. Wait, he can do it too. Max is like me.

There was something I had to do years ago. I didn't know why, but I had to do it. Max is no different. It's no different than a jockey riding to the finish, or climbing Mount Everest, or going over nineteen feet in a pole vault. You do it because it's there to do. You're a person in the process of becoming. Who said it was easy? But you can learn with understanding because you've been there.

I had to do it. Max has to do it now.

25

The Center for Special Education was a uniquely designed building in the fifties. Ramps led up along each stairwell. There were special rails for the blind. The school was painted with bright rainbows. Sarah Randolf was the principal. She was warm and comforting, a wonderful and easy overweight woman in her forties. Her eyes were soft from many years of kindness.

"I'm a friend of Max Shapiro's, Mrs. Randolf. We've been having discussions about the track meet involving all the New York schools."

"Yes."

"I just want to know if the Center for Special Education is a public school."

"Yes it is."

"Then your students are qualified to enter the New York field trials."

"I suppose we can, but we never have."

"Max wants to enter. I think he should. And anyone else who wants to."

A look unfolded into a wonderful smile. "Well, why not?"

The following day, a note was posted on the bulletin board: "All students wishing to enter the field-and-track competition, report to Room Five Friday at three o'clock."

There was a group of students in the room when I came in.

"It's going to be a field event," a pretty student aide translated my words into sign language for the three deaf boys with winglike fluttering hands.

The deaf kids looked intently at my lips when I talked, every syllable. They looked with their feelings and insight.

Then, the blind girl, feeling instead of looking. Reaching out with care.

"Would you repeat that more slowly," she asked, "and exaggerate the movements of your lips? They can understand you."

"There will be a field-and-track event—running, broad jump, relay races, javelin. How many of you would like to enter?"

They all raised their hands.

"Before we make any selections," I said, "we're going to train four afternoons a week. You will need sneakers or running shoes and warm-up shorts."

Max rode home with me. "Jonathan," he said, "this is going to be great. How did you do it? Jiminy, this is great!"

The school had an old yellow Volkswagen van that I used to pick up the children. Up over Riverside Drive, across Ninety-sixth Street, down to the Village and back up to Central Park. We took long walks, then a little running—walk a bit, run a bit. The blind kids were assigned a sentry, as pair of eyes, who ran alongside them, slowly, building their confidence. Kids from the school in wheelchairs followed, pushing themselves over the gentle knolls and running paths. I had inherited a band of handicapped ragamuffins.

I made the following notes in my ledger of impressions:

Melissa, age eight. Tall, proud. She wore braces on her teeth but not on her arms, for she had none.

Stanley had multiple sclerosis and was confined to his wheelchair because of partial paralysis. He looked at me through his glasses, always trying to smile, making awkward grimaces when he tried to speak.

Josh and Jimmy, twins, age eight, both were deaf. Freckled and blond and smudged, they dressed alike in corduroy slacks.

Mary Sue was a black girl with wonderful white teeth. She wore a red sweater sporting a big Peanuts badge. She was blind, age eleven.

Steven, legally blind, frail, shining dark hair, quiet.

Matthew, an oversized, overweight black child. Even though he was fourteen, his intelligence level was that of a six- or seven-year-old. Some said he was retarded. He was like a big hippopotamus, waddling around the park with his weight thrown forward on his toes. The kids called him Big Mac. He was full of love, always embracing the children, almost squishing them.

And Max, short for his ten years, and never still. Strong arms, good physique. Sandy hair, always cheerful.

They looked like typical kids from a New York public school smiling for a class picture. They could have been from Des Moines or Tallahassee. The only difference between these kids and any others was that they had more courage.

Through the autumn leaves and days gray with rain, we practiced. Sarah Randolf found a track at a private school in Riverdale that we could use. I read every book on field and track. What I didn't know, I faked.

Matthew followed me everywhere I went. I made him equipment manager. He did pretty well with his responsibility. He never forgot where anything was.

"Max, you just have one leg, and I know you want to run, but why don't you consider the pole vault or the javelin? You can skip, gain momentum, and go over."

"All right, Jonathan," he agreed. "I never thought of that."

"Jimmy and Josh, you're naturals to run the hundred yards. But Steven wants to run it, too, and he can win. So you two have to be his eyes. He's going to hold on to your arms and run between you around the track."

Around the track they went, Steven hesitant at first, then running, full out between them. Melissa was going to enter the cross-country event. I made Stanley my assistant coach. He couldn't talk too well, and it took time to understand him. But he could watch Mary Sue, and when she reached her mark, he'd blow a whistle, and up she would go, first four feet, then six. She could fly through the air. It was a remarkable team. They never wanted to stop practice. [Every day— the four days became every day.] We practiced for a month, and I knew we could make a respectable showing at the competition.

One afternoon, toward the end of practice, Max said to me, "I have a secret weapon."

"Let me see it."

"No, I can't."

"Hey, I'm your coach. I've got to see the weapon."

"You won't let me use it if I show it to you."

224

"You better show it to me."

"It's a surprise."

"Is it legal?"

"I don't know. But I can't tell you. It wouldn't be secret anymore."

Max had shown such courage and stamina, I figured whatever it was would be all right. He could pole-vault six feet, but he kept raising the bar higher and higher. He missed a lot of the time and lifted himself by sheer will and determination and enthusiasm. And most of the time he had dauntless self-confidence. It didn't matter if he didn't go over every time. Just being on a team and entering the competition was what counted.

Big Mac ran over and hugged each member of the team as they finished practice. He put away their equipment happily. I wondered what would happen to him when the kids grew up.

In the evening, I continued my quotidian task of writing reports and covering the shows in "Shubert Alley" for Michael Mann. I was reading a script when the telephone rang. It was KRON-TV in San Francisco. They were offering me a newscasting job with a lot of autonomy. It sounded great. San Francisco was a good, cosmopolitan town. I thought how nice it would be to live there, with instant flashes of Nob Hill, Sausalito, and Tiburon. Cronkite had recommended me. It was a lot more active than critiquing scripts and plays. But there was a catch. They needed someone right away. That was nonnegotiable. It was impossible for me even though I wanted the job. I had made a commitment to the kids. The news director I was speaking with couldn't understand that. He interpreted my refusal to come to San Francisco as standoffish and difficult, and I couldn't do anything about it. The competition came first.

There were a few difficulties at practice. I worried about Max pole-vaulting. Not so much going over the pole as landing on his artificial leg. Steven had the idea of putting a large air mattress over the sawdust to cushion his fall. It made a lot of sense.

Melissa sometimes slipped when she ran. She had trouble with balance.

She was down and disappointed, and she was giving up.

"Come, Melissa, you're not trying," I said to her.

She just looked at me from a distance. Quiet. Silent. Angry.

A few days later I was working with Max at the pole vault. Melissa was running around the track, and this time she fell and wouldn't get up.

I went over to her. "You feeling okay?"

"Yeah."

"Well, what's wrong?"

"I can't get up. I don't want to be on the team."

"Come on, get up," I said. "You can do it."

She yelled at me, "I'm not."

I replied with responsive firmness, "Yes, you are. Now, get moving—up."

"I can't," she said again.

"You can!"

"What do you know about getting up?" she said. "You don't know what it's like. I feel helpless." When I heard that note in her voice, I knew where she was because I had been there too.

"I know what you think," I said softly. "And I know what it's like—not having arms."

"But you have arms."

"So, I have a couple of arms. You have it a little tougher, that's all."

"Tough," she said. "You can't imagine what it's like not being able to feel with hands—to write, to eat, to talk with gestures."

I put my arms around her. "I'll be your arms, Melissa. Let me tell you something. I couldn't talk when I was little. I couldn't even tell somebody I didn't have arms. Just think, you can sing and laugh and even yell—I couldn't even do that."

She looked at me sideways, not believing me.

"I learned to talk."

"Honest?" she asked.

"Honest."

"Really, Jonathan?"

"Really, Melissa. I had to learn, just like you have to."

I told her more how it was for me when I was a kid, and all of a sudden she rolled over and wriggled and finally her

226

contorted body strained and managed to get up—alone; then she tripped, but she started the whole process again. Finally up. She was standing, and she started to run again.

The next day, when Max was having trouble and Steven's confidence was waning, I overheard Melissa encouraging them.

"You can do it—you really can. Jonathan did."

"What do you mean?" they asked.

"He couldn't talk when he was our age. He told me about it."

"Is that really true?" Steven wanted to know.

"It's really true."

They all needed someone to look up to—they needed an Andrew in their life. And from that time on, I knew they had a different feeling and respect for me.

The weeks passed quickly. The competition was just days away. I wondered how we would do. We needed a little luck. Michael Mann wanted five more reports on Broadway shows. I decided I would try to cover at least three that night. I was running across Forty-sixth Street after seeing *The Sound of Music,* to catch the second act of *Music Man.* What the hell, it paid the rent. After the track meet I was going to England to be with April. The *Express* might offer me a job, or maybe Time-Life would soon hire me.

"Jonathan," a voice called out. "Saw you on the news. Great to see you."

It was Fritz.

"It's good to see you, Fritz." We talked about old times.

"Can you have lunch tomorrow?"

"Sure."

"Good. I've got an important story for you. The Metropolitan Club at one, okay?"

The club was one of New York's oldest. Just off Fifth Avenue at Sixtieth Street, it was an enormous palatial white marble building.

Fritz and I sat in the formal oak dining room. He was dressed in a conservative gray flannel suit looking quite well put together.

"I never thanked you for looking after me at Oxford," he said.

"Well, Fritz, what are friends for?"

We remembered. Avon. The *Queen*. Molly. He spoke
clearly about his life. He was busy supervising his stocks and
bonds.

Then he leaned over and spoke in a hushed voice. "I bought
a schooner, Jonathan. It's beautiful."

"That sounds really nice."

"It's my ark. I'm outfitting it with two of everything to
replenish the world. Do you know where I can find a female
giraffe? It's very hard to get the animals. I've got people
working on it to get some in Africa, but it's taking too long.
I've got to go. There's not much time."

Oh, Christ, I thought, he's serious.

"Given up on the world, Fritz?"

"We all must find our own sanctuary while there's still
time."

Maybe he was no crazier than anyone else, I thought.

26

It seemed like a good morale-builder for the team to get together for dinner at my apartment the evening before the meet. That day, everything went wrong. The uniforms I managed to have donated weren't ready and were then lost before they were finally found. Max narrowly avoided a major accident in the afternoon when he stumbled crossing Fifty-seventh Street and was almost hit by a car. Then the Volkswagen bus broke down and had to be towed back to the school.

There was a lot of tension.

"Do you think we're ready, Jonathan?" Jimmy, one of the deaf kids, asked. He spoke in a monotone, not distinguishing syllables or sounds.

"You bet we're ready," I said confidently.

I was riddled with anxiety. I didn't even know if Carmichael would let us register when we arrived at the stadium. I had sent the forms in and there was a box to check if there were any abnormalities or medical history the athletic board should know about. I had not checked the box.

Stanley was agitated and excited. Tempers broke out when he charged into Jimmy. "I didn't hear you coming," Jimmy said.

"Well, you can see me," Stanley replied.

"Calm down. Calm. Calm. I have some uniforms. For a while I thought we lost them, but here they are." I gave each of the kids their shirts. They were blue with CSE, Center for Special Education, stamped on the front. Each shirt was individual, printed with each name and number.

The kids' eyes lit up.

"This is it. Tomorrow's the big event."

Oh, Christ, I thought to myself. What is going to happen? Stanley wheeled up to me. It was hard for him to talk through dripping saliva because of his deteriorating nerve disease. "Thank you, Jonathan," he said slowly. "For the shirt. I love my shirt."

Mary Sue interrupted, "Hey, coach, can my parents come tomorrow?"

"Sure. Tell them to be at Columbia Field at twelve o'clock. And the rest of you kids be ready to be picked up between nine-thirty and ten. Got it? Now, let's chow down."

I prepared grilled cheese sandwiches, tomato soup, Ritz crackers, Coca-Cola, and some Hershey bars.

The training table was in the kitchen, and we sat around eating. Jimmy helped Melissa with her food. Everyone talked at once.

Sarah Randolf arrived with a lemon meringue pie.

"This is great, Sarah. This balances our high-protein, high-carbohydrate, high-energy diet."

She laughed.

There was a special on television. A new group from England called the Beatles that the kids wanted to watch. Sarah helped me clean up. I was pacing back and forth.

"I thought I'd better come over and calm you down, Jonathan."

"I'm calm. I'm calm," I said.

"Good luck tomorrow."

"Thank you, Sarah."

"Jonathan, that's quite a team you've got there."

"I know."

"Tell me, why are you doing this?"

"I'm not doing anything, they are."

"No, Jonathan, why?"

"Sarah, you've done this most of your life, haven't you?"

Sarah looked at me warmly. "Yes."

"Then to use your line, why not? I only wish my girl were here. April would love to see these kids. She works in a London clinic with children. She's been very ill herself, but she's getting better."

"Nothing serious, I hope."

"Well, it was serious. She had multiple myeloma."

"I've always heard that's a very difficult disease, Jonathan. It's rare. I think one of our students has it. We aren't sure."

"Well, there is a cure. Hansen's work in Sweden at Karolinska has been remarkable. They gave her massive doses of immune globulin and hydrocortisone, and she is recovering."

"I'd like to know more about the treatment. There is a child at school who is suffering very much."

"Absolutely. I can give you Trevor Hopkins' address in London. He's the expert in the field."

"Thank you, Jonathan. April sounds very special."

"She is, Sarah. She really is."

Later that evening, I drove the kids home, embracing each one as I said good night. A warm steaming mist collected on our faces.

Max was the last. He drove back with me. "You know, Jonathan," he said, "at first I thought you were just helping me because I asked you. And you really didn't want to do it. Then I thought you were helping us because you wanted to be a big shot for some other reason. I feel badly that I thought that. Now I know you are doing this just for all of us."

"You're right, Max."

He was right on all counts.

"See you tomorrow," he said as he went in his apartment. He had made a hell of a judgment call.

I went into my apartment alone. I tried to sleep. Hours passed. The rain was falling hard now. I lay in bed in the dark, alone, waiting for tomorrow. And then I heard a cricket, a sound of a cricket clicking outside my window, distant and far away.

"Crick-it, crick-it," and then a long interval. And then it came again, louder and faster.

I jumped up and walked to the window.

"Crick-it," again.

I looked down across the park. It was empty, a three-o'clock-in-the-morning emptiness. And slowly my eyes rested on a streetlamp at Sixtieth Street below my window. Fourteen floors down across the street, with light falling all around him, was a black man . . .

"Crick-it."

. . . looking up. And then a smile.

"Crick-it."

It was the King of the Crickets. For Christ's sake, it was Andrew, snapping a gold cricket.

I raced to the elevator to a hollow ring, the sound of

clanging doors, and a slow humming. I couldn't wait. I ran, leaping down flights of stairs to the lobby, past deco gates, past the doorman into the street.

"Crick-it." Faster, louder, "Crick-it, crick-it, *crick-it*."

I reached out and cried to Andrew. He waved. I was intercepted by a passing taxi. I crossed the street, running, returning to Andrew standing there alone in that pool of light. A faltering bus passed my view, and in a moment, without a word or sound, he had disappeared. All was empty.

But he was there. I saw him. I saw that smile of smiles. That smile embraced kindness. I heard the cricket.

I stood there, lost. Was it just in my mind? Was Andrew in this world?

Finally I went back into the building and into my apartment, wondering if my mind had played tricks. I had finally found Andrew. But he had never really left. He was a part of me.

I went to one of my drawers where I kept my cufflinks, watch, and old coins. At the bottom of my jewelry box was a gold cricket. The one Andrew had given to me. I had forgotten was there. I took it out and polished it on my sleeve. It gleamed. Tomorrow it would bring us luck.

Tomorrow was the day.

27

It was a sunny morning, the air crisp, a fall football day. A day for the outdoors, fresh-washed sky, clean clouds, a day which seemed to anticipate the event.

On the way to Morningside Heights, Max asked me, "Can we really register? What will happen if Mr. Carmichael doesn't let us?"

"Don't worry, Max, we'll register."

"But that man, Carmichael—"

"Max, save your energy for the meet."

I picked up the team. We swerved in and out of traffic, up the East Side Drive. We were an hour away from the first event.

"Well, gang, here we are. On to victory."

They were proudly wearing their blue uniforms with white letters. They felt like all the other kids. The normal kids without handicaps. The tension was there. Even more than the night before. I was scared as hell. The kids had the innocent confidence and determination that I had long since forgotten.

We pulled into the track-and-field building at Columbia. It was built with pillars, like a coliseum. The lift of the van lowered Stanley, and the team followed me onto the track, where we joined eighteen other teams from New York public schools. Twenty-five thousand people sat in the stands around the field. Jimmy and Josh carried a large box.

"Hey, what's in the box?" I asked.

"My secret weapon," Max replied.

At the registration desk, Carmichael looked up at me. "I told you, Landau, this is not an event for handicapped kids."

"What handicap?" I asked. "We're from the Center for Special Education."

"This meet is only open to New York public schools."

"Good. We're in the right place, Max. CPE is part of the New York public-school system."

Then a judge standing near Carmichael noticed me. "Aren't you on the news? Jonathan Landau, right?"

"Right." What the hell, if that helps, you bet.

There was a hurried conference, and we were officially entered.

"Criminy, Jonathan," Max said. "You did it."

"Easy, Max. Let's go and win."

We were assigned our section on the field. It was next to the bar-jump and hurdle area. It was time for a pep talk. "Now, listen, team. We've practiced for four weeks, and you're ready. I want you kids to win, get it? No excuses will be accepted. Play fair, be proud. Get in there and fight." I used every cliché I could think of. It was my best Knute Rockne Notre Dame halftime speech. Tough. Convincing. They were defending the honor and glory of the school. I really didn't have to say anything. They were revved up and ready. We were either courageous or stupid.

The meet began. Our first event was the broad jump. I led Mary Sue to the starting mark. Stanley wheeled into his position. There's were twelve contestants entered, and Mary Sue was sixth in line. Her turn came. She left, and down the track she ran, straight ahead, without wavering, without fear. Stanley blew the whistle. She jumped instantly, with total confidence. Seven feet, three inches. Good enough for fourth place. My God, she placed! The kids gathered around, congratulating her, and Steven, who was also blind, touched her smile. We were off to a fine start.

The crowd could not know Mary Sue was blind, but they did know we were a strange-looking team, Stanley slobbering in his wheelchair, a girl without arms, a kid in a brace with an artificial leg, deaf boys who only read lips, and an oversized equipment manager who smiled a lot.

Steven, left alone for a moment, tripped over a bench, and there was some laughter from the crowd. An athlete tripping over a bench! The laughter soon quieted when Max asked for the pole for the vault to be set for nine feet. The pole-vaulting contestants were going over nine feet with ease. One youngster from **P.S.** 41 went over at ten feet, which was a junior record.

"Max," I said, "you can't be putting that bar up at nine feet. You'd better stick with eight."

"I can do nine."

"Like hell you can. You only have two chances. Try at eight first. Don't be so confident."

"Look," Max said. "I've waited a long time for this, and I'm going over at nine." He hobbled away with his brace, a brave, skinny one-legged wonder. Down the track he went, slowly, skipping and hopping. He stopped. What was happening? He picked something off the track and threw it aside. Then he went back to his starting mark. All eyes looked at him. Especially the other teams. He ran as best he could down the lane, pushing a little faster now, holding his pole. Then his arms pulled and pushed his frail body up in the air. He skimmed the bar at nine feet. He made it. He had missed every time in practice. But this time he did it. The loud-speaker announced his name. "Max Shapiro has cleared nine feet, one inch." The crowd applauded and then cheered.

"Son of a bitch. This is going to be a runaway. Criminy," I said to Max. "All right!"

"Now you want to see my secret weapon? Just watch." The bar was set at eleven feet.

"Oh, no, not eleven feet, Max."

He went down to the end of the track again and pulled a red wagon from the box, stood in it, and the twins pushed him down the track, faster and faster, Max balancing with his pole steadied. Poised. Arched. An English knight, jostling. Son of a bitch. Faster they went, until they reached his mark. He placed his pole and went over at eleven feet. There was laughter and good-hearted applause from the crowd as whistles blew furiously.

A track official came over to me. "We can count the first jump, but that is clearly illegal, Mr. Landau."

"Max, get over here. Put that secret weapon away forever. You trying to get us thrown out of the meet?"

"Well, I was just trying an experiment," he said.

I walked away, shaking my head. I was amused, but I couldn't show it.

Next, Melissa ran the six-mile cross-country. It was a long, grueling, exhausting test of stamina. I felt for her. Please don't slip. Off the track and into the streets they went. The minutes seemed like hours. We waited. Then the crowd exploded in cheers. They had returned. I looked for Melissa. She appeared. Out of forty runners, she came in twelfth. Only eighteen finished. I had never timed her. I had no idea what she could do. But she was a stunning sight when she ran back onto the field with the other runners, especially with her empty sleeves flapping in the breeze, a running flag of courage.

Then came the half-mile. Seventeen runners ran the track. Jimmy and Josh with Steven sandwiched in the middle. The threesome jumped up and down and warmed up. To their places, on their mark, go! They paced themselves with the pack. Around the track they went like synchronized trotters. The two of them guiding Steven. And in the last twenty-five yards, Steven left them, broke through on the straightaway, and ran. God, did he run! Across the finish line first. And he kept running. I shouted as he passed the bench. "Slow down! Slow down, Stevie. You won!"

A couple of the contestants complained. A runner holding on to another runner was an infraction. But the judges refused to listen. They awarded Stevie the first-place medal, which he gave to Stanley in the wheelchair. The kids jumped and hugged each other. They had done more than win. The other team led a cheer. "Two, four, six, eight. Who do we appreciate? CSE!"

I looked at those goddamned kids. What a victory. I would never forget.

"Sure did enjoy the track meet, Mr. Carmichael."

"Yeah, Mr. Carmichael," Max said. "Sure did enjoy the meet. We only won one event, but we'll be back next year."

We walked off the field in single file, followed by Matthew and Stanley in his wheelchair, rolling along, holding his medal.

I tried calling April that night. I couldn't get through.

The next morning Sarah Randolf called. "Jonathan, the children love you. You've given them so much pride."

"Thank you, Sarah."

"Can you come around? I'd like to see you."

"I'm going to England," I replied. I couldn't wait to see April.

"I was still hoping you might consider teaching with us. We could have a track meet every year. I've been thinking of something like a special Olympics."

What a wonderful idea, I thought. I had wanted to impress April. In the beginning I was helping the children more for April than for them or for myself. Along the way, it changed. I did something wonderful for the children, and something good for me.

"Jonathan, are you still there?" My thought was interrupted.

"Yes, thanks anyway, Sarah. I'll be glad to help you from time to time."

"When you get back, we'll be up in Vermont, in Stowe. The Center has a lovely house there and we'll be taking the children up for a month. Visit us if you have a chance."

Deep down, I knew that I wouldn't.

I saw several modules being moved across the hall from Michael Mann's office that day. Two, to be exact.

Mann looked up at me. "They're making an office for you now, Jonathan. And I've been reading your reports. Let's meet next week. I need a complete update. There's a box of program submissions over there." He pointed to a new box with some thirty scripts and proposals.

"Can I take a week off and read?"

"Sure, Jonathan."

"I can read better in London. It's important."

"Take them with you to London. Cover London while you're there. See if we can steal any good ideas from the BBC."

Mann stood in the center of his office, preoccupied. "These are the weapons, and this is the strategy for manipulating the environment."

Around his office were large charts that indicated all the network shows in greens, reds, and yellow. Mann had several assistants who followed him everywhere. Each one was assigned to monitor a different network. ABC, CBS, NBC, with time slots, and on each board, the stars, type of show, and numbers were indicated. Often Mann slid the shows around.

If ABC was doing particularly well in a particular time slot, CBS would pick their best two shows and put them opposite that one. "If they're getting a fifty share, then shove in *Gunsmoke* Sunday night." It was a constant battle, back and forth. It was a battle of ratings, a programming war. With pawns and knights and bishops moving in battle. And the only password was "win."

"I'm gonna blow those fuckers outta the box," Mann said.

28

The plane touched down early. Up through London, morning traffic was beginning to form. Belisha beacons flashing orange signals, past Chelsea pensioners displaying quiet pride, guards walking in the dappled sunlight of a mall. Cockneys having a bit of horseplay at the Smithfield meat market. Past the flower market at Chelsea, baskets of posies, daffodils, and yellow and white tulips. Everywhere, signs of Britain's crown; royal emblems on buildings, banners and lamps, post offices and telephone boxes. Cabbies waited respectfully as a cavalry detachment, dressed in royal blue and red, marched in regimented steps across the park, toward Whitehall. Gleaming brass plates and black horses. Across the Burlington Arcade, all the shops just opening.

Traffic boomed a ceremonial cannonade as we drove toward the Addison Road. I smelled the morning air, finally, in London.

Up past familiar green squares and houses. I knew how it would be. At the clinic, at ten o'clock when the children broke joyously into the yard, April would follow. I would see her, across the courtyard, with the children, pointing the way, understanding their insecurity, encouraging their curiosity, receptive to their confidence. She would look up and see me. We'll smile at each other and know we have what we've always wanted—each other.

As I approached 18 Addison Road, a few nannies pushed old-fashioned carriages on their early-morning rounds. A constable nodded. "Good morning, sir." I opened the Huxleys' gate and saw on the door, just before me, a wreath with a black ribbon.

Time stopped.

The moment froze.

Everything was ice.

It was a shock, a terrible shock. A black wreath. It appeared so suddenly. I stood numb, in disbelief, dazed. It can't be. I started to open the door and go inside the gate. I stopped and looked at the brass numbers again. Eighteen Addison Road. And all of a sudden I turned and ran away, running as fast as I could past a blur of passersby. I ran away, and the feelings that were deep down—hurt, loneliness, abandonment—they surfaced. They welled up and in an instant exploded inside me. I stopped running and I wept.

I wept through Knightsbridge, past painted iron railings and pink petunias, past the wide front doors with brass doorknobs, past the familiar streets, following the familiar footsteps that April and I had walked.

April seemed to be with me. Of course. She was part of me. "Isn't this a superb park?" she asked softly. "It was designed by a man with an extraordinary name, Capability Brown."

Capability Brown took us down a path echoing the softness of the surrounding countryside. To a bridge, a lake, where in the distance the cupolas and Italian palaces at Whitehall blend. Children played with their colorful sailboats. Then on into Kensington Gardens.

I sat alone on a park bench. In the distance there was a graceful, canopied bandstand with a wrought-iron balustrade. Deck chairs, blue and beige stripes, orange and green, red and white, surrounded an open gazebo. A little farther, pink and red peonies cascaded over the walkways. Overhead was a cloud-streaked ultramarine sky.

Then I heard a regimental band. Didn't I? Maybe a morning concert. Yes, the orchestra was on the bandstand. I looked closer and saw Andrew, the King of the Crickets, smiling, his teeth gleaming, in full English regimental dress, red tunic, brass buttons and gold-striped pants. He took out his cricket and clicked it several times. The orchestra took their positions. He saluted me with his baton and the band played "A Room With a View." There was my mother, in a Lily Daché hat, putting on lipstick, a darker shade of red, looking at her reflection in a compact; my father standing close by, in white flannels, carrying a golf bag. I stared and blinked. Daddy

Grace raised his hands and actually said, "Close your eyes and visualize."

Falling off the balustrade was Butch McCoy, Lady Meredith laughing. And, wouldn't you know, Mr. Balmain stepped on the bandstand and placed his metronome on the piano. It clicked back and forth in front of Andrew. It was the same sound as a cricket. Responding in perfect harmony. The Red Caps sat on a bench watching, and a Coldstream Guard stood at attention in front of the bandstand, Sergeant Footer. And in the deck chairs, sunning themselves, were Grandpa Honour and Grandma Rachel. Uncle Moe passed smartly by in his plaid suit. "Nice music, eh, Jonathan?"

Jamie Fitzpatrick waved wildly. "Hey, Jonathan," he cried out. "I'm sorry."

There, standing in front of the bandstand were some of "Sunday's people," all enjoying the concert.

And, next to me, was April in a pale, soft gown. She held my hand and smiled.

"April, you were supposed to get better. You had an even chance. What happened? What in God's name happened?"

But she just looked at me with a smile of destiny.

"Let me tell you about the kids. You should have seen Max."

Was I alone? I saw the pavilion, over next to the orange trees. I remembered the day we came down from Oxford when the sun was warm.

Then there was Lily, shaking her head. "We can't always put it into words." From a deck chair, Peter turned away from Anna and spoke to me. "Sometimes we lose what we love. Nothing is forever, Jonathan."

The pain, Jesus, it hurt. God, it was real. Just like when I was a kid. The feelings were still there. Memory traces. Where are you, Andrew? I need you. Goddammit, Andrew, what happened to the happy ending? Somebody make it all right.

Hemingway stepped down from the gazebo. "Luck wasn't with you this time, Jonathan." He sat down in a deck chair with the Paris edition of the New York *Herald Tribune*. "Jonathan," he said, "write it down."

Fritzie walked through the deck chairs in a vendor's outfit shouting, "Get your fresh bananas."

The clock was chiming now. They all started to leave, except April. I reached out, and she disappeared.

Evans stood next to me. "Very good show, sir." Ten o'clock —I must go over to the clinic. April will be waiting.

The band played softer. It stopped. The park was empty. They had all vanished. Big Ben towering above the Houses of Parliament, finished chiming. It was time to go. I tried to hear the ticking.

I wanted to hear the even, unalterable rhythm of the huge clock. I couldn't hear it, but I knew it would keep time forever.

That night I lay in bed. I was devastated. I would never forget April. I didn't know what I was going to do. I couldn't accept the fact that April was no more. Just like that. She died. I was so convinced that she was going to live. She promised me. Even Trevor Hopkins told me that she could make it. Except for Lily, I had not been involved in death in a personal way with someone I truly loved. And I had believed with all hope, against all odds, that April had a fifty-fifty chance. Those numbers just didn't seem to come up on the wheel. I was alone, but I knew that we are all alone. Yet April was going to make everything all right. She was the myth to fill the emptiness, the void. It was a warm and loving companionship. I wondered if everything had an ending. April had fought with quiet courage. There must be a lesson in that for me. She taught me how to love. She loved the children, and she loved the child in me. I couldn't pity myself because she gave me more than courage. She brought my life into perspective. Maybe I had found a place.

I thought about the patterns of my life. I didn't always understand why people came into my life when they did. Like when Andrew came. He came with hope and humanity. He was special and he seemed destined for me. And I didn't always understand the events. My palate and the operations, the mimicry, the hurt, the painful anger, the absurdity of it all. Luck, fate, chance.

Pain came from thinking that I wasn't all right. People always let me know that I was different, except for Andrew and April. I was outside, always running, looking for some way to be inside. I talked my way through life. Better than anyone else. Just as I had promised myself I would a long time ago.

But I ran away from the pain. I ran with nonconformity and anger and defiance and outrageous actions. It was another way of being accepted. I never believed all my success. I was making an impression on others and trying to be someone else rather than being me. I ran until I did not need to run anymore, until I found a comfortable place where I could live, and then, lost my place again.

Could we be like "Sunday's people" in the play? Coming together by design, sometimes with grace, and when we least expect it, we change.

That weekend I flew back to New York. My apartment was dusty. There was a note for me to call Time-Life. I knew they had a job for me, but, again, I just wasn't ready. I knew what I had to do. What I wanted to do. In a rented car I drove up through New York State into the green farmlands of Vermont, I arrived at Stowe. I found my way to the Center easily. Willow Pond House on Willow Pond Road. Without asking directions, I found the beautiful white Georgian farmhouse with green shutters high on a hill surrounded by tall weeping trees and even rolling hills. It was dark when I arrived. Bright warm windows illuminated the night. I walked up to the porch, and inside were the kids. Josh, Big Mac, Melissa, Jimmy, Steven. All of them. Max ran up and leaped into my arms in surprise. He was shouting and laughing and crying all at the same time. The children surrounded me. They surrounded me with love. And Sarah Randolf smiled welcome. Perhaps for just a little while, but a wonderful welcome.

It was nice to be home, I thought. Outside, yellow light from the windows framed the darkness. Outside, I heard crickets. They were there to remind me of humanity. They were there to remind me that all would be right with the world.